What people are saying about …

SCREEN PLAY

"Fans are going to love Chris Coppernoll's latest novel. *Screen Play* is an inspiring tale of friendship and faith set amidst the complexities of Hollywood and cleverly combined with an uplifting love story reminiscent of *Sleepless in Seattle.*"

Tina Ann Forkner, author of *Rose House* and *Ruby Among Us*

"*Screen Play* brings you front-row seats to Broadway, delivers back-stage passes to friendship and ambition, and shouts 'bravo!' to the longest-running show on earth—the unexpected love story

Ray Blackston, author of *Flabbergasted*

"With *Screen Play,* Coppernoll establishes himself as a man in touch with his time. It's a poignant love story, beautifully told within the context of an honest relationship with God. The characters will stay with you—and so will the relevant spiritual insights."

Gwen Faulkenberry, speaker, author of *Love Finds You in Romeo, Colorado, A Beautiful Life, and A Beautiful Day*

"As I sat back and read this gripping inspirational and emotional story, I saw my own life woven throughout the pages. This isn't just one woman's journey of struggles and triumphs. If you've ever hit rock bottom, felt worthless, questioned God's will for your life, and prayed for Him to rescue you, then you will see yourself throughout these pages too. *Screen Play* made me want to start writing the next chapter of my life *today* and realize that if we'll take the limits off of God and release our faith in uncommon ways, then we will begin to see God do uncommon things. What you thought was the end is going to turn out to be a new beginning."

Tammy Trent, recording artist, speaker, and author of *Learning to Breathe Again*

"This is more than a romance. Chris Coppernoll subtly develops his own deepening themes of community, isolation, and trust. He deftly shows us how God both uses His people right where they are and moves them to places they could have never reached without Him. *Screen Play* will leave readers satisfied with Harper's love story—but transformed by God's love story playing out within the pages of this novel."

Christa Parrish, author of *Home Another Way* and *Watch Over Me*

"You will be captured by the characters and story in this book. Chris Coppernoll skillfully composes a symphony full of the elements of life: romance, disappointment, surprise, and ultimately hope."

Anne Jackson, speaker and author of *Mad Church Disease* and *Permission to Speak Freely*

SCREEN PLAY

SCREEN PLAY

a novel

Chris Coppernoll

David C. Cook®

transforming lives together

SCREEN PLAY
Published by David C. Cook
4050 Lee Vance View
Colorado Springs, CO 80918 U.S.A.

David C. Cook Distribution Canada
55 Woodslee Avenue, Paris, Ontario, Canada N3L 3E5

David C. Cook U.K., Kingsway Communications
Eastbourne, East Sussex BN23 6NT, England

David C. Cook and the graphic circle C logo
are registered trademarks of Cook Communications Ministries.

This story is a work of fiction. All characters and events are the product of
the author's imagination. Any resemblance to any person, living or dead,
is coincidental. LoveSetMatch.com is a fictitious Web site imagined by
the author. As of this book's publication date, no such site existed.

LCCN 2009910527
ISBN 978-1-4347-6482-9
eISBN 978-0-7814-0372-6

The Team: Andrea Christian, Steve Parolini, Sarah
Schultz, Caitlyn York, Karen Athen
Cover design: Amy Kiechlin
Cover images: iStockPhoto.com, royalty-free

Printed in the United States of America
First Edition 2010

1 2 3 4 5 6 7 8 9 10

102909

To Gray,
always

ACKNOWLEDGMENTS

An author friend says writing the novel's acknowledgment page is its most formidable task. How can everyone responsible for bringing a novel to fruition be recognized? A special thanks goes to my agent, mentor, and friend, Chip MacGregor of MacGregor Literary, for representing my writing and for his sage counsel regarding all matters literary. I'd like to acknowledge Don Pape, Terry Behimer, and everyone at David C. Cook for the opportunity to write stories. Significant recognition is due my editor, Stephen Parolini, for his creative contribution to *Providence, A Beautiful Fall,* and *Screen Play.* Thanks to Caitlyn York, for her eye for detail and energy. I'd like to thank my daughter, Gray, for her love and inspiration, and Christa, without qualifiers, for allowing Him to inspire her to slip a silly little card into a package with her book that started our brand-new adventure. And finally, our Lord, Jesus Christ, who closes old doors and makes all things new.

CC

*"How'd ya like to spend Christmas
on Christmas Island?"*

Lyle Moraine, "Christmas Island"

*"There are motives I cannot discover,
dreams I cannot realize. My God, search me."*

Oswald Chambers, *My Utmost for His Highest*

~ ONE ~

I absolutely *had* to be in New York by 1:30 p.m. Did my life depend upon it? Yes, as a matter of fact, it did. Just the thought of calling Ben or Avril with bad news from O'Hare churned my stomach and made my face prickle with a dizzying fear. I joined a sea of travelers bundled in parkas, hoods, hats, and gloves; they stretched out in front of me, pressing in and wresting me through a queue of red velvet theater ropes.

All of Chicago wanted to flee the blizzard they'd awakened to. Sometime after midnight the sky exploded with snowflakes. Icy white parachutists fell from their celestial perch as innocently as doves. The year's last snowstorm tucked the city in with a white blanket knitted through the long winter's night.

When I reached the American Airlines check-in, I hoisted one of my two black canvas bags onto the scale for the ticket agent.

"Harper Gray?" she asked, confirming my reservation.

"Yes."

She returned my driver's license, dropping her gaze to the workstation and tapping my information into the system. At the kiosk next to me, a large Texan with a silver rodeo buckle typed on his iPhone with his thumbs, mumbling something about checking the weather in Dallas.

Computers, I thought. *What don't we use them for?*

It was obvious how many of my fellow travelers were heading somewhere for the New Year's Eve festivities. I couldn't help but eavesdrop on a cluster of merry college students reveling in their Christmas break. They joked and chattered, mentioning Times Square, unbothered by long lines or the imminent threat of weather delays. At thirty, almost thirty-one, I could no longer relate to their carefree lifestyle. Too much water under the bridge, most of it dark and all of it numbing.

"Here you are," the ticket agent said, handing me a boarding pass still warm from the printer. I fumbled with my things, stuffing my photo ID into my wallet as a mother and her young son squeezed in next to me. The crowd current swept me away from the ticket counter, denying me a chance to ask the agent the one question I most wanted answered.

Is anyone flying out of here this morning?

I rolled my carry-on through the main concourse. I'd used the small black Samsonite for so many trips, I thought the airlines should paste labels on it like an old vaudevillian's steamer trunk. A row of display monitors hung from a galvanized pipe, cobalt blue icicles glowing all the brighter in the dark and windowless hallway. I joined a beleaguered crowd of gawkers studying the departure screens. Their collective moans of frustration confirmed what I already knew. My flight—indeed, all flights out of O'Hare—was:

DELAYED

I pinched my eyes shut. This was *not* what I needed. Not today, not today of all days. I absolutely *had* to be in New York by 1:30 p.m. Did my life depend upon it? Yes, as a matter of fact, it did.

~ TWO ~

When my travel alarm jolted me from dead slumber that morning, I'd climbed out of my warm bed and stepped into a cold shower, after which I pulled on jeans in a dimly lit two-bedroom apartment. The walls were bare, stripped of framed artwork, curio shelves, and knickknacks. The kitchen was cleared of dishes, pots, pans, and silver. The last piece of cozy furniture, my double bed and headboard, remained only because my landlady said she'd take possession of it after I was gone.

I'd booked the 6:05 a.m. direct flight to LaGuardia the day Ben called with his blessed invitation. He'd offered to purchase my ticket, saving me the embarrassment of asking him for money since there was no way on earth I could afford airfare on my own. I attributed the good fortune to God's provision, solely based on the timing of Ben's call, coming as it did after I'd sent skyward my own blizzard of fervent prayers. These were desperate prayers, all punctuated with the exclamation point "Help me!"

I slipped out of the apartment, locking the door behind me for the last time, wheeled my suitcases quietly down an empty hallway, and dropped my keys through the brass letter slot belonging to the building supervisor. Apartment 319.

It had been only a year but felt like a thousand since Avril and

I had shared this place together. Those were *amazing times*. We were both working, making good money, and I'd fallen in love.

But life can change on a dime, leaving you with little more than a nickel. Work ended in those first weeks of January. Avril abruptly left for Newbury, Massachusetts, *thrilled* to be working on a new project in the Bay State, while I wouldn't earn a paycheck for the next twelve months. Capping the ugliest January on record, Sam had reserved a quiet table for two at La Maison Rouge to celebrate my thirtieth birthday. Avril was certain I'd receive a gift I could wear on my left ring finger, but Sam presented me with news; he was moving to Los Angeles. A week later Sam departed, never asking if I'd like to go with him or even if I'd be okay without him.

The next day I woke up to the unmistakable sensation of drowning.

My charmed life had been interrupted by sudden impact with an iceberg. I cracked, filling up with the relentless rush of water until all buoyancy was gone. I spent the next year alone, unemployed and unloved, watching my life fall apart piece by piece until all of it fit into two black canvas bags.

That early morning as I wrestled two unwieldy suitcases out the front entrance and down icy concrete steps, I felt fragile, agoraphobic. The cold seeped through my thin leather flats; mine were the only prints in the freshly fallen snow. Easy, weightless flakes swirled through the air, and I said another prayer, an apology for entertaining thoughts of the cab driver finding me hypothermic when he arrived, and how it might all be easier that way.

It had crossed my mind. Yes, *that* thought. The idea of taking my own life, however repugnant, carried with it the promise of solving everything. It was a false promise that rattled me, clueing me in that I needed rescue. When the checkered taxicab picked me up, I felt like I was boarding one of those orange-and-white coast guard choppers they use to pull stranded victims from the icy waters.

To the other passengers at Gate 12 killing time on their laptops or thumbing through the latest Christa Parrish novel, I must have looked like any other stranded traveler balancing a paper coffee cup on her knee. But inside? I was the memory keeper, a woman bearing the scars of a naive walk onto an icy lake, hearing the frightening sounds of cracking ice, and then feeling the unthinkable plunge into frozen darkness.

~ THREE ~

For two hours, we watched the snowplows scrape the runways, listened to colicky babies cry, and waited for a breakthrough. I thought of calling my mom in Orlando, or my dad in Elizabethtown, but after a year of telling them things were fine when they weren't, I decided to forego the playacting.

The first beam appeared from the burning yellow sun. It cut through the sky, puncturing holes in the cobweb clouds. A stressed-out gate agent announced our boarding over the intercom, happy to uncork the exits and let people drain out into planes.

The flight was packed. I wedged myself into a seat between a man who started snoring before takeoff and a surgeon talking on her cell phone about organ transplantation. I slid a dog-eared copy of *Apartment 19*, the classic American play by Arthur Mouldain, out of my carry-on. I'd found it in a used bookstore on Michigan Avenue the day I received the blessed call. I cracked open the paperback once again, pouring the words into my mind like hot cocoa into a thermos. I reread Bella's note, too, folded between the pages. She offered just thirteen words of encouragement, but they meant the world to me.

I believe in you. God has a purpose
and plan for your life. Bella

At one fifteen, I pulled open the elegant pane-glass doors of the Carney Theatre on West Forty-fourth Street and let myself inside. Angels, not the heavenly sort, but kindhearted benefactors, had recently donated millions toward renovating the 702-seat Carney. I'd read about it online at a Chicago public library on State Street.

I tiptoed across a sprawling sea of bright red carpet toward two open doors on the other side of the lobby and entered the darkened theater. Before my eyes adjusted completely to the room's murky darkness, I parked my luggage against the back wall and quietly pulled open the clamshell seat so as not to disturb the actors rehearsing onstage, or any of the half-dozen strangers scattered around the theater. My breathing felt rushed, a result of speed-walking and nerves, so I tried drawing in long, deep breaths while transitioning into a strange, new world. I recognized the play's director, Ben Hughes, even in silhouette, sitting ahead of me in the shadows, but then I'd know him anywhere. I couldn't identify the stranger sitting next to him, a woman leaning in, whispering as two actresses rehearsed on the lighted Carney stage. I wondered how well she knew him.

Everyone knew the two actresses onstage—everyone familiar with the New York theater world and network television, anyway.

Avril LaCorria—my blonde-haired, easily thin, twenty-eight-year-old best friend, who I hadn't laid eyes on since our year together in Chicago—and Helen Payne.

I'd never met Helen, but it was impossible not to know the legend. Her hit TV show, *Mystery Detected*, had aired each Sunday night for ten years in every home in America, including my own. I'd watched it countless times with my mother while I was growing up. Helen was sixty, I guessed, with a robust build and the confident poise of a Broadway star. She'd dressed for rehearsal in a dark sword-pleated skirt, frilly white blouse, and unbuttoned tan cardigan to chase away the chill of the large Broadway theater.

"I come on stage left," Helen said, walking through her moves. "Stand at center stage and ... where will she be?" Helen asked, pointing over at Avril in a way that suggested even after four weeks of rehearsals she didn't yet know Avril's name.

"Right where she is now," Ben said. He stood, reestablishing his directorial authority.

I leaned forward in the back row, resting my arms over the theater seat in front of me. It was my first look at the much-touted revival of *Apartment 19.*

"Shouldn't she be further back, Ben?" Helen asked, as if it were the only position that truly made any sense. "Or if she were even sitting when I came in, I could just give my first line—*Why are you still here in the apartment?*—to myself rather than asking her directly. The audience will think I don't know she's even there."

"Helen, I'm fine with that, but let's just walk through this once again with Avril at the front of the stage. The audience will get the tension that she's supposed to have left, but she's still in the apartment with you."

Judging by Helen's expression, a brief but contemptuous stare, she didn't much care for Ben rejecting her suggestion. Without further rebuttal, Helen exited the stage, tapping her heels sharply as she returned to the wings.

"From the top again," Ben said, slipping back into the obscurity of his theater seat. A moment later Helen reentered, this time in character. Even without benefit of a costume, props, or theater makeup, her transformation into Audrey Bradford was utterly mesmerizing.

She took her mark at center stage, glaring at Avril's character, Roxy Dupree, the eccentric and emotionally unbalanced tenant who rents a single room in the wealthy widow's large New York apartment. With neurotic contempt exuding from her large presence, Helen Payne delivered her line.

Why are you still here in the apartment?

Avril looked as though the pent-up tension in Helen's question had knocked the answer clean out of her head. She stammered.

I wanted to speak with you. I was afraid we got off on the wrong foot.

Helen pointed a sharpened finger into the wings at stage right. *I want you out of this apartment, now!* Avril reacted like she'd been Tasered, her body crippled by an electric shock. The intensity onstage was palpable. Prima donna or not, Helen Payne knew her stuff. Each line she delivered sent chills up my spine. The method actor moved with purpose around the stage, a caged tiger, every subtle gesture underlining what a monster her character was.

In front of me in the dimness, I detected a slight movement and shifted my line of sight. The thirty-something woman sitting next to Ben—her raven hair cut blunt at her chin—turned her head to look at me. She stared, her eyes detached and expressionless, studying or sizing me up. A beam of auxiliary stage light flickered across the woman's eyes, as thin as the cold blade of a saber, and I felt a sudden chill. The flap of her charcoal hoodie had fallen around her shoulders, making her look like a poisonous crone from a Grimm's fairy tale. I fixed my eyes on hers, unable to peel them away. She turned back toward Ben, scribbling something onto a clipboard in front of her, and tilted it toward him just as the scene broke onstage.

"Okay, let's stop there. Very good, everyone," Ben said, rising up from his theater seat to the height of his six-foot-two frame. "Can we get the houselights up, please?"

The unseen hand of the lighting director amplified the soft glow inside the Carney from half past midnight to noonday sun. A sea of ruby seats, hundreds of closed clamshells, uniform and perfect, came to life before me. The scarlet curtains framing the proscenium brushed downward in vertical lines like a woman's hair. Upper and lower box seats, once the symbol of luxury in Broadway's grand old days, were recessed into each sidewall, garlanded with ornamental gold leafing. But the heart of the Carney Theatre was the grand crystal chandelier suspended in the center of the room. It looked like a bell made of diamonds, cascading light like water splashing from a fountain.

Twenty or so actors, stage grips, and crew once concealed in the dark drifted out onto the stage. Ben addressed everyone from his spot in the fifth row.

"All right, everyone. We've got the makings of a truly great show on our hands, but as you can see from rehearsal, we're not ready yet. But we will be. After all, we still have four days."

Ben glanced at his wristwatch, the consummate Broadway director, responsible for every detail of the show.

"I've got just after one thirty now. Let's break for an hour lunch. Rehearsal will go no later than six—however, I'll need you all back here at the Carney tomorrow morning at 10 a.m. Please do not make tonight your ultimate New Year's Eve to remember."

Ben's gaze searched the theater, finally catching sight of me sitting in the back row.

"Oh, one more thing," he said. "Harper, would you stand up, please?"

I stood as the rest of the cast and crew turned to stare at me.

"Everyone, please say hello to Harper Gray. Harper is here from Chicago to fill the role of Helen's understudy since our darling Miss Molly left for Hollywood to make her movie. Please make Harper feel welcome, especially since she ..."

Ben turned back toward the stage. The Russell Crowe look-alike, with brown hair slightly lower than his shirt collar, laid the flat of his hand across his eyes like the bill of a baseball cap, searching for Helen in the bright houselights.

"Helen, how long has it been since you had to use an understudy?"

The actress returned to the stage, her star shining just as brightly without the presence of stage lighting. She stepped with a balanced gait, playing her other character, the real-life Broadway diva Helen Payne.

"I'm not sure—but I believe the last time, Ben, was in 1983."

A howl broke out among the cast and crew. It was the sound of showbiz people recognizing humor in another's pathetically comical lot in life. I cringed inside.

Helen Payne had given thousands of performances over the past twenty-five years, which meant I basically had a thousand-to-one shot of ever being called upon to grace the footlights in *Apartment 19*.

Standing alone at the back row of the gloriously refurbished Carney Theatre, I bit my lip, lifting the corners of my mouth into the shape of a smile, the most natural I could muster. I was pretending—acting, if you will, that I didn't look grubby on the outside from a long, frustrating day of airports, shuttle rides, delays, and crowds. Or worn out on the inside from bruises accumulated over a long, bumpy year. And that the star of the show hadn't just completely humiliated me in front of a group of strangers.

I smiled, feeling the last ounce of my self-esteem shatter into a million pieces. This was the water at my chin finally flooding above my nose, suffocating and submerging the old me to a watery grave.

My eyes lifted until they met Helen's powerful stare where she stood, the Trident Queen, in the center of that magnificent stage. She appeared to be grinning through me, with her award-winning TV persona, her four-decades-long Broadway pedigree sizing up and dismissing me in an instant.

She posed on the high stage above me, a modern day Cruella De Vil, with one arm wrapped around her middle like a belt of flesh and the other jutting away like the chiseled lines of a cold, Roman numeral. Her burning cigarette balanced at the end of her hand as a lifeless thread of smoke ascended in retreat.

Clearly, she enjoyed the cast's laughter. Helen was a born performer onstage and off. Her demure posturing told everyone that this Broadway production had only one star. She would give up her stage to an understudy the day William Shakespeare returned, holding in his quivering, bony hands the sequel to *Hamlet* written with Helen in mind.

"So everybody, make Harper feel right at home in our little family," Ben said. "And I want to see everyone back here in one hour."

Helen floated out of sight, presumably to her private dressing room backstage. I clutched the rough upholstery of the theater seat in front of me, shaking off the cold beam of narcissism Helen had shot at me.

The old cliché "nothing left to lose" didn't begin to scratch the surface. I felt like a child does when a fever breaks, or when a witch's spell is broken in a fairy tale. This sensation didn't *dawn* on me; it slammed me like a hit-and-run driver. I felt *reset*, released, and fighting mad. After a year of falling, I'd come to New York City and found rock bottom. It took a beloved TV star to meet me there and press me down with the heel of her foot. But I also realized I wouldn't stay there. Touching the bottom meant I finally had a push-off point to find my way back to the surface.

~ Four ~

My favorite LA actor sat on the Carney's stage, her legs dangling over the edge. She wore faded blue jeans and a white embroidered hippie top, no doubt from a California boutique on Rodeo Drive. Avril LaCorria smiled, waving to me with wiggling fingers, looking like a beauty pageant winner riding in the back of a convertible in the Rose Parade.

She eased herself off the stage. No longer in the mind-set of Roxy Dupree, Avril put on another character, clowning her way down the center aisle toward me. She approached bashfully, her hands tucked into the front pockets of her blue jeans, her shoulders drawn up tight as if she were a puppeteer's marionette. When the space between us had dwindled sufficiently, Avril let out a sudden squeal of excitement and threw her arms around me in crazy delight.

"Oh, my gosh! I've missed you!" Avril swallowed me up in her rocking embrace. "I can't believe you're here!"

We both lost our balance and came crashing down into the theater seat beneath us.

"I missed you, too," I said into her armpit, conscious and thankful of the message her flamboyant hug sent to everyone in the room. If one star didn't accept me, at least another one did.

"We are going to have the best time in New York! Oh, my gosh, I can't believe how well this all came together."

Avril squeezed me again, chirping the musical utterances she voiced when everything was right in her perfect world. Cast members shuffled past us on their way out, slowing enough to joke with Avril and the new girl, my comic fate threatening no one.

Ben retraced the path Avril walked, sidestepping the exiting actors, comfortable enough in his own skin to wear J. Crew—denim, brown plaid, and construction boots. With his wire glasses and short, sandy beard, Ben looked as ready to go hiking as direct a Broadway play. He slid into the row of seats ahead of us, and Avril climbed off me so I could stand up.

"Welcome, Harper. Glad to see you were able to make it safely to New York." Ben extended his hand over the seats, and I took hold of it. Strong and warm, his hand shook mine at first, then held on while he spoke. "I hope your flight was good. I hear there's been weather."

"The flight was fine, but the timing of your call was perfect, Ben. I can't thank you enough for offering me this role."

"It's Avril you should thank," he said, letting go of my hand and gesturing to her. "When Molly gave us her news on Monday, it was Avril who reminded me of *Grease* last year in Chicago. That cast gelled together quickly. I said, 'If there's any way Harper's available, let's ask if she'll come do this for us.'"

I smiled. It was nice of Ben to make it appear that I was the one doing him a favor. I hadn't forgotten that about him. His humility and kindness were still fresh on my mind since that was also the last time I'd worked.

"You didn't have the biggest role in the show, but obviously I know what you're capable of."

"Thanks, Ben."

"And you know me, I like working with actors I trust," he said, his green eyes peering at me through the wire-rim glasses. Everyone around us might have interpreted his gesture as an appeal for my loyalty, but I didn't. I knew exactly what Ben meant, and answered him with my own silent nod. It wouldn't be the first time he'd trusted me.

"The situation's just as I described over the phone. It's unlikely you'll see stage time, but we're obligated for insurance purposes to have an understudy. The Mouldain estate has granted us a very limited license for *Apartment 19*—a short forty-two performances over the next six weeks. And you probably know this, but the role of Audrey Bradford has never been portrayed by a younger actor. So, if you ever do get the call, we'll show the critics just how innovative we can be. Let's get you up and running after lunch today, okay?"

Ben clapped his hands, punctuating the end of his speech before stepping away, on to his next directorial task. I told him thanks one more time, and Avril bowed low like an obliging servant.

"We are but lowly actors, m'lord. Humbly at your service."

Like the famous TV detective Columbo, Ben turned back toward us in the aisle.

"Oh, and one more thing. Did you get the script and video of rehearsals we Fed Exed you?"

"Yes," I said. "I was able to get my lines down before leaving Chicago."

"Memorized?" Ben asked, taken somewhat aback. "That's fantastic, and one less last-minute detail to manage. Good work, Harper."

It was true. I had my lines down, but not because of any video. Had the script and DVD arrived on time (I didn't bother mentioning neither had arrived until the day before my flight), it wouldn't have mattered much because my apartment lacked a television set, DVD player, *and* electricity. .

"Our stage production director, Tabby Walker, will be working with you. She'll go over basic stage blocking in rehearsals this afternoon."

Arriving on cue, the raven-haired woman I'd seen next to Ben joined us, attaching herself to Ben's side.

"I'm looking forward to it," Tabby said, her high-school hall-monitor clipboard cross-armed over her chest like a shield.

"Good," Ben said, checking his large silver wristwatch. "We'll see you back here at two thirty."

Tabby said nothing more. She simply spun on her heel and followed Ben out of the theater.

I turned to Avril. "What's up with her?"

"Oh, don't mind Tabby," Avril said, moving toward the main exit. "There are all kinds of people in the land of make-believe. Tabby's world only works when she's in charge of everyone in it."

"Bet I'm in for a very interesting day."

"Only after a very interesting lunch. Are you hungry?"

"Ravenous," I said.

"There are five thousand restaurants in midtown Manhattan. What are you in the mood for? A kosher deli, Italian, Taiwanese, Chicken McNuggets?"

"I can't choose. It all sounds so good."

My stomach growled. I pressed my arm through the sleeve of my leather jacket as we walked through the sea of theater seats. I gathered my *one* small bag from the back wall.

"Harper, how is it you only brought one suitcase with you from Chicago?"

"My other bag wanted to go to Philly."

Avril laughed. "Why do the funniest things always happen to you?"

I didn't know the answer, didn't care. I was thankful that anything was happening in my life.

Pedestrians filled West Forty-fourth Street as we broke through the front doors leaving the Carney's placid world behind. The cold city air blew against my face, calming my nerves. I inhaled it in huge gulps, like a reef diver breaking the ocean's surface.

"Oh, I just got the best idea! I *have* to take you shopping tonight after rehearsal," Avril said, excited about everything. "It will be my way of welcoming you to Broadway."

"You don't have to do that, Avril."

"Harp, there's *no way* your other bag is showing up in New York on New Year's Day. Of course, I want to celebrate you being here, but you have to have clothes to wear too."

She smiled, and I felt good about our friendship. With Avril, out of sight meant (mostly) out of mind, but when we were together, it was, "Do you have clothes to wear? Do you have food to eat?" I treasured her friendship.

For lunch, Avril recommended Bongiorno, an Italian eatery near the Theater District. Inside, the walls were exposed brick, the floors, hardwood, and tables covered with red cloths under white paper, a bottle of San Pellegrino on every one.

"Okay, last time, I *promise*—but, I'm so glad you're here," Avril said, once we'd been seated. She squeezed my hands across the table like we were a sister act reunited, Rosemary Clooney and Vera-Ellen in *White Christmas*. "Life's so perfect. Have you ever noticed that, Harper? We shared an apartment at Northwestern, had the flat in Chicago while we worked on *Grease*, and now we'll keep a two bedroom in the Village while we go to the Carney every night and dazzle Broadway."

"*Apartment 19*."

Avril rolled her eyes, puffing a burst of air from her lips.

"You don't like it?" I asked.

"It's just not realistic. A small-town chick moves to the big city and rents a room from the diabolical and very weird Audrey Bradford. Hey, I've got an idea—live somewhere else."

"It's supposed to be a story about surviving a difficult situation," I said, the script still fresh on my mind. "Your character, Roxy Dupree, doesn't feel like she has much choice. She's trying to do the right thing, and it takes all the courage she has."

"Oh, whatever. I just want my next project to be set in LA, preferably at the beach, with one of those *SNL* comedians making the whole thing funny."

"*Baywatch: The Movie*—starring Will Ferrell?"

"Perfect. Now, just attach a six-figure paycheck and send the plane ticket to my iPhone."

The waiter brought out our lunch plates. Speaking only Italian, he announced the name of the dish we'd both gotten—insalata caprese con pollo—and set our plates on the table in front of us, then split back to the kitchen.

"I can actually see you making that movie," I said. "You look great, Avril. New York suits you. If I didn't know you so well, I'd say the Big Apple is your kind of town."

"Despite living in Chicago, New York, Toronto, and Boston— I'm LA through and through. New York robbed me of my tan. That's nearly unforgivable," she joked. "I'll never fall in love with New York, Harper, but that doesn't mean it's the wrong city to fall in love *in*."

Avril took a small bite of her salad, smiling and teasing like she had a secret. I took a bite of mine, and the flavors exploded on my tongue. *How long had it been since I'd tasted food like this?*

"Is there something you'd like to tell me?" I asked, both of us waving off our server when the pepper mill appeared.

"He's a lawyer here in Manhattan. Very good looking, short hair. He works out all the time so even his Armani business shirts look like Nike athletic wear."

"Okay, I get it," I said, marveling at her gift for kismet. "Does this paragon have a name? How did the two of you meet?"

"His name is Jon," Avril said, suddenly coy. "I hesitate telling you how we met. It's not my favorite part of the story."

"What do you mean?" I asked.

She set down her utensils and stalled for a moment, taking a sip from her water glass and wiping a bashful grin away with her napkin.

"Jon and I met online through an Internet dating service," she finally said, leaning in to await my reaction.

"Huh."

"Yeah, that's what I thought too at first, but I've been dying to tell someone because I feel"—Avril tilted her face upward, as if looking for the words stenciled on the ceiling—"like I bought a dollar raffle ticket and won a brand-new Mercedes. I mean, honestly, online dating is the *last* thing in the world I would do. It all started as a joke when I was out with a friend of mine, Penny, and her friend Jill. We were hanging out one night when Jill confessed, pathetically, that she was an online dater. Of course, we *made* her log on so she could show us all her matches. She tells the most hilarious stories of the guys she's met online. Well, an hour later Penny and I were signed up, uploading crazy head shots of each other from our cell phones, laughing the whole time."

"Avril, you were on TV every week for three years."

"Yeah, I know, but you couldn't really tell it was me in the photo. I wore a large floppy hat. Anyway, Jon was one of the guys I got matched with, and I decided to go out with him."

"A TV star?"

"He only knows I'm an actress in New York, of which there are thousands, and nothing more. It's actually been nice going out with someone who doesn't know anything about me. I can be more myself this way. I don't have to worry Jon's only interested because he fell in love with the character I played every Tuesday night at nine, or that he wants to break into the business, or see his picture splashed across the front page of a tabloid."

I shook my head in disbelief. "What's the name of the site?"

"LoveSetMatch.com. And I will so kill you if you tell anyone," Avril kidded. "But honestly, who cares? It totally worked because Jon is so cool."

I raised the white napkin from my lap, erasing any trace of insalata caprese from my lips.

"So you haven't told him what you do for a living?"

"I haven't exactly been *completely* up front with him yet. He wasn't a teeny bopper TV watcher, so he has no clue."

"LoveSetMatch.com."

Avril stared over the tabletop at me, happy as could be. "So what about you, sister? Anyone fill Sam's shoes after his infamous disappearing act?"

Sam's shoes. I flashed for a moment, remembering his habit of leaving his shoes lined up inside the door of his apartment. His nine-to-five office shoes, his Adidas for basketball league, the tasseled loafers he wore Sunday afternoons on his parents' boat. He had a pair of shoes for everything important in his world. Maybe his flip-flops best represented us. I wondered which pair he put on the day he decided to walk away.

I shook my head—"This wasn't a good year for romance." A good year for romance? It hadn't been a good year for getting out of bed in the morning.

"Harper, it's a new year in a new city, and that city just happens to be Manhattan. If you have the desire, and you're willing to fall in love, Cupid will find you with that little arrow of his."

I laughed out loud.

"Wait, you think I'm single because I'm not *willing* to fall in love? Avril, I've been waiting my whole life for a missing person to suddenly make an entrance, to walk on stage left and surprise me with a knock at my door."

"So put out an open casting call. There are four million men on the island of Manhattan. If you can't find someone here, where will you?"

"I don't know, but Sam taught me I don't just want someone, I want *the one*. Sam was only half there. I tried pretending the missing half didn't matter, but ultimately that was the half that mattered most."

"Finding Mr. Perfect is going to be more of a challenge than just finding someone to love," Avril said, sounding like one of those "results may vary" disclaimers on TV. "Then again, I found mine."

Avril beamed her "life always works out better than expected" smile, the central truism she lived by, and I thought I could see a halo of bliss sparkling around her head. She removed a gold American Express card from her wallet and laid it face up on the table. Our waiter swooped by to pick it up.

"Lunch is on me today. Now that you're working in theater again, it's time to go to work on your love life. Speaking of which, you look terrific. What have you been doing over the past year, starving yourself?"

~ FIVE ~

Avril and I finished lunch and were back at the Carney Theatre before two thirty. I'd planned to arrive long before Tabby Walker, but waiting in the shadow of the neon marquee was the woman with the blunt-cut raven hair, holding a tall coffee, steam venting through its lid. She wore the same ice sculpture look from earlier on her face, peering down at her watch when she saw us as if we were campers returning to our cabins past curfew.

"Harper, I didn't get a chance to introduce myself before. I'm Tabby Walker, *Apartment 19's* stage production director and Ben's P.A. Ben's asked me to go over the entire show with you this afternoon, so I hope you're ready."

"I think so," I said, holding out my hand for Tabby to shake. I shouldn't have bothered; hers wasn't coming.

"Okay, follow me."

Tabby turned and walked down West Forty-fourth Street without me. Avril and I threw each other looks, and I turned to follow Tabby, leaving Avril standing in front of the Carney.

"I thought we were going to do a walk-through?" I said, catching up with her.

"We are. Just not at the theater. We're going to be working on the second floor of a dance studio we've reserved a half block down West Forty-fourth."

At a nondescript metal door, Tabby jangled a ring of keys from her pocket and, finding the one she wanted from the ring of twenty, drove it into the doorknob. She turned it counterclockwise, and the door scraped open on its hinges.

Above the doorway hung a small sign that read "A Chorus Line Dance Studio." Judging from the boxy sign's cracked face, exposed wiring, and missing light bulbs, I guessed it had been a while since A Chorus Line had dazzled anybody with its own marquee. Tabby halted before going inside.

"Harper, it's critical that you have *all* the stage blocking and script memorized by day's end. You can do that, can't you?"

She moved ahead without waiting for my answer. I felt an uneasy feeling rise up like a ringing warning alarm. We stepped onto the landing inside the doorway, little more than a cramped two-by-two space, and I followed Tabby up a narrow slat-board staircase that led to the second floor. The not-for-the-claustrophobic stairwell grew colder, darker as we climbed, and I listened to the reverberation of our shoes.

Tabby flipped on a bank of ceiling lights when we arrived on the second floor, bringing the dance studio more or less to life.

The studio was a grand, simple room—a rectangular matchbox with a well-worn, once-beautiful hardwood floor dark as burnt gold. Around the edges, time had shadowed its original stain, making the border of the floor look like a giant picture frame. The floor revealed its scars, a million scuff marks from rhythmic tap dancers, strictly ballroom beginners, and modern jazz stylists.

Tabby attempted to turn on the heat by adjusting an ancient thermostat bracketed to the wall just above an old upright piano. She unbuttoned her coat, unwinding the dark scarf she had wrapped around her neck, and hung it on a hook in the corner.

A shaft of light poured in from a row of windows where the wall met the high ceiling, and sunlight painted a foursquare court in the center of the dance floor.

I removed my own hat, coat, and gloves. From behind me, I could hear Tabby muttering, saying something garbled underneath her breath, and I turned to see her shake her head in disgust.

"Is anything wrong?" I asked. Tabby pursed her lips.

"Molly put us in a real bind. I don't have time to start from scratch, walking the new understudy through basic blocking for the show. Sorry, I just don't."

I looked up at a round schoolhouse clock with black casing hanging above the door. Its loud ticking filled the space. Two forty. This was going to be a very long day.

"And don't take it the wrong way," Tabby continued, "but I don't think you were the best choice for understudy. I want to be up front about that. I know twenty actresses in New York who could walk in off the street and nail this role. But I wasn't there when Ben made the call. *Avril* was. I was putting out production fires somewhere else when she got him all excited, and you got your lucky break."

Tabby rubbed her hands together, stepping away from me as if brushing off one order of business before moving on to the next.

Inside me, something snapped. Maybe a year spent languishing in Chicago had scraped my emotions raw, but Tabby's words struck. Had she confined her slander to me, I might have just let it go, but she didn't and now I couldn't. I walked across the battered dance studio until Tabby was in arms' reach. She turned, caught off guard by my confrontation, reading anger in my face.

"I was hired by the show's director, Tabby, so my being here is legit whether you see it that way or not. You can judge my ability against twenty or two hundred actresses if you want, but until you've seen me act, frankly, you don't know what you're talking about."

I stepped in closer, close enough to see Tabby's eyes widen and her nerves flinch beneath porous skin. She crossed her arms, involuntarily shielding herself like I'd seen her do with the clipboard.

"But what I really want you to remember, Tabby," I said, "is that Avril is like a sister to me, and I would seriously go after anyone who tried to hurt her or tarnish her reputation. Likewise, my respect for Ben is *huge*, and I stick up for my friends. You can say whatever you want about me, but you're going to regret it if you make even one more snide remark about Ben or Avril."

I turned and walked back to my corner, wiping away the spontaneous tears that came with my sudden eruption of emotions. I could feel my heart throbbing in my chest, banging away like it was trying to pound its way out. I felt the sharp sting of remorse because I was suppose to be *different* now, a Christian, a follower of the Prince of Peace. What had gotten into me?

Instantly, His Spirit nudged and I squinted my eyes to listen. He'd given me His forgiveness, so shouldn't I be willing to extend some to Tabby?

The thought sickened me. Chewing Tabby out one minute, only to turn around the next and tell her how sorry I was. But I did turn around. Tabby hadn't budged. Her cold, emotionless face, however, was finally showing some color: red. Her eyes had thinned, narrowing to a steely squint, and I lost the words to my apology.

"I doubt you'll be around long enough to make me regret anything," she said. "Ben's under the impression you have your lines memorized. I happen to know your script wasn't even delivered until yesterday."

Tabby collected herself. She ambled over to a stack of folding chairs leaning against the wall, clasping onto one and dragging it back across the dance floor. I moved a few feet closer, certain my window for apology had closed. Tabby removed the copy of the director's script from her shoulder bag and opened it before sitting.

"So, we're going to have you read through the whole script, Scene 1 until the finale, and you can show Broadway how you memorized an entire play in twenty-four hours while you boxed up all your belongings, said good-bye to friends, and moved yourself cross-country to New York. This should be easy for a talented actor like you."

♫

As promised, Ben released the cast and crew to enjoy the New Year's Eve festivities just before six. Avril's idea of celebrating began with a shopping spree, all part of her plan to roll out the red carpet and welcome me to New York.

She knew all the pricey Manhattan boutiques and jewelry stores, including a small clothing emporium on the Upper West Side called Odessa that resembled a silk merchant's shop and smelled like patchouli.

Avril insisted on buying me something "New Yorkish" to wear to rehearsals and chose a black fitted chemise. I tried it on in one of Odessa's two fitting rooms, a space smaller than an airplane bathroom. Its only privacy came from a paisley pull curtain that, even when closed, still exposed me from the knee down. I peeked at the price tag: $185. Avril insisted we get it, and after a few minutes in an argument I knew I would lose, I left Odessa with the black chemise.

We walked along crowded streets back toward Times Square, our stomachs full of pepper chicken, veggies, and brown rice from an upscale Cuban Chinese restaurant on upper Broadway. I was tired from my ordeal at the airport, two exhausting hours spent in the company of Tabby Walker, and the late hour. Times Square was jam-packed with New Year's Eve revelers and heavily garbed tourists standing behind blue police barriers. Over the sound of noisemakers, we could hear music from a rock band playing further down in the square, and see the sparkling ball Dick Clark planned to drop at the stroke of midnight.

"Let's get a closer look!"

Avril took my hand, one mittened glove clutching another, and led us careening through the raucous crowd. We stopped beneath a lamppost on the corner of Forty-fourth and Broadway. I could see fogging breath escape from every face into the bitterly cold night. The rocking of the mass made me dizzy, and I tipped backward only to be held up by the throng.

A digital countdown clock in Times Square ticked down, and for the first time I noticed how truly late it was. The strangest feeling hit me at one minute to midnight: the sensation that we were all gathering on a street corner in New York to watch the death of one year and the birth of another. The last seconds of my terrible year were passing away, and a new year was beginning. *A new beginning.* The ball started its slow decent, the crowd chanted the countdown. They might as well have been counting down the end of the old me and the rebirth of the new.

The idea revived me, like cold wind in my face. It was symbolic, ceremonial. God had taken me from one world, Chicago, and placed me here in another, New York. From friendless to reunion with Avril, from jobless to work, from faithless to belief, and from lifeless to life.

The frantic crowd noise splashed in my ears. Above us, brilliant and beautiful fireworks went off in the skies over Manhattan. Revelers shouted with holiday cheers as tears streamed down my face. Next to me Avril stood laughing and happy as she'd been a year ago.

We stood in the din of a whirling moment, the wind blushing Avril's cheeks scarlet. Then the New York sky opened up and all around us fell the graceful, dreamlike snow of angels. A billion specks of ashen ticker tape fluttered into Times Square. Twirling and tumbling, they landed on our coat sleeves in icy white dots. Snowfall speckled Avril's red wool cap and the tips of her blonde hair. She screamed something to me, but the words were lost in the noise of the celebrating crowd.

"Happy new year," she shouted again, closer to my ear, and I wondered if the moment was as surreal to her.

"It's time to go," I shouted.

"Wait, wait. Let me take your picture!" Avril lifted her cell phone, excited by the moment. I turned my back to Times Square and smiled a sleepy, long-day smile, and Avril clicked the shutter, giggling.

"Okay, I'm sending this to your cell phone," she said, using her thumbs to text into her phone. "You can show all the folks back home you've finally made it in New York."

Past the stroke of midnight, we were off to find a taxi, running like Cinderella afraid the spell would break. We hailed a cab two blocks from the square and climbed into the heated back seat where I collapsed from exhaustion.

Riding in the cozy darkness of a heated New York City cab, I watched out the window as we wove through Midtown South to Greenwich Village. New York's neon lights rolled past us in a blur of blue and orange and purple. I realized then that I was a survivor, pulled from the icy waters by the mysterious hand of a stranger, my gown still dripping, my open mouth taking in a deep, rich, life-saving breaths.

"Thank You," I whispered to the Lord. Avril rested her arm across my shoulders, and I could feel sleep wrapping around me like a coil. My final thought ... a shapeless, silent gratitude for the miraculous appearing in my life.

~ Six ~

Avril brushed a fallen lock of blonde hair back in place as she stepped into the kitchen and opened the refrigerator door. Inside, she found a green and silver foil bag of gourmet coffee that looked like a Christmas present and proceeded to pour a heap of the dark brown coffee beans into a Braun grinder sitting next to an automatic espresso machine.

"Get any sleep last night?" she asked.

"I would have loved getting nine hours instead of six, but I'm more or less recharged to go another round with Tabby. Yesterday was brutal."

Avril pressed the button on the coffee grinder, drowning out all hope of further conversation. I picked myself up from the bar stool at the kitchen island and walked into the living room as she tap-tap-tapped, grinding the beans to a perfect consistency.

It was a small apartment, less than eight hundred square feet, but the morning sunlight filled it with the optimism of a new year. The tones were cool and brown; they reminded me of the sands of Malibu. On one wall were bookshelves filled with a brainy collection of hardcover classics, silver-framed photographs of Avril and her parents, and Chinese pottery. A small blue water globe no larger than a baseball caught my eye. I touched it with my fingers, causing the earth to bobble slightly on its stand. When it settled, I could see the United States, from New York to California, making the country look small from sea to shining sea.

I watched Avril pour a bottle of Evian water into the coffeemaker and flip the switch to brew. She joined me in the living room, where I was sitting in a comfy brown chair facing the bookshelves and a fireplace with white painted bricks. A moment later the sound of percolating coffee filled the apartment like a relaxing fountain. The aroma of French roast soon followed, and we soaked it up like the meditational comfort of a weekend spa.

"As soon as I heard Molly was leaving, I thought how perfect you'd be in this role," said Avril, dovetailing one conversation into another. "Ben's choice of Helen is obvious because she's box-office gold on Broadway, and the character of Audrey Bradford has always been played by an older woman. But his casting choice of Molly as a younger Audrey Bradford was kind of interesting, don't you think? Ben told me he believes there could be an even greater potential for drama if Audrey is played by a younger actress. Of course, he'd never say that around Helen. You should have seen her face the day Molly was introduced as her understudy. Well, I guess you didn't have to—you caught some of that vibe yesterday."

"But wouldn't it be weird if Helen could only do the first act, and a younger Audrey Bradford came out for the rest of the show?"

"I wondered the same thing. But Ben is pretty confident that *if* Helen couldn't perform, he'd know well in advance of her ever taking the stage. And with only forty-two performances, the odds of her becoming ill during the show are minimal. She agreed to a physical with her doctor, and I guess passed with flying colors."

The coffeemaker puffed its last gasp. Avril proceeded behind the island to pour us each a cup of day starter. She returned carrying two mugs to the living room with poise, and handed one to me. I blew delicately across its surface before setting it down to cool.

"I meant to ask you," Avril said, "does Sydney know you're here in New York?"

Sydney Bloom, our beloved theatrical agent, our wise and witty mother hen, had loved actors all of her fifty-plus years, Avril and me for the last seven. She was equally at home talking shop over lunch at a kosher deli on Fifty-first Street, or a wheat grass bar on Santa Monica Boulevard. I loved to picture her in the place she loved best, her beach house in Monterey.

"I left Sydney a message," I said. "Just told her I was flying to New York, but I didn't say why. I didn't want to share my news over voice mail."

I'd fallen in love with acting the day I stepped into a crowded theater class at Northwestern in Chicago. At first, The Fundamentals of Acting was just a freshman elective, a stop on the road to my English degree and nothing more. But by the end of the semester, I was no longer content simply to *read* Shakespeare's *Romeo and Juliet*—I wanted to *be* Juliet. The next fall, I switched my major to drama and theater and began soaking up the art form with other theater students, including Avril and a bumbling young theater major named Ben Hughes who discovered his talent lay not in acting but directing. We dubbed ourselves "The Misfits" after the 1961 John Huston movie starring Clark Gable and Marilyn Monroe, mostly because none of us felt like we fit in anywhere else. We were a tight-knit group in and out of the classroom, writing and performing student productions, blocking our scenes, and trying our hand at improvisation. We pooled together our meager dollars to root through vintage clothing stores in Chicago for authentic costumes and crazy props.

We fought off butterflies fluttering in our underfed stomachs each opening night, peering through the thick black curtain and counting heads under the houselights of the campus theater. We were young romantics, dreaming of somehow making a career out of pretending.

What's the best part of acting? It's the indescribable feeling of being someone you are and someone you're not, all at the same time. Acting is finding a character that's in you, forgetting yourself, and then bringing out this whole other person. Character is all that matters when you're onstage.

"I never do this," Sydney told me one night outside Chicago's Lookingglass Theatre after a midseason performance of Tennessee Williams's *The Glass Menagerie*. She handed me her business card, which I was understandably leery to take. We stood outside the theater chatting, wrapped in heavy wool scarves and thick winter coats to stave off Lake Michigan's bitter winds. Her cheeks were pink from the chill, and I remember thinking she wasn't made for exposure to the elements. Her trademark designer glasses, oversized purple frames, fogged with every breath that puffed out of her round face.

"Call me next week if you think you can stand talking to a real agent," Sydney said, as if there were hardly a worse thing a person could do.

"Sydney will be thrilled you've landed a role in the first New York revival of *Apartment 19* in thirty years," Avril said now.

"I know, but I've wanted to avoid 'the conversation.'"

"Which conversation?"

"The one that follows a thirty-year-old actress who hasn't worked in a year. The gentle pep talk your agent gives you when she knows your career is over."

Avril waved my argument away with a brush of her delicate hand. "You're crazy. Sydney will be thrilled you're here. You should call her this morning to let her know."

"Avril, Sydney and I haven't spoken in six months," I confessed. "We stopped talking after *Grease* ended, when there wasn't a job out there for me and we both felt awkward with her 'something will turn up' talks."

"But all that's changed now. You're back on your feet, on Broadway no less. Sydney will love hearing the news."

I blew across the surface of my coffee again before taking a sip. The flavor was strong and black, and by the time I took my second sip, I realized that Avril was right. Sure, I was broke, and going back into the world of unemployment in six weeks, and my acting job didn't involve any real stage acting. And, yeah, I was single without prospects and almost every stitch of clothing I owned was still locked away in my checked suitcase, lost somewhere in the dungeons of LaGuardia or maybe Philly. But I wasn't going to worry, and not just because I had a good cup of coffee and a temporary roof over my head. I had at least two other incalculably good things going for me: my vivid memory of God's well-timed rescue, and my belief He could do it again whenever He pleased.

"I'll call her," I said, clinking my cup to hers.

"Happy new year."

I showered in a tiny white-tiled bathroom Avril had "colorized" by adding a yellow daisy curtain, a matching floor rug, and photographs of wildflowers arranged on the wall beside the medicine cabinet.

I dressed in dark slacks I'd stuffed in my carry-on and buttoned up the black chemise Avril had purchased for me the night before, wearing it untucked. Judging from the full-length mirror in the bedroom, everything fit the look of a New York winter: basic flats, a red wool scarf I borrowed from Avril, and finally, my made-for-Manhattan leather jacket.

"Can you get yourself back to the subway?" Avril asked as I cut across the living room and rattled open the latches and chain locks on the apartment door.

"Think so. See you at the Carney later, right?"

"Right after your rehearsal with Tabby," Avril said, teasing me as she refilled her coffee. I gave her a friendly "oh, shut up" look before closing the door behind me.

Life had been so easy in Chicago with Avril, and our yearlong stint in *Grease* was the icing on the cake. Avril played the female lead, Sandy, and I was one of the sassy (but nameless) Pink Ladies. It didn't matter that my name wasn't written in lights on a marquee, and I really didn't think much about it. I was happy to be working in a career field known for an 85 percent unemployment rate.

What kept me financially afloat was a commercial I shot for a nighttime cold medicine, Drowz-U-Tab. That one-day commercial shoot rewarded me with $8,500 per quarter in residuals, a "performance" fee paid to actors whenever the commercial aired on TV.

$30,000 for one day of sitting up in bed and pretending to suffer the insomnia associated with a runny nose. The truth was, after that first check arrived, I never slept more like a baby.

But all good things must come to an end. The last Drowz-U-Tab check arrived the week after the plush red curtains closed on Ben Hughes's all-that-and-a-milkshake production of *Grease*. That's when Avril boarded a jet to Boston for the next act in her breezy, triumphant career, and I was set adrift in a sea of icebergs.

I stepped off the subway car in midtown Manhattan, a short twenty-minute ride. The smell of hot tar and diesel fuel thickened the air like the breath of a dragon. I walked the remaining blocks to the dance studio, studying the faces of New Yorkers on the street. It was time for Scene 2 with Tabby Walker. I prayed I'd do better this time, hold my tongue, and be the person my faith said I was.

With closed eyes I recited my lines, practicing a Zen-like concentration. I stood in the middle of the makeshift stage Tabby and I had constructed using folding chairs and an Asian rug we found rolled up in a closet. I juggled the recitation of Audrey Bradford's words with hitting my mark or remembering to bolt out of a chair when I recited a certain line in Act 1. After I'd surprised Tabby by knowing the script *off book* the day before, she'd decided to up the ante on New Year's Day, running me through *all* the stage blocking for Act 1 and 2 in a single morning. *What was her problem?*

Tabby threw a line to me from her do-it-yourself director's chair, Ben's master script open on her lap like a fifty-state road atlas. I began to perspire as I concentrated on my lines and moved to the correct stage positions Tabby had marked out on the rug and the studio floor. I thought about the difference watching Ben's rehearsal DVD would have made, but it was too late for that now. I also ignored the dirty looks Tabby gave me when I messed up, and just did the best I could.

After a long monologue, I stood in character, eyes still closed, waiting for Tabby to throw me my next cue. Silence. I opened my eyes to find Tabby lost in a text message on her cell phone. I cleared my throat.

"Okay, we've been at this long enough," she said. "It's almost eleven thirty. Someone is supposed to bring lunch here so we don't have to leave. Since she's not here, I suggest we take a break while I go see what the problem is."

Tabby slid off her perch on the wooden bar stool, dropped her master script to the floor, and rounded the corner out of sight.

I let the weight of concentration fall off my shoulders like a pack from a mule and wandered off the improvised stage, taking a dancer's towel from a folded stack near the doorway to dab my face and fore-head. How long had it been since I'd worked so hard and sweated like this? On the wall opposite the mirrors, I took a sip from an old turn-wheel drinking fountain like I hadn't seen since grade school. I grasped the star-shaped gear, turned it away from me, and bent down to taste the cool water arcing from its spigot.

From my position at the drinking fountain, I could hear Tabby talking on her cell phone around the corner.

"I walked her through the script and we're working on block-ing … like I said, not great. I mean, I respect your decision, Ben, but we both know we could have called in Tira Bancroft, Melanie Catsburn, Elizabeth Benton—any one of them could have nailed this, and they're all local. What? I guess, but Ben, I'm basically teaching a rudimentary acting class today. Harper's so far behind the rest of the cast she isn't ... yes, she knows her lines, but ... yes, she's hitting the blocking, but ..."

Tabby's voice rose and fell like waves in a sea of churning drama. It was clear that Tabby didn't care if I overheard her.

"Whatever you say, Ben. I was a professional when I woke up this morning, and I'll ... right, if you want her to work, I'll make Harper work."

It was the last I heard of their conversation. Tabby's heavy footsteps descended the stairwell to the street below, where I heard the outside metal door hit the wall with a smack.

I took liberty with the break, lying down on the rug to catch my breath. I slowed my breathing and tried to relax every aching muscle in my body. God had showed Himself again, protecting me from Tabby's sniper fire. I thanked Him, like I'd done the night before, for bringing me to New York. And for sending Bella to run into me at the used bookstore on Michigan Avenue in Chicago when my life was a mess.

Bella had invited me to the stone church on LaSalle Street. She'd held my hands when they trembled, sat with me on the back row in the church. Listened quietly while I cried, and prayed with me when I told her how hard life was, how hopeless I felt. She shared her faith with me, told me she didn't believe everything was hopeless, and asked if I believed Jesus had risen from the dead, and "was anything impossible for God?"

Two months before Christmas I'd been baptized. Bella flew home to North Dakota before Christmas break, and Ben called to invite me to New York just days after Christmas. Just like that, things had fallen into place after a year of telephones that wouldn't ring. I felt like a blind trapeze artist, somehow catching the bar with chalky hands at the peak of its swing. I had no clue how the trick was done, only that I wasn't the one doing it.

Ten minutes later, Tabby returned with sandwiches. I sat up on the rug, then stood to my feet and made my way toward her in the doorway.

"That took a few minutes," she said. "I had to sharpen my teeth in someone's hide."

Tabby dropped a brown deli sack on top of the upright piano. I heard one of the low notes vibrate inside the wooden shell.

"Is something wrong?" I asked.

Tabby snorted. "In my job, there's always something wrong. I explicitly told her to bring the sandwiches to the studio, *not the theater*. So, what does she do? She takes the sandwiches to the theater. Unbelievable."

"I overheard your conversation with Ben," I said, because I couldn't pretend I hadn't.

She darted her eyes toward me.

"So," she remarked. "Ben wants you as Helen's backup, that's the way it goes."

Tabby wadded up her sandwich bag into a tight ball. She tossed it at the small trash basket near the door, and her shot hit the rim and ricocheted out the studio door.

Thoughts of Bella's care for me were still fresh on my mind, as was a trace of regret for not apologizing to Tabby the day before. I decided to extend an olive branch, hoping she wouldn't snap it off with her teeth.

"Tabby, I was surprised when I got Ben's phone call too," I said. "But I think things happen for a reason. I appreciate the time you've devoted these last two days, and I hope as the show moves forward, you and I can learn to get along."

She recoiled, flashing a look that was something between condescension and total dismissal.

"Harper, you and I are *not* going to be friends. It's my job to make sure you can take Helen's place for a night in the unlikely event we have to send you out onstage. But thankfully, it's not in my job description to be your buddy because I don't have the time or the interest."

She picked up her cell phone, eyes scanning up and down the screen like she was reading another text message. I wanted to say something kind and brilliant, like Bella could. I wanted us to be friends, not adversaries, but my mind was a blank.

"Let's eat," Tabby said. "I want to wrap up as quickly as possible this afternoon. I have to get back to the theater. It's the first day of dress rehearsal, and I can think of a hundred other things I'd rather be doing."

♫

By two o'clock on New Year's Day, the show's costume designer, Phyllis Holcromb, had fitted all eleven cast members into their costumes with the help of her assistant, Mira.

My exhaustive morning rehearsal with Tabby over, I milled about backstage marveling at the transformation of the cast wearing their costumes. Harriet Greene pointed back with her thumb as she exited the fitting room.

"Harper, I think Phyllis is looking for you. She has costumes for you to try on."

Harriet was wearing her landlord's costume, a man's tan slacks and vest over a white business shirt. Though the role was originally written for a man, Ben recast the landlord, Mr. Hedges, with a rotund African-American woman, Ms. Hedges. I'd seen Harriet at rehearsal the day before, joking around with some of the other actors.

"Thanks," I said, entering the wardrobe room.

"There you are," Phyllis said, as if she'd been looking for me all morning. She spoke with two pins pressed together in her mouth, hemming a costume at a sewing machine. She took the pins out. "Your costumes are over there, Harper. Ben gave me your sizes and sent me shopping, but you'll have to try everything on. You're the last I have today."

Phyllis pointed to a rolling wardrobe rack half filled with costume changes. An elegant black evening dress caught my eye, hung on the rack's end with a string of gaudy large pearls looped over the hanger.

"Size six, right?"

"I'm a size four," I told her.

Phyllis stopped the sewing machine.

"Shoes, dear. Size six."

She pointed to four cardboard shoeboxes sitting on the bottom rack below my wardrobe. I crouched down and shimmied the lid off the box on top. Inside, a hot pair of black designer heels rested in a bundle of thin white packing paper.

"These shoes are amazing," I said. I felt the soft Italian leather against my fingertips, remembering the life I'd once lived.

I stood up to thumb through my costumes. A vintage 1950s black cocktail dress, the evening gown, black wet-leather pants like a rock star might wear, a frilly chemise as red as bloody roses. Phyllis joined me to admire the eccentric collection.

"Well, what do you think?" Phyllis asked.

"They're beautiful," I said, holding up the short cocktail skirt against me, admiring it in the large oval of mirror on a stand. Phyllis looked pleased with her work.

"I found that at Gargoyle, a vintage clothing store off Broadway. Ben called me and specifically asked for a drastically different look for you than he wanted for Helen."

"What do you mean?"

"He said he wanted Helen's Audrey Bradford to look like she rarely goes out, and your Audrey Bradford to look like she never stays in."

Phyllis pulled the plastic cover off the dress for me in one quick motion. "You'll look and feel gorgeous in this gown, Harper. It's Versace."

"Oh my. It's too bad I'll never wear it."

"Well"—Phyllis tilted her head sympathetically—"it's a funny last-minute detail, but Ben gets these ideas, and he calls me at odd hours from the back of taxi cabs or wherever he might be. I just jot down his impressions for costumes and hit the boutiques."

I ducked behind the changing screen and emerged minutes later in the long black Versace gown. Even in bare feet it was gorgeous, and powerful. I felt like I was someone else watching me in the mirror. Tabby stopped dead when she entered the fitting room and saw me.

"Do you like it?" I asked Tabby.

She hesitated, poker-faced. "It looks fine," she finally said. "When you're finished, see Laura in makeup. She'll need to try out some looks on you. Wear the dress so she can see what you'll be wearing. Oh, and make sure nothing gets on it."

Tabby disappeared around the corner before she'd finished her sentence, off to corral other actors for the start of dress rehearsal, I presumed. I left the shoes in their box, making my way down the long backstage hall toward makeup. Helen appeared from her dressing room just as I passed by her door and halted when she saw me.

"What is *that* they've got you wearing?" she said in a voice every bit as disapproving as Audrey Bradford herself.

"It's one of my costumes," I said. "I was just trying it on …"

Helen frowned at the dress, her eyes darting to mine, then back down to the dress. She turned without speaking, then snapped down the narrow hallway, her patent leather flats striking the floor like she was giving it a spanking.

♪◌

"Dinner?" Avril offered.

"Yes, please."

"You look tired," she said, sitting next to me in the back row of the Carney following the first dress rehearsal. The houselights had been lowered like a Christmas candlelight service, and the effect was calming. Avril crossed one leg over the other. She'd cast off her Roxy Dupree costume and come home to her Avril clothes, always more California than New York.

Maybe it was the lighting, but it suddenly struck me just what a star she was becoming. Watching Avril bring Roxy Dupree to life on the Carney stage, seeing her languid and beautiful now after rehearsal, so easy with this vagabond life, it felt like catching a glimpse of someone just before the inevitable moment arrives when stardom catapults them into the stratosphere. Soon Avril would be one of those celebrities who dons dark sunglasses to dodge paparazzi, drives incognito behind the tinted windows of her Escalade, and walks Hollywood's red carpet on Oscar night with cameras flashing. Hollywood's fast lane would one day whisk her away.

Harriet and another actor, Melissa Ginch, approached us, taking silent steps up the long aisle toward the exit.

"Time to check out the new girl," Harriet said in jest. She and Melissa drew closer.

"I hope Tabby didn't wear you out today. Molly couldn't get out of here fast enough."

"Still here," I said, reaching up to shake Harriet's hand, which she offered without hesitation. It almost felt like a high five. "We ran the entire show this morning."

"Sounds like you're doing the same thing we're doing, but it took us all day to get through dress rehearsal."

"I think it's going to be a marvelous show," Avril said, her voice a confident arbiter of unseen possibilities. "One more full rehearsal tomorrow, then we open."

Marshall Graham joined us. Now the landlord, the witness in apartment 20, and the police detective—their respective roles in the show—formed a semicircle around Avril and me.

"So, what's the verdict? Are we going out for drinks?" Marshall asked, draping one arm around Harriet's neck and the other around Melissa's. "After all, it is both Friday night and New Year's Day."

"Oh, here we go," Harriet said. "Time to corrupt the new girl."

"Harriet, I'm sure Harper's been around theater long enough. She knows acting is just a ruse, an excuse to go out for cocktails afterwards," Melissa said.

"Absolutely," Marshall said. "We're part of a long and distinguished tradition."

Avril turned to me, raising her eyebrows for my vote. This put a wrinkle in our dinner plans, but acting is by its nature a social affair, and I could tell she wanted to go. All I needed to do was say yes, and the five of us would be off to the nearest Manhattan watering hole. The bar would be nice too, a ritzy lounge in a five-star hotel within easy walking distance of the Theater District. The tables would be a polished dark mahogany, glossy even in dim lighting. There'd be brass rails running along the bar for elbows and matching foot rails beneath for tired feet. Bottles of colorful booze, stacked in layers of different shapes and sizes, would be displayed behind the mirrored bar. We would all bond and exchange backstage gossip and share the real scoop on what it was like working with the great Helen Payne.

But I'd waited so long to hear His voice. *And now He was speaking.*

Since leaving Chicago I'd waited to hear something, anything from the God Bella affectionately referred to as "Abba" and whom I knew best as the Rescuer who made my phone ring. I recognized His voice instantly, soft and gentle as a reed in the sand, but it boomed against my spirit like the breaking of an ocean wave on the shore.

He wanted me to tell the truth. In the past, I'd never had any trouble telling half-truths. But my Rescuer wasn't keen on half-truths. In fact, He had nothing to do with them.

Avril swiveled toward me in her seat, an obvious cue. I paused to think about the night of Ben's phone call back in Chicago and what I'd been mulling over in my mind before that call. How I'd been begging God for a miracle when He suddenly carved a narrow passageway out of my despair with Ben's voice: *Would you like to come to New York and be in my show?*

"Actually," I said, surprised to hear myself saying the words, "I was thinking I'd catch a church service tonight after dinner. There's a beautiful old church I saw on my way to the Carney yesterday. I noticed they're having a special New Year's Day service."

Harriet's eyes widened. Melissa reacted with the look of someone repulsed, and Marshall extended his chin as if deliberating the words of a village idiot. Now they all knew: Helen's new understudy was "religious." If they'd lacked something to gossip about over drinks before, they lacked no more.

"Okay, well that sounds like a big *no*," Melissa said, backing her way out from Marshall's arm. Avril looked embarrassed and watched the rest of the cast mates peel off toward the door.

"We'll catch up with you later," Marshall said as they disappeared under the red glowing EXIT sign.

Avril stared at me.

"I never expected that out of you. A church service? Maybe a little warning next time?"

"I meant to ask you earlier about the service, but it's been so crazy I hadn't had a chance."

Avril got up from her chair without making eye contact with me. "I think it's fine, but you didn't have to scare everybody off. I don't even remember you *going* to church when we lived in Chicago."

"I didn't then, but I *really* want to go," I said, touching her arm. "And I want you to come with me. A stranger in a strange city and all that. Will you?" I lifted my eyebrows into an obvious *please*.

"It's not even Sunday."

"Avril, you'll love it. It's a beautiful old church with a Roman arch doorway in front, and they've hung a wreath in the middle and strung it with Christmas lights."

"You're talking about the one on West Forty-seventh?"

"I think that's it. What if we just went to dinner, then spent some time in a quiet church reflecting on the past and praying for the future?"

I wondered what was going on in Avril's head as she paused to think. Maybe she grasped that church was a sanctuary, a sacred place of prayer. Maybe she'd say yes for her love of me, or because Jon had already called her to say he was busy. Maybe she'd think it could be fun, that church was just another kind of show in different part of Broadway.

"Okay, I'll go," she finally said. Whatever her reason, I felt an understated but indescribable sensation of joy. I'd done what He'd asked, and we weren't following the gang to the bar as we always had in Chicago. We were following the Spirit to church.

~ SEVEN ~

A Gothic stained-glass window glowed bright with yellows and blues, like a medieval rainbow in front of the Fellowship Community Church. We stood motionless on the sidewalk, feeling nervous about entering and yet warmly received by its invitation to find sanctuary and rest inside.

"It's beautiful," Avril said. A reverence for the sacred had softened her voice

I thought of Hollywood's old black-and-white movies *The Bishop's Wife* and *It's a Wonderful Life* and how the stone chapel seemed to welcome Avril and me like small-town memories of a place we'd never been.

I took hold of the metal pipe handrail running up the center of the steps, cold even through my gloves, and together we climbed five stone stairs to the entrance.

Avril reached for the black wrought iron handle on the wooden door. She pushed the lever down with her thumb, and we stepped into a well-lit vestibule.

Two women greeted us in a small reception area; a volunteer wearing a name tag that read "Tabitha," and a college-age girl whose name I didn't catch. They invited us to hang up our things on a row of wall pegs or drape them on box cubbies below already piled over with coats, scarves, and hats.

Avril and I shed our winter coats and walked into the sanctuary. The room was larger than I'd expected, illuminated with ceiling lights above a long aisle. Church pews arranged in symmetrical rows on either side faced a slightly elevated pulpit. The gathered crowd of sixty or so seemed unabashedly friendly. They stood together in groups of two and three, smiling and engaged in animated conversations.

A petite, plain-looking woman reached out to us with a small, delicate hand.

"Hi, I'm Katie," she said, a soft Midwesterner's accent rounding out some of her words. I took her hand and shook it. Katie's looks were striking in their innocence. Her face projected an uncomplicated brightness, like fresh snowfall on farmland, and her eyes were like two islands floating on the surface of a deep blue ocean. She dressed in casual blue jeans and a beautiful duck white button-up that told she didn't lose much sleep over what the fashionable crowd at Odessa was wearing.

"Hi, I'm Harper. This is my friend Avril."

"Is this your first time visiting Fellowship Community Church?"

"Yes."

"Welcome," she said, letting go of my hand to shake Avril's. "We're not sure what to expect for turnout tonight, because we've never done a New Year's Day service before, but we're glad you came."

A young man hurried to Katie's side, giving off the same impression of youthfulness with his cropped hair and a thin beard he looked barely old enough to grow.

"Hi, I'm David," he said. "First, welcome. Second, can I interrupt your conversation for just a second?" He turned to Katie.

"Has Ruthann come in yet?"

"I haven't seen her," Katie said.

David chewed at his bottom lip as if sorting through a problem.

"Okay, well … I'll figure something out," he said before dashing off. A few feet away, David turned back as if remembering his manners and waved to us. "Nice meeting you."

"That's David, my husband," Katie said, looking won over by even his clumsy moves. "Ruthann's one of the students who's supposed to lead worship tonight, but it looks like she's not going to make it."

"Oh dear," Avril said.

"Don't worry. David will find a replacement."

"Is David a pastor here?" I asked, hoping I didn't sound judgmental. They both just seemed so young. Early, maybe mid-twenties, but certainly no older.

"Well, he's the *only* pastor." Katie laughed. "We're a new church plant still in our first year."

I thought Avril would say "Oh dear" again, but maybe it was just me who was thinking it.

"It looks like the service is about to start," Katie said, looking up at David, who was behind a microphone on the platform. "If you'd like to find a seat, we can talk again after."

We sat on the right-side pews where most of the group had congregated. College students mainly, probably from NYU and Columbia University, Avril guessed. A third of the group was made up of Asian students. There was also a surprising number of older folks sprinkled throughout, giving the church an open-to-all feel.

"If I can have everyone's attention," David said, drawing our eyes to the stage. "I want to thank everybody for coming out tonight.

We're going to start this first New Year's Day service with prayer and worship. I've asked Bobby Mars to kind of jump in here at the last second. So why don't we go to the Lord in prayer while Bobby gets set up."

An unassuming dark-haired man, thirty-something, started making his way to the elevated platform. Bobby looked like the kind of guy who probably collected *Star Wars* action figures in junior high. He wore a black T-shirt and black jeans, and his pale, skinny arms jutted out of his shirt sleeves like pretzel sticks. He picked up a shiny Martin guitar the color of caramel and tuned it quietly while David led us in prayer.

When I opened my eyes, David stepped down from the pulpit, and Bobby invited the crowd to stand. He stood before the microphone, strummed the first guitar chord, and opened his mouth to sing. Out of the mouth of this skinny white guy poured the soulful voice of a black gospel singer. His first note shocked the heart of the stone cathedral until the room began to beat with the rhythm of a Southern-fried Tennessee tent revival. People stood to clap their hands, lifting them up in praise.

Bobby closed his eyes as he sang, emotion welling up in his taut face. He sang hymn after hymn, song after song, one rolling into another. His voice was pitch perfect, and he never once looked for lyrics or glanced at sheet music.

I've seen lots of performers in my life, professional actors who knew how to milk a crowd and play to their emotions, but Bobby didn't look or sound like he was merely performing. He looked like a blues singer turned out in worship to God. Avril and I sang along with the unfamiliar songs as best we could, trying to read the lyric sheet left for us on the pew, a pointless exercise since Bobby didn't follow it anyway. On the last song, a guitar string snapped and hung limp from the instrument like a fallen contestant in a game of endurance.

Bobby hit a high note and held it, arching his head back, his eyes closed behind thick, black-framed glasses. Sweat rolled off his forehead, trailing past his temples, and dampened the ends of his bangs. The church fell silent, watching color bleed into his face. Bobby looked like he was in pain, a flagellant holding his scarring hand over an open flame. His head rolled from side to side as he contorted his mouth to wring out every drop of his soul. Finally, when his frail body had exhausted its strength and breath, Bobby stopped singing, and the music was gone.

A few in the congregation clapped their hands, but most were too emotionally stirred to move. A weird electricity surged in the air. Bobby muttered a few unintelligible words of thanks and praise to the heavenly Father, pointing heavenward with his index finger. He left the guitar onstage, leaning it against an amplifier, and returned to his seat.

"Thanks, Bobby," David said, drawing a deep breath. "That was amazing. It's been a while since you've been up here, so … whoa, thank you."

Avril leaned in and whispered, "We should find out if his songs are available on iTunes." I nodded, keeping my eyes on David.

"Since it's New Year's Day, I thought instead of having a regular message, we would break into small groups and just take time to reflect, get to know each other a little better, and pray for one another. So you guys can just get into groups however you feel led."

Clusters of people began moving around the room, drawing together in groups of four or five. Avril and I were absorbed into the small group nearest us.

I was glad to see Katie sit down in the pew directly ahead of us, making ours a group of six, including two female college students, an older woman, Avril, and me.

"I'm glad David decided to do this," Katie said, once we'd settled in. "We can talk about anything. The idea is just to get to know each other better, and if you're looking for a religious reason, well, we want church to be a place for real, authentic relationships. We don't want anyone to feel they have to wear a mask and put on a show. Since it's New Year's Day, I thought we could start by reflecting on the past. Was there anything that *didn't* happen last year that you hope will happen this year?"

Where should I begin? I'd spent the last year living like a blind woman in an Andrew Wyeth painting, frozen on a bleak, reedy hillside, crawling toward a house I could never reach.

Katie searched the group for a volunteer to start. She found me and nodded with the gentleness of a kindergarten teacher that I could go first.

"What do I hope?" I said aloud, the words falling from my mouth riddled with uncertainty. "I don't know, I hope for love and dream of everything working out in my life. Sometimes I feel like I'm lost, and I want someone to find me and place me where I belong. But more than anything, I want to see God working in my life because if this last year taught me anything, it was that I can't do anything by myself."

"Do you think God wants to provide those things for you?" Katie asked.

"Yes, I know He does, but it's so hard waiting for them."

Emotion cracked my voice and Avril crossed her hands in her lap, uncomfortable with my sudden transparency. We were actors-for-hire after all. We told other people's stories, not our own.

"I take it you've had a hard year. Someone once said if we feel there's a purpose, we can get through anything. Do you think there's been a purpose behind it?" Katie asked, her voice soothing like Bella's.

"Yes, but I feel like I've been smashed flat. Completely pulverized. At times, even my bones ached, and just when I doubted it was possible to go on, God scraped me up and brought me to New York."

"Harper, Scripture says we're like wet clay whirling on a potter's wheel. God takes hold of those He loves. He examines us, our flaws and imperfections, our blemishes and defects, and if necessary, He presses us against the spinning wheel, tearing down the old us, so He can build us as a new person, one without the flaws we had before."

Was that the purpose of the Chicago year, being smashed against a spinning wheel, flattened like a pancake? Did my being in New York signal God was building me up now?

"My husband would have said he was clay in God's hands," the older woman said. "He started out as a trumpet player in a theater orchestra, but he went on to be a dancer and Broadway actor. He could do it all."

"I didn't know James played the trumpet, Mrs. Gruens," Katie said.

"He gave it up before you met him, but James began his career as a trumpet player. He loved acting most of all, and he became quite good at it."

"We're actors," Avril told Mrs. Gruens. "We open at the Carney this month."

"Oh, that's wonderful, dear. What show?"

"*Apartment 19* with Helen Payne."

"You know, I attended the premiere for *Apartment 19* on Broadway in 1958," Mrs. Gruens said. "*Marvelous play*, but oh, the theater can be such a vagabond life. James spent part of the year in Boston, summers in the Catskills, and he traveled by train to Baltimore and Toronto looking for theater work too. If we hadn't married so young, I doubt we'd have ever found each other. I hope the footlights haven't kept you girls from meeting someone special."

"I'm not presently dating," I said naturally, as if the words had been lifted from page three of my five-year plan. In reality, it was a toss-up which pursuit I'd been less successful in, show business or my life love. My one starring role had been in a Drowz-U-Tab commercial as a woman so tired she couldn't find rest. Ironic.

"Take it from someone who's loved actors for more than sixty years, don't wait to fall in love or until the timing's right to start a family. No matter how high your star rises over Broadway, when the grips pull the velvet curtain closed for the night, everybody needs someone to go home to."

"If only men like James could be picked from the trees, Mrs. Gruens," I said.

"Well, when you're ready, God provides. You girls should talk to my sister, Elvira. She's got a true gift for matchmaking."

Katie smiled. "I know three girlfriends who are into Internet dating. Have you ever heard of that, Mrs. Gruens? I don't know if I could do it, but they seem to love it. Well, two of them do."

Mrs. Gruens looked as if she'd bitten into a tart lemon. "Computer dating? No, if it didn't work for Doris Day with all of those punch cards, I doubt it works any better today."

The group laughed. I counted heads. Based on ages and fingers without wedding rings, I guessed at least four in our group of six were single.

"I'm not really ready to do something like that," I said. "Not yet anyway."

"You're both beautiful girls," Mrs. Gruens assured us. "I'll bet God has someone very special picked out for each of you, and He doesn't need a computer to do it."

Avril just smiled.

~ EIGHT ~

Apartment 19 was one of three works written by the prominent twentieth-century playwright Arthur Mouldain. Before his death at age thirty, Mouldain poured a hot, black cup of sobering realism into the minds of American theatergoers along with such postwar contemporaries as Eugene O'Neill and Tennessee Williams. His plays gripped New York audiences, and critics found in Mouldain a playwright who exceeded their ideals and imaginations. It was his wife, Theodora, who at sunrise one morning found Mouldain collapsed at his work desk in the light of open French windows facing Central Park. A heart defect caught him, silencing his brilliance only days after he finished his masterwork, *Apartment 19*. The black pen with which he wrote revisions was still gripped in his right hand.

The night he died, all of Broadway dimmed their lights in Mouldain's honor. They posthumously awarded him with Broadway's highest accolades and, in 1960, a Pulitzer Prize for drama. *Apartment 19* is considered one of the greatest plays of the twentieth century, but the turbulence of the 1960s unpopularized Mouldain's work in favor of a more avant-garde movement in American theater. Productions like *Hair* and *Combat* drew ticket sales at the box office, the attention of theater reviewers, and investors. *Apartment 19* wasn't performed again on Broadway until 1979 in a production starring famed Hitchcock actress Leigh McDowell. The brief run received critical praise but was a commercial disaster.

The Mouldain estate took the flop personally, blaming the show's producers for its failure. Throughout the 1980s and '90s, they denied all performance licensing, whether professional or collegian, virtually silencing Mouldain's work. Thirty years would pass before an American audience would see any of Mouldain's plays again.

Ben Hughes had spearheaded a four-year-long campaign to bring *Apartment 19* back to Broadway. He spent two days in Hartford, Connecticut, meeting with the Mouldain Society, rallying support for his claim that it was indeed time to revive Mouldain. Ben flew to London to meet with Mouldain's daughter, Elisa, to cast his vision, seeking her blessing and the granting of the necessary performance license. Eventually Elisa Mouldain relented, giving Ben the first performance license for *Apartment 19* in thirty years—but with the unusual condition of a "sunset clause." Protective and eccentric, Elisa Mouldain would limit the number of performances, whether the play was a hit or a miss, to forty-two and no more.

Elisa's restriction made the prospects of *Apartment 19* turning a profit more problematic than usual. Ben's nervous business partners would invest three million dollars in the venture, but only if Ben agreed to raise ticket prices. *Apartment 19* would have to virtually sell out the 702-seat Carney Theatre *every show* to turn a profit. But were Broadway audiences willing to shell out the ticket price of a Disney musical to see a fifty-year-old Arthur Mouldain play?

Apartment 19's cast knew the pressure Ben was under; everyone did. New York theater critics' expectations had blown up over thirty years into the stuff of legend. Ben's production had to stoke the imaginations of reviewers, wow new audiences, return a profit in forty-two nights, and satisfy Elisa Mouldain that she hadn't made a terrible mistake in trusting him. I found myself praying for Ben.

"Harper, you've made Saturday morning the easiest part of the day," Ben said, finishing his bagel and coffee. "No actor likes working at 7 a.m., but it's the only time I had open. Thank you for coming to the studio so I could see your Audrey Bradford."

"It's no problem, Ben."

"A director loves knowing at least something in his show is going right. You've got enough under your belt, dare I say, you could open for us tomorrow night."

Ben straddled a folding chair turned backward, his arms resting on the top. He rubbed at his eyes, jostling his wire-rimmed glasses out of place.

"What's it been like working with Tabby?" he asked, getting up from his chair.

"We went through the show once on the first day, twice on the second. In the afternoons, she has me watch rehearsals and make notes on any changes you introduce to the show."

Ben seemed surprised. "So, you've gone through the entire show three times already?"

"Yes."

Ben crossed his arms, tapped his index finger against his lips. "I'm curious, Harper. You seem to want to bust out of some of my staging at times. I remember that about you, your flair for improvisation. If I asked you to expand on a scene, where do you think you could take it?"

Ben was right. I had wanted to break out of the box, expand on the creative ideas that flooded my imagination whenever I got into Audrey Bradford's character. But I just couldn't respond to Ben's question with a menu of choices. Instead, I returned to my mark on the rug, setting my toe like a dancer's onto the piece of masking tape still there from Tabby's original mark-up on day one. I took a moment, letting his question stir my own creative curiosity.

"How expanded do you want it?" I asked, looking up at him.

"Very," he said, returning to his folding chair.

I closed my eyes. I felt like a dancer in this studio, just seconds before the burst of motion and fluid expression. I uttered a prayer underneath my breath and waited for the downbeat of the conductor's baton.

It was spontaneous, an instant flash of inspiration. Everything clicked and I could *feel* the intuition showing me how to move. Ben's original blocking worked fantastically, but there were a million and one ways to play Audrey Bradford. Mouldain had written layers into his play. There were depths to plumb in his work, harmony notes that vibrated both beneath and above the melody line. Savvy actors and directors could pluck a moment like the strings of a harp and turn a scene on its edge.

My eyes opened, and I could almost see the red velvet curtain opening in front of me, hearing the guide wheels squeaking along their track as the grips pulled its fraying rope. Around me, a three-walled apartment belonging to the deranged Audrey Bradford decorated my imagination. In front of me, a red-cushioned sea of theater seats, the ocean floor, waited.

I tossed aside Ben's blocking, moving left instead of right, making up my own marks as I triggered Audrey's words and phrases. My turns were crisp and fluid. The rubber soles of my shoes squeaked like a basketball player pivoting on the court.

I saw two young dancers arrive early to the studio for their lesson. They watched me from the doorway, their energy and presence feeding my performance. The rhythm and cadence of Audrey Bradford's words snapped from my mouth like icy branches in a winter's storm.

Helen always played the scene's emotional finale by piercing the audience with a near shriek of her voice. I could feel the pressure too now, building inside of me, but I *lowered* the tone of my voice and the gaze of my stare to a spot just above Ben's forehead. Audrey Bradford's words came out with startling transparency and emotion, a whisper under pressure that sent a chill up my spine when I spoke.

I waited for Ben to say something, anything, aware that my heart was beating like I'd just finished an aerobic workout. I exhaled a huge sigh to wash away the scene.

Ben sat motionless, his feet planted, lips pursed. He nodded his head ever so slightly, with his chin perched on top of his curled fists. Eventually, a sly smile bent the left side of his mouth slightly higher than the right.

"That's *exactly* why I wanted to do Mouldain. He's such a *genius*." Ben stood up again, reanimated and talking faster. "You get all the layers in his script, don't you, Harper?"

"Yeah, I guess so. I see the possibilities."

Ben scoffed. "Yes, *possibilities*. You'd think as director I'd have the freedom to portray some of those possibilities and do whatever I wanted creatively. But with only forty-two shows, and having to promise my partners we'd *at least* break even, I've had to roll this production straight up the middle. Don't repeat this, Harper, but while we have a really strong, good show—we don't have a *great* show, not yet anyway. A great show requires taking great risks."

"From what I understand, this production's been all about risk taking."

"Offstage, yes. But onstage, I've only succeeded at bringing the show out of storage, dressing the stage more or less the way it was done fifty years ago," Ben said. "I just didn't have the time, money, or clout to both revive *and* reinvent Mouldain in the same production."

Ben dropped his head and shook it like he'd worked himself to the point of exhaustion for four years only to miss the game-winning shot at the final buzzer. He raised his eyes to look at me. "But thank you, Harper, for at least showing me what might have been."

"Thanks, Ben. That means a lot, more than you know." So far, I'd felt like the production's family dog. Allowed to come in from the cold, but not an equal member.

Ben glanced at his watch again, suddenly aware of the time. "If it's any consolation, you've also helped me work out one of my staging quandaries with Helen. So this has been fruitful in several ways."

He picked up the leather satchel leaning against his chair leg. "I need to get back to the theater. And, Harper, remember to come by the office. There's some paperwork for you to fill out. We need to start getting you paid."

Ben crossed the dance studio quickly, parting the assembling clique of dance students waiting in the doorway, and disappeared down the stairwell to the street. I picked up a chair and carried it to the stack by the dancer's bar, cleaning up the studio for the incoming class. A few minutes later, I, too, pushed open the steel door at street level and stepped onto West Forty-fourth Street. The city air was biting and cold, scented with diesel fuel. I didn't care; I was feeling great about finally making a contribution to the show, however small.

A block down West Forty-fourth Street, I noticed a truck unloading stage equipment in the covered alley beside the Carney. The door leading backstage was propped open, so I took the shortcut, striding down the tapered walkway and tugging open the faded red door someone had wedged open with a stopper.

Despite the million-dollar renovations out front, backstage the historic Carney still looked like it belonged in a 1940s showbiz picture starring Mickey Rooney and Judy Garland. Ropes and rigging that moved staging panels were tied to a wooden railing. *Apartment 19's* set pieces, made to look like Manhattan of the 1950s, rested on wheeled dollies so stagehands could quickly strike the stage. Above me, a metal-grated catwalk was just visible in the dimness and pixie dust.

There was a public call-board mounted on the wall by the electrical circuit board, listing rehearsal instructions until opening night. Further down the half-lit hallway, I could see the office door was ajar. Pale light streamed out from the florescent overhead fixtures.

"Can you make sure everyone gets into wardrobe and makeup as soon as they come in this morning?" I heard Ben ask as I approached.

"I'll get everyone in place, Ben."

Tabby appeared from the office door, nearly bumping into me. She gave me a quick look but said nothing, carrying out her mission to rustle up actors as they moseyed in on an early Saturday morning.

I peeked around the door into the production office to find Ben searching for something on the large, cluttered desk.

"I'm trying to find those papers for you," he said, once he'd realized I'd wandered in and we were alone in the office.

I leaned into the doorframe, giving him enough space inside the cramped back office that was half-consumed by the oversized desk. Ben continued rummaging. I didn't react when he opened the bottom tub drawer to reveal a very large, mostly empty bottle of Scotch rolling around inside.

"It's going to be great," I said.

"What?" Ben asked.

"The show," I said. "It's going to be amazing."

"We shall see." Ben replied like his mind was somewhere else. "Ah, here it is."

He pulled out a simple manila folder from underneath an issue of *Variety* magazine, and when he held it up to his face I noticed that his hand was shaking. A sticky note the color of robin's egg blue fluttered as he opened it.

"Just fill out whatever's in there and get it to Tabby, okay?"

"Sure," I said, taking the folder. I started to walk away, then paused. "Ben, do you remember when we used to do all this for free? All of us, working night and day, trying to get everything just right? We did it for the love of theater, and that's exactly why an audience will show up here tomorrow night. They won't know what it all could have been. They'll just appreciate the special gift you've given to them."

Ben stopped shuffling papers and looked up at me.

"But *I'll* know, Harper. The most chilling words in all the human vocabulary are *could have been.*" Ben straightened his back, no longer hunched over the desk. "And if we got it wrong, Harper, what was the cost back then? A bad grade? A snarky review in the student newspaper? We never gambled with somebody else's millions, or our reputations, or invested months, years, making our families sacrifice," Ben said, drifting into a dark place. There was a pause, then a deep sigh. "I'm sorry. I'm just about out of gasoline here. Good thing there's just one more day." He turned and smiled, reaching up for my hand. "It *was* easier once, wasn't it, Harper? We had to go and ruin it by chasing our dreams, then catching them."

"Maybe the best is yet to come."

I let go of Ben's hand and said a silent prayer on my way out. It was quiet backstage, the truck unloaded, the hallway absent of actors and busyness. I headed for the stage in search of a little hang-out time with Avril before she went into makeup.

Helen's dressing room door was partly open, so I glanced inside as I passed. Helen was sitting upright on a silk love seat the color of soft money, like the queen of England awaiting visitors. She looked up at me.

"You there," she called out. I stopped, shuffling back to her dressing room.

"Did you want something?" I asked. She gestured to me with her finger, curling it toward herself twice like she wanted me to come closer. It was a command, not a request.

"I hope you've got your lines down for tomorrow night, just in case," she said, holding back a chuckle.

"Yes," I said, playing along, albeit uncomfortably. "Just in case."

Helen allowed herself to laugh. "Oh, don't worry. You won't be called upon anytime soon, but I do think it's good training for an actor to be ready for anything."

I nodded in vague agreement and began backing myself out her door.

"There is a certain romance to the role of understudy, don't you think?" she asked. "You serve no purpose whatsoever, lend nothing to the success of the show, and no one in the audience even cares to know your name—*unless* the star cannot, for some reason, perform. Then you must take the stage without the benefit of a dress rehearsal, and knock everyone's socks off."

Helen stared at me from her love seat. She was wearing a large Egyptian necklace, a scarab resting at the base of her throat. I thought about Mrs. Gruens at that moment, picturing her standing in a frosted window, watching for James to return by train from a winter stint in Boston years ago when he was acting, greeting him with a bowl of hot clam chowder, happy to make him feel like a king in one world, even if he were only a serf in another.

"I'm sure it won't be necessary for me to fill in your shoes, Ms. Payne. You said it yourself, you never miss a show."

"Oh, come now. Don't play goody-goody. Every actress wants a shot at knocking the star down a notch or two," she said in a voice both sweet and accusing. "The legendary Bette Davis said it best: 'The person who wants to make it has to sweat…. And you've got to have the guts to be hated.'"

Helen sipped from the water glass on a table in front of her and set it down again, leaving dark rose-colored lipstick in a crescent moon on the rim. "I was aggressive at your age," she said, rising to her feet. "Ready to do whatever was required to get on that stage—to be the best in the world."

Helen's voice grew louder. I thought I saw some of her Audrey Bradford escaping through the seams of her tightly stitched personality. "I wasn't going back to Hartford, not after feeling the heat of Broadway lights. I would do *whatever* it took to keep myself here, and I'm sure you're the very same way."

"I don't think I'm like that," I said, trying to give deference, not correct her. "I'm only the understudy, but I want to feel gratitude for what I have."

Helen crinkled her face like I was certifiable.

"Gratitude? But darling, you haven't got anything!" She laughed, popping and hissing like a coffeemaker finishing its brew. "Oh, that's delicious. Now why don't you run along and play with the others?"

Helen shooed me out of her dressing room, shutting the door behind me. I stood backstage for a moment, staggered by the woman's gloating, her haughty rub-my-face-in-it snootiness. Discouragement fell on me like a sudden rain shower. Every encounter with Helen was unpleasant. I was still unsure how to deal with Tabby's predisposition to dislike me. I'd made the cast recoil when I'd turned down drinks with them for an hour of worship, and I was concerned about Ben. Mostly, I was frustrated, or at least confused—why had God graciously rescued me from my pit in Chicago only to drop me in the middle of so much enmity? I was beginning to question whether this break was God's will.

I walked out of the wings onto the Carney stage to find Avril dancing by herself at center stage as the lighting team adjusted the gels and spotlights around her. She was dressed in faded blue jeans, a sleeveless white shirt that showed off toned arms, and a long maroon scarf around her neck she twirled with her hands while she danced. She looked like a happy little girl.

I smiled when I saw her, and she took me by the hands, spinning me around, her laughter surprised and delighted. She waltzed us around the polished, wooden floor, dancing to a melody she made up on the spot.

"I take it you've heard from Jon today," I said.

"Surprised me, with roses, my love," she sang in three-quarter time.

"You look like you're in love."

"Maybe I am," she said, stopping our dance to whisper. Avril's real life was grander than most people dare to dream.

"Avril, I need you in makeup. You and Helen," Tabby called out, standing in the center aisle, lights dimming up and down around her. Marshall Graham walked in through the lobby doors, wearing a navy blue varsity jacket with white leather sleeves. He joined the other actors, Melissa and Harriet among them.

I climbed down from the stage. The show's set designer, Mark Blane, had collaborated with Richard Mulican, *Apartment 19's* lighting director, to fine-tune everything to luminescent perfection. The stage dimmed and brightened, awash in a fantastic display of daylight radiance. Suddenly, it was summertime in New York onstage.

I walked down the center aisle to the middle of the theater, taking in the full spectrum of the opening set. Mark had done a masterful job. Onstage was a recreation of midtown Manhattan in the 1950s. The painted backdrops looked like an exhibition on realism worthy of hanging in the Metropolitan Museum of Fine Art. The newsstand and coffee shop looked like Edward Hopper's

Nighthawks come to life. The sleek silver buildings of the Manhattan skyline stretched upward behind them, reinforcing the American steel workers' optimism for the world of tomorrow. An elevated subway station practically hummed on the canvas backdrop, anticipating the next arriving car. The muted color palate—plum, browns, burnt yellows, and charcoal black—made our stage feel as if Danny Kaye or Gene Kelly might step out at any minute and swing around a city lamppost.

The actors had all gone into hiding. I caught a glimpse of Harriet warming up backstage waiting for Tabby's cue to walk on. She looked nervous, and I found myself praying for her, for Ben, and for ticket sales. I thought about Mrs. Gruens, too, for some inexplicable reason, wondering why I'd never wondered until then whether her husband was still alive.

♫

A dress rehearsal should run exactly as the audience will see the show on opening night. I took my unassigned position, a seat on the back row, as the houselights dimmed around us.

For the next two hours, Ben, Tabby, the crew, and the show's financial backers and producers sat silently in the darkened Carney Theatre watching a play no one else had seen in America in over thirty years.

Each set looked perfect. An enormous round moon hung on invisible lines. It looked like a luminous sun whenever hot yellow lights were thrown on it, and cooled into a silver evening whenever Richard hit it with twilight hues. Even I was buying the illusion.

We watched like critics, scrutinizing the show's pacing, its transitions and flow. We didn't laugh at its humor or applaud the spectacle, and no one gasped on seven separate occasions when lines were forgotten or stumbled over. In the second act, Avril's microphone went dead, and Helen looked as if she was going to have a fit. In one scene, the automated lighting board suddenly flooded an indoor night scene with bright daylight. When one of the crew's cell phones rang backstage, Helen broke character and shouted out, "If it's the *New York Times* theater critic, tell him we'll call him back later!"

After the curtain closed, Ben called everyone back to the stage.

"You all know how this works: good dress rehearsal, bad show. Bad dress rehearsal, *great* show. We've got a couple of technical bugs to work out and a few missed lines, but also some very promising stuff. It's three o'clock. Principal actors, take an hour lunch. I'd like to see you back here at four to fix a staging issue I sorted out this morning while I was working with Harper. Everyone else, we'll see you here tomorrow for opening night."

~ NINE ~

Too busy to fall in love?

Let LoveSetMatch.com do the work for you!

Convenient, online dating at the click of a mouse.

For on-the-go professionals, falling in
love has never been easier.

Find the love you've always been looking for

and leave the matchmaking to us!

Avril's Manhattan attorney, Jon, worked seven days a week and twenty-eight nights of every month. Holidays were a coin toss. Perhaps this was the allure of LoveSetMatch.com for him and every other busy Manhattan professional. Online dating allowed him access to what he couldn't find any other way. Love and connection.

My heart softened to the idea of online dating when I caught up with Avril in the Carney's grand lobby following Saturday afternoon's late rehearsal. I found her leaning inside in a cozy nook between the lobby wall and a lighted poster box, her cell phone resting against her ear. A golden light from the promotional poster for *Apartment 19* cast a soft glow over her. Whatever Jon was saying on the other end, she loved it.

"Yes, I know what day it is," Avril said, still holding the bouquet of red roses Jon had had delivered after lunch.

"No," she giggled, "I don't think it's silly to celebrate our six week anniversary."

Harriet, the actress who joked she was Queen Latifah's twin, walked up beside me as I waited to say good night to Avril.

"What's she doing?" Harriet asked.

"She's talking to her boyfriend, Jon. He's the one who sent the flowers."

Harriet let a couple of beats pass before she responded. "Is it just me, or does Avril always look exactly like Miss America to you?"

"It's probably the roses," I said. "But we can ask her later if 'world peace' is the one thing she wants most."

Avril overheard us and made eye contact, but it only brought a larger smile to her face. She turned away, seeking a little privacy, but I could still hear her as Avril told Jon she loved him. She closed the cover on her little pink phone.

"Oh, bliss …"

Avril collapsed against the wall, closing her eyelids as if nocturnal dreams were her only rest from the weight of continual happiness. She blew out a contented sigh.

"Someone around here's happy," Harriet said.

Avril opened her eyes. "Friends, neighbors, countrymen and -women, if it were in my power to bestow upon each of you one quarter of the happiness I feel at this moment, I would gladly do it."

I laughed, happy for her being so in love, but envious, too. Not the pity-party garden variety, but the kind that prods you into taking action. I wanted what Avril had, but in a way that was meant for me.

Avril smiled, showing off white movie-star teeth and moving toward us across the bright red Broadway carpet. I could imagine flashbulbs popping all around her like the Hollywood press did for Marilyn Monroe. Maybe she *was* Miss America.

"I'd love to stay with you all," Avril said. "But alas, I'm off to catch a checkered chariot to whisk me away to my love. It's our anniversary."

"I think what you got may be some kind of illness," Harriet said.

Avril, still enchanted, stepped closer to Harriet, lowering her own voice to a whisper. *"Don't cure me,"* she said.

Avril glided across the lobby and through the front doors, holding her bouquet of roses like a trophy. Harriet and I watched her hail a cab under a shower of brilliant marquee lights. A moment later, a yellow taxi pulled up to the curb, and Avril opened the backseat door and slid in. The taxi dashed away, merging into midtown traffic where it disappeared in the rush of trucks and cars. She was off to enjoy a sumptuous dinner at one of New York's five-star restaurants.

"There goes the most beautiful woman in New York," Harriet said.

"And the happiest."

"Must be nice."

Harriet turned her attention to me.

"So, Miss Harper Gray, did you enjoy your church service last night?"

I looked up at her, checking to see if she was making fun of me. I was still a little bruised and paranoid after Helen's pep talk. Harriet appeared guileless.

"Yes, I did. You should have come with us. We met some very nice people," I said, trying to imitate the kindness Bella had once shown me.

"I thought about it, but I don't know. Next time, maybe."

Like Avril, Harriet had show-business charisma, an appealing quality that invites trust. I sensed she was a deep soul, someone able to understand the world around her better than most. She put it to use in her performance as the landlord. It gave her character—essentially a witness who sees some of the peculiar happenings in the apartment—a palpable empathy toward Roxy.

"Any plans for dinner?" I asked.

"I have to get back to Brooklyn. My son's waiting for me," Harriet said, fishing through her shoulder bag and retrieving her cell phone. "He's not used to his mom having to work on Saturdays. Thankfully, his grandmother lives with us."

"What's his name?"

"Darius. He's nine and absolutely brilliant, a genius. Tonight we're going to watch Animal Planet and eat Moose Tracks ice cream."

"Sounds like a big time," I told her. "Will you bring Darius to see you in the premiere?"

"Probably not. He has cerebral palsy, and it's just hard to bring him here. I'd need to request a special van, and it's a long way from Brooklyn and a long show for him to sit through. Plus, I don't think I could act if I looked down and saw him in his wheelchair. I'd be like, 'Darius, how you doin', baby? Soon as we kill off Miss Audrey Bradford, mama'll be done and we can go home and watch basketball.' My baby loves the NBA."

Harriet and I exited the Carney Theatre, walking up West Forty-fourth Street through a biting wind to the subway. When we could travel together no further, we bid each other good night, and I boarded the D train to the Village.

Sitting in a seat facing sideways, I shuffled through hundreds of songs on my iPod, but nothing seemed to match my mood. I chose the Yellowjackets as a fallback, instrumental jazz to massage my soul. It was my first time alone again, and I thought about calling Katie Tylers. She'd graciously offered to be my listening ear if I ever needed one. After chitchatting with Harriet and watching Avril float away for her romantic date, I was feeling just a little blue.

But by the time I deboarded the train in Greenwich Village, I'd decided to spare Katie the tedium of listening to my whining. Still, I knew Avril wouldn't be home for hours, and the prospects of a dull night hanging around the apartment alone seemed pathetically similar to my old life in Chicago.

I jostled my apartment key into the dead bolt, unlocking the door with a loud click. Inside the rooms were dark and quiet. I turned on the small lamp Avril kept in the kitchen next to a fern on the counter. The stereo remote was on the kitchen island, so I picked it up, tuning in some music on Avril's satellite radio from across the room.

For dinner, I heated a can of tomato basil soup and crumbled a few Ritz crackers over the top. After cleaning up the kitchen, I could have easily just gone to bed, but it was only 8 p.m.

I browsed Avril's bookshelves for something interesting, but my blasé attitude prohibited me finding anything. Finally, I sat at the small alcove desk—a contemporary two-level lit by a retro '70s reading lamp with stringy purple tassels. I smelled a real daisy peeking out of a small light blue vase next to the computer and wondered where Avril had picked it up. I began searching for the Power button, which I found hidden at the back of the Mac, and switched both it and the lamp on.

I clicked around online for a while, checking emails, browsing Facebook for the first time since coming to New York, and awaiting the inevitable arrival of boredom.

Then I closed my eyes, returning to prayer in hopes that God would choose this moment to speak again, but the only thing that came to mind was a picture of Avril sitting with Mr. Wonderful at a candlelit table with Manhattan's diamond skyline in the background. Avril was *so* in love. How did that happen? She'd always been a go-getter, willing to take risks and try new things.

Like Internet dating.

I typed in a Google search for "Internet dating." In seconds, 4,136,087 matches appeared on the screen. I reasoned this gave the weird social practice some kind of legitimacy. Then I did a second search, this time for Avril's dating site, the one that produced the kind of love that came with a dozen roses—LoveSetMatch.com.

I clicked again and watched the LoveSetMatch.com Web site load onto my screen. A photo of a happy thirty-something couple greeted me on the home page, a rugged, manly-type guy holding an attractive auburn-haired woman. They were beautiful in an average sort of way, and I understood its message instantly: *This could be you*.

I snooped around LoveSetMatch.com for a minute or two, feeling curious and incredulous all at the same time. The site boasted an impressive 12 million members worldwide, and proudly proclaimed that LoveSetMatch.com couples walked the aisles of matrimony to the tune of eight-five every day.

There was a science to it, the site assured me, and that science required everyone to fill out a personality questionnaire before they could find their fabulously compatible partner.

It all seemed so dubious and computer cold. Falling in love by algorithm? Then again, it was where Princess Avril had found her Prince Charming (and at least six weeks of complete bliss and happiness). Maybe LoveSetMatch.com was just a modern-day version of old-world matchmaking, the likes of which Mrs. Gruens's sister, Elvira, could only dream of.

The last hook? The LoveSetMatch personality test was totally, 100 percent free. I could take their two-hundred-question love survey, find out what personality type I was uniquely compatible with, and never spend a nickel. If ever there was a night to waste time on such a trivial distraction, this was it. A perfect remedy, or *match*, for my boredom. And who knows, maybe it would also be a scratch-an-itch lottery ticket leading me to my highly compatible soul mate. *Be prepared*, LoveSetMatch warned. The compatibility survey would take at least an hour to complete.

Perfect.

I left the computer alcove for the kitchen and pulled out an unopened carton of orange juice from the fridge, giving it a robust shake. I grabbed a heavy crystal juice glass, one of a set Avril told me she'd purchased in Soho, and filled it. Back at the computer alcove, I took a small sip and wondered if I was really going to do this. The "Let's Get Started" button blinked on-screen, an enticing invitation, and I clicked on it.

Step 1: Create a username and password.

I typed in the first thing that popped in my mind.

Username: H*E*P*B*U*R*N.

A spinning icon appeared as the system processed the information I'd just fed into it. When it stopped spinning, the page refreshed with a set of questions.

Question 1—If I were at a party in a room full of strangers, would I:

(a) Stand by myself and not talk to a living soul?

(b) Scour the room introducing myself to strangers?

(c) Sign on as understudy in the Broadway revival of a lost Arthur Mouldain play?

(I added that last one.)

Question 2—What kind of evening do I consider romantic?

(a) Cooking dinner at home with my partner.

(b) Fine dining in a five-star restaurant.

(c) Not spending a year alone in Chicago.

(I added that last one too.)

I answered multiple questions, taking them seriously. My answers came quickly, probably because of all those personality tests I'd taken in the back of magazines during college.

By 9:20 p.m., I'd lost track of how many questions I'd answered. The LoveSetMatch.com icon continued to spin on the screen. It refreshed one last time, and then there were no more questions. LoveSetMatch.com wanted me to upload a recent picture of myself.

It was raising the ante.

Was I willing to upload my photo? Did I even have one? It wasn't like I'd moved my photo albums with me to New York. Any pictures I did have were sitting in plastic storage tubs in my dad's basement in Elizabethtown, and everything in them would be outdated anyway. Except …

I slid back the wooden chair from the desk, making a scraping sound as I lurched into the bedroom looking for my cell phone. I picked it up from the charger on the nightstand, powering it to life with the push of a button. Its smiling face greeted me with sing-song chimes.

I shuffled through the new messages until I came upon HARPER IN NYC, and sent the photo to my email account without ever opening it.

Technology.

By the time I sat down, HARPER IN NYC had already materialized in my in-box. Another click, and I watched as the color image expanded to full size on the computer screen.

It was the first time I'd seen the photo. My smile looked a little sleepy, but satisfied. Even my coffee-brown hair had decided to cooperate, for once. Behind me, Times Square appeared in a breathtaking display of fireworks, and blazing neon blurred around me out of focus. The camera even caught snowflakes reflecting the bright lights of Times Square. Avril's shot captured my story in a single frame, a woman standing still while the rest of the crazy world spun out of control around her.

It wasn't a bad photo, but was I willing to share it with the gawkers on LoveSetMatch.com?

Evidently yes, because I uploaded it and for one last time watched the wheel flip round and round like a fan in the hands of a dancer.

Somewhere in Silicon Valley, I pictured a colossal supercomputer handling my personal, romantic data, juggling then comparing it against all the compatible matches in their 12–million-member database.

A final screen appeared. This one didn't want to know any more about my personal likes and dislikes. This screen wanted money.

"Congratulations," the page announced. LoveSetMatch.com had found *highly compatible matches* for me, but before I could *see* my matches, I'd first need to become a member of the most respected, reliable, and scientific online dating system available in the modern world.

This privilege would cost me seventy-five dollars for three months.

What's the children's story about a boy who takes the last of his family's money and buys magic beans? The story vaguely crossed my mind as I searched my leather wallet for my one credit card, not sure if it would take one more purchase. I'd like to say I prayed about the decision, but I didn't. It was an impulsive, spontaneous, reckless, and too-late-to-turn-back-now decision.

I thought of Avril and how she sparkled and purred at the thought of Jon. I thought about how everything went so well for her and how this was exactly the kind of thing she would do—in fact, had done.

I tapped my Visa number in, using the keypad. The timepiece turned around one more time before my personal page went up, showing my Times Square photo and all the public information I'd made accessible. I saw the impossible-to-miss "New Matches" tab under my name and a bold number "2" embossed over it.

Two matches.

I tilted back in my chair, chuckling at the foolish amount of time and money I'd poured into this rabbit hole. Just two matches from their 12–million-member database? For this I paid seventy-five dollars?

It was only morbid curiosity that compelled me to examine their profiles. According to LoveSetMatch.com's unparalleled scientific compatibility service, my two perfect soul mates were Gus, a husky fifty-seven-year-old farmer from Lima, Ohio, and Jimbo, a forty-three-year-old live-bait salesman currently residing in Baton Rouge, Louisiana.

I shut off the computer and apartment lights, brushed my teeth, and laughed at how I'd allowed myself to be swept up in the fantasy. In bed, I switched off the bedside lamp and pulled my blankets over my head. I was no longer laughing.

How long would it take to meet someone and genuinely fall in love? The answer depressed me. Even if I met my soul mate tomorrow, would we recognize each other? Wouldn't it take months or even years to know beyond a shadow of a doubt that he was "the one"?

I rolled over, burrowing into my pillow. God could do anything, *anything*. But the question was, *What did He want to do?*

~ TEN ~

When Ben had overheard me asking Avril if she wanted to go to church on Sunday morning, he half-jokingly asked me to say a prayer for opening night. I looked for derision in Ben's question, saw it in the faces of both Marshall and Melissa, but not in Ben. He seemed to welcome any heavenly backing. I walked away certain I was getting a reputation as the oddball cast member who prays.

Early Sunday morning, I stood outside Avril's bedroom door, knocking softly. When she didn't answer, I cracked open her door and asked if she'd like to go with me to church. From beneath a thick layer of winter bedding, the mop of blonde hair sticking out of the blankets politely declined.

I assembled what seemed like suitable church clothes for a down-town worship experience in New York City, an understated green dress and flats. Attire had been casual at the weeknight service, but I didn't know what to expect on a Sunday morning. Thankfully, my other suitcase had arrived late Saturday afternoon.

The trip to Fellowship Community Church was uneventful, a welcomed island of calm in an otherwise hectic two days in the city. The sun was bright and clear, the sky overhead a perfect patch of blue. Another subway ride, the drawn faces of three-dozen strangers traveling alone in the dark. I got off at the Forty-second Street

Station in Times Square, climbed the cement stairs back to street level, then walked the remaining four blocks to the church.

"Twice in one week," David said, greeting me at the door of the sanctuary.

He offered me his hand, which felt warm to my own since I'd forgotten my gloves and my hands were freezing.

"I couldn't resist after everyone was so friendly."

"That's our specialty. By the way, sorry if I was a little abrupt on Friday night when I ran into you. Katie said I might want to work on my social skills."

"No worries," I told him, becoming aware of how relaxed I felt whenever I stepped into the church building. "Where is Katie?"

"Right behind you," David said, pointing over my shoulder.

I turned to see Katie standing inches behind me as people made their way past us to the sanctuary.

By the way she was dressed—dark blue jeans and a claret-colored sweater pulled over her white oxford—I gathered she'd just come up from downstairs, the children's area, and not from the icy outdoors. A pair of brown penny loafers complemented a very preppy look. She took hold of both my hands.

"I hoped I'd see you today. Do you have someone to sit with?"

"Not really." I shook my head.

"Can we sit together?" Katie asked.

I was vaguely aware of David disappearing behind us, drawn away by the details of leading a Sunday morning service. There were two hundred or so people gathered in the church, a room made doubly warm by the bold morning sunlight filtering through the colorful stained glass windows.

"I'd like that."

Katie led us to seats on the third row, left side. I wondered if this was the preacher's wife section, then flashed back to the Carney where I'd been planting myself on the last row for the past two days. I did a quick search for Mrs. Gruens, just to say hi, but didn't see her or the worship leader Bobby Mars.

"I'm glad you're here, Harper. I really enjoyed meeting you and Avril on Friday night, and ... I don't know, there was just something about you I liked instantly. David says I have a knack for reading people, an intuition, but I just think it's appreciation for others."

"I loved Friday night's service. I've been thinking about getting back here ever since. I tried waking Avril, but she was exhausted, and tonight's a big night for her."

"Anything you can talk about?"

"The play we're in—*Apartment 19*—opens. Avril has one of the leads."

"What role do you play?"

"Funny you should say it like that. Technically, I'm understudy for Helen Payne, but since it's unlikely I'll ever be onstage, I've been asking myself that very question."

"How long do you plan to stay in New York?"

"About six weeks. That's the entire run of the show, forty-two performances. After that, we're back on the streets." I smiled, cuing her that I was making a joke. Katie only stared back, reading my face so closely I wondered if I'd see her lips move.

"Mind if I pray about that?"

"My staying in New York?"

"No, that you'll see what God wants you to do, in the show, and wherever else He's working in your life."

"Sure," I said, thinking that sounded exactly like something Bella would say.

The service was sweet. Ruthann, the student missing from Friday night, led the worship. She couldn't have been more than twenty, standing in front of microphone strumming her guitar, wearing a simple brown peasant dress with a strand of Indian beads around her neck. A second female student accompanied her on guitar and vocals.

David spoke his message in a style so casual, I didn't realize he'd started until he said something about "wrapping up." The kingdom of heaven, he said, is where "people do the right thing. It's where people forgive, sacrifice, live, and support each other. Most of all, it's a place where all people love one another."

The simplicity spoke to me.

Before I knew it, the hour had ended. Katie reached over to me, squeezing my hand and making me promise to call her for lunch the following week. I took the lilac-colored card she gave me, her name and cell number printed on one side, just before she was pulled away into a group of older ladies in pretty church dresses.

I glanced around the sanctuary, wondering on the off chance I'd know somebody, from the Carney, I guess.

Bobby Mars stuck out from the crowd this time, sitting on the back pew, his hair now dyed an impulsive shade of punk rocker blue, the natural black locks on the back and sides surviving the home dye job. I wove through the crowd, winding down the center aisle. I expected we'd make eye contact as I approached and slipped into the row in front of him, but that didn't happen. His eyes were in a dreamy, faraway place. He was wearing dungarees marked up with a black ink pen—a spiderweb design—and a fading black T-shirt bearing a silkscreen image of Yoda and the words "May the Force be with you." I peeked over the pew between us, curious if he was wearing shoes.

"Bobby?" I said. "I'm Harper. I was here on Friday night when you sang? Sorry if I'm interrupting, but I just wanted to tell you how much I'd enjoyed your music the other night."

Bobby nodded, bobbing his head, as if to say, "Thank you very much, I'm glad you enjoyed it," but there were no words to accompany his gestures.

"I'm sorry to bother you. I just wanted to say 'hello.'"

"It's no problem," he said, hoisting his right foot up onto his left knee, jostling his body into a more upright position against the hardback wooden pew. "I kind of dig it when people say they like my music. I know it's like an ego thing, but I think people need to hear it sometimes when they do something that's okay with somebody else."

"Well, sure," I said, agreeing with him. "Do you lead the music here at church very often?"

"I have, sometimes," he said, biting the nail on his right pinky. "What I like to do is just be here, 'cause this church is pretty much what keeps me alive. I don't have a lot to say, you know, but what the people here have done for me has kept me off the street."

"Where do you live?" I asked.

"Downstairs. David and Katie made a couple rooms down there, and they gave one to me."

Bobby's face contorted as if he were holding back tears or feeling a sharp pain in his side.

"Are you all right?" I asked.

"I've got nowhere else to go," he said, not really answering my question. "I've been busted three times, spent two and half years in jail. I've got a kid in California I've never seen. I'm a drug addict, alcoholic, you name it, and there are lots of times I cry out to Jesus for just the strength to breathe."

Bobby seemed to catch his breath, the contractions that troubled his body subsiding for the moment. He exhaled slowly, as if practicing a relaxation technique he'd learned somewhere.

"You wouldn't know it to look at me, but I used to have a lot of money. My grandfather left me $150,000 when I was twenty. It was supposed to get me through college and everything, but I blew through it in a couple of years. Thank God He gave me a voice. I used to be in a band that did quite well back in the 1990s, but I didn't care about it. Half my life is wasted, and that's only if I live to be sixty. Now I sing here and down at the mission. I always tell people the old me died someplace out on the road, and I got reborn as a poor gospel singer in New York City."

Bobby laughed. Of course, that's how I felt too, the old me dying somewhere in an empty Chicago apartment building while the world outside went on its way without me. Unemployed, unmarried actress didn't sound nearly as heartrending as a homeless drug addict, but I knew where I'd be without God's intervention.

The pain in Bobby's side seemed to have returned, and he closed his eyes, ending our conversation. The church was almost empty now; most of the people had wandered outside where it was cold but sunny. I saw David waiting to talk to Bobby, so I smiled at him and headed for the exit.

ℰ

Avril called my cell phone as I was leaving church to ask if I'd like to meet her and Jon for ice-skating at Rockefeller Center, lunch included. My opportunity to meet the mysterious Jon. I agreed and strolled toward Broadway underneath a sky as clear and blue as heaven.

"I'm sorry I didn't get up and join you at church," Avril said over the phone. "But I was so tired. Let me make it up to you."

"Avril, you don't have anything to make up to me. Are you with Jon now?"

"Yes, I want you to meet him. He's so amazing! I've been telling him he works too hard, and how it's my job to help him slow down and enjoy himself more. So this morning he called me to say he was taking Sunday off and surprised me with tickets to go ice-skating at Rock Center. I've got one for you, too."

"You must be having a positive effect on him."

"Harper, Jon's the whole package. You'll see it when you meet him. Around twelve thirty?"

After going home to change, I found my way to Rockefeller Center and began rummaging through the crowds looking for Jon and Avril. The Glenn Miller Band and other romantic music of the 1940s swing era poured through outdoor loudspeakers. A waist-high wooden fence surrounded the plaza, but I spotted Avril, already on the ice, in a white ski jacket with sporty turquoise armbands and a headband that kept her ears warm, her hair in a ponytail. She waved when she saw me and skated near the fence to talk.

"Hey, here's your ticket. Just come around the other side and join us on the ice."

Avril handed me a ticket, which looked like something you'd exchange for a half pint of milk in elementary school. I walked around to the other side of the ice-skating rink; the line was shorter than expected, and within ten minutes I was strapping on skates.

Jon seemed nice enough—quiet, affectionate. He had a rugged look, partly because he hadn't shaved, a detail that brought to mind the long hours he spent working. Avril didn't seem bothered by his stubble. She glided across the ice, beaming like the guest of honor at a birthday party.

When he saw a buddy he knew standing at the fence, Jon skated away from our trio. Avril filled the space between us, skating closer, wrapping her warm hand around my cold one. I could feel her strength through the knitted mitten.

"So, what do you think?"

"He's nice."

Avril smiled. "He's amazing. Whenever I think there's a problem in our relationship, like his being a workaholic, Jon calls to say he's taking the day off. I can't believe I found him through online dating. Talk about a needle in a haystack."

"It is kind of amazing."

"There are millions of single men in New York City, and that little dating site honed in and picked him out just for me."

"How do you do it?" I asked, watching an afternoon gust charm her hair like special effects in a movie. "How do you get everything to always work out for you?"

I could tell by the way she looked at me that Avril knew she lived a blessed life. I listened for her secret. "Harper, think about it. There's always something to do in New York. We're actresses, the most coveted job in the world, and I'm totally in love. You've already got two out of three. You just need to find someone who loves you. It will change your whole outlook."

"I have a confession to make," I said. "I signed up for LoveSetMatch.com, but I'm not sure it will work the same. It only gave me two matches."

"Harper, you have to give the whole process twenty-four hours to sort your information," Avril said, laughing.

"You mean there's more than just two?"

Avril rolled her eyes. "*Yeah,* they give everyone a couple of matches the first day just to show them how it works. Give it a day or so and you'll start getting the good ones."

Jon rejoined us, and we skated off as a group. After a few times around, watching other couples falling, and falling in *love,* on the ice, I split off on my own. But a half hour of skating and watching Jon and Avril circle the ice hand in hand was enough for me. I navigated the icy rink a few more times, then turned in my white rental skates. Ben had asked everyone to be at the theater by four, and even though I wouldn't be performing, I wanted to focus on opening night.

"Hey, are you finished already?" Jon and Avril skated up to me on the lacing platform. I stood up, back in my church flats.

"I thought I'd go to the apartment. Do you know when you'll be back?" I asked, careful to keep from letting slip Avril's alter-identity.

"We're going to skate a little more, and then go uptown for a late dinner. Why don't you come along?"

A late dinner? I wanted to ask if she'd forgotten about something. *A premiere?*

"You go ahead," I said. "I've got something to do this afternoon."

"I'll let you two say good-bye. It was nice meeting you," Jon said, practicing his backwards moves, shifting into the tide of skaters, careful not to bump into anyone before stopping in the center of the ice.

Avril looked to me for confirmation.

"You do remember the opening, right?" I asked.

"I'm not *that* lovesick, Harper. Not yet anyway."

She pulled her pink cell phone out of her coat pocket and glanced at the hour. "It's still early. Call time is hours away. See, Harper? It all fits together. One thing into another. All you have to do is go with the flow."

Smiling her happy-girl smile, Avril twisted the blade of her white skates and pushed off against the ice in a smooth arch, gliding away from me like a beautiful bird into the arms of her love.

♫

Back in our warm apartment, I boiled water in a stainless-steel tea-kettle at the stove. I'd intended to brew blueberry tea but dumped in a package of hot cocoa powder instead, swept up in a sudden craving for sugar.

After whipping up a tuna salad to go with the hot chocolate, I carried my late lunch over to the alcove and carved out a resting place for my bowl.

I restarted Avril's computer and nibbled on lunch while the site ran me through its page prompts, entering my user name and password. Once my personal page uploaded, I was astonished at what greeted me:

NEW MATCHES: 14

A wave of optimism akin to finding a buried treasure swept over me. I double-clicked on the first match to investigate, feeling weirdly excited and curious.

Match 1 was a twenty-four-year-old NYU grad student named Mark and resembled a high-school freshman who'd just gotten his driver's license. I read through his profile sheet, reminding myself that this was a time to remain open minded. Within minutes, it was obvious that Mark from NYU was probably better off being LoveSetMatched with someone else.

Match 2 was a thirty-eight-year-old architect named James. Currently city of residence? San Diego, California, a mere ten states and three thousand miles away from the island of Manhattan. His stat page indicated he was the father of two young sons, five and six. I scrolled further down his profile page until I found a section titled "My Story" and read the heartbreaking tale of losing his wife to breast cancer.

Tears welled in my eyes. I hadn't expected to actually *feel* anything at an online dating site beyond attraction to the opposite sex.

I clicked on James's photo tab and studied his collection of family pictures. Snapshots of himself with the boys, a family portrait that included his beautiful wife, and finally one of James standing alone with the Pacific Ocean at sunset behind him. The emotion I felt was *empathy*, not desire. I clicked back to his family photos and looked into each set of eyes, the younger boy with sandy blond hair, the defiant older brother looking so much like his father. I said a quiet prayer that God would give them whatever they needed to make their lives whole again and went back to surfing my matches. It was too much sorrow.

Match 3 had already logged in and checked out, assessing my worth as a fixture in his world and finding me lacking. Melvin, a forty-seven-year-old civil servant from St. Paul, Minnesota, had closed out our match. True love lost before its chance to bloom. I noticed the "Close Out Match" tab at the bottom of the page, returned to Match 1 and closed it, then made my way down the list of fourteen.

I moved the mouse to click on Match 4, but slipped and clicked 5 by mistake. Roger was a forty-two-year-old firefighter from Cleveland, Ohio, who'd posted a picture of himself in a blue T-shirt and pants, standing with the guys in front of the company's red fire truck. The photo made me laugh. I could imagine Roger as the last single guy among a group of married firefighters. By the grins on the other men's faces, it looked like they meant to do something about Roger's singleness: one less fire to put out.

The rest of my first matches fell into categories of once, twice, or thrice divorced and just-could-tells. I closed most, if they hadn't reached the same conclusion already. They all seemed like good guys, but with the exception of Mark, the student from NYU, they all lived far away.

Avril had asked me if I were open to a real relationship. Sometimes I'd settle for a cup of coffee and an hour of good conversation, or maybe a few laps skating around Rockefeller Center. But what I really wanted was for God to package up my soul mate and stamp "overnight airmail delivery" on the box.

There'd be no love connection today. I slouched down in the cushioned chair and slid the mouse over to log off LoveSetMatch.com, then realized I'd missed Match 4. A sudden chill prickled up the back of my neck. I wanted Match 4 to be someone special. I whispered a small prayer, then doubled clicked the tab.

Bachelor #4 turned out to be yet another ineligible long-distance single. Luke was a thirty-four-year-old bush pilot living and working in the wilderness of our nation's forty-ninth state. I shook my head, laughing at the lunacy. Didn't I just *pray* for closer? Luke couldn't be farther away if he lived on the seventh ring of Saturn. He listed himself as never married, no children, and employed full time in the lumber industry.

Luke from Alaska was a flying lumberjack.

Wow.

I shut off Avril's computer, even less impressed with my second encounter with good old LoveSetMatch.com. *What a waste of time.* I'd set my hopes too high. But instead of whining, which is what I felt like doing, I found myself *kneeling* beside Avril's desk as clouds outside parked in front of the sun, dimming both the living room and the alcove. I closed my eyes and prayed for James in San Diego, and his two boys.

My gosh, surely it was better to have never loved than to go through the loneliness, find true love, and then lose it. I prayed for Roger and the firefighters, pals who only wanted the best for their friend. I prayed for all the lonely singles in the world, including me. I prayed for every woman seated at the dinner table across from an empty chair, and for every man sleeping in a half-full double. I even prayed for flying lumberjacks.

It was quiet in the small office, as it had been in the Chicago church chapel when I arrived before anyone else and waited for Bella. There my prayers had always centered around me. I was poor and broken, my reservoir of strength like three copper pennies rattling around in the bottom of a mason jar.

"Please help" was the only prayer I'd memorized, and that only because I'd said it so much, with "save me" coming in a close second.

I took a long, hot shower and dressed for the theater. This was the night. One of the students at church had mentioned seeing an advertisement for *Apartment 19* in the *New York Times,* along with a story in the Theater section. I still hadn't asked about ticket sales. Could we sell 702 tickets tonight for an Arthur Mouldain drama no one had seen in thirty years? I hadn't a clue. I was only sure of two things: I wouldn't be acting at the Carney Theatre on opening night, and when my thirty-first birthday arrived in three weeks, I would still be alone.

~ Eleven ~

The three-sided marquee in front of the Carney Theatre dazzled West Forty-fourth Street with its wide backlit panels framed in oversized blue and yellow bulbs. From the opposite side of the street I read the name of the show in black letters that looked three feet tall.

APARTMENT 19

starring Helen Payne

Two newly potted trees decorated the Carney Theatre's front doors like bookends on either side. When I crossed the street, I saw that someone had power-washed every speck of dirt and stuck-on chewing gum from the sidewalk for twenty feet in either direction.

Entering the house through the main lobby, I pushed down the bottom of my theater seat and eased myself quietly into it. Even two hours before opening curtain, a controlled frenzy of activity and excitement crackled in the air.

Helen Payne brought her yapping Pomeranian out from backstage, adding to the chaos. It yammered in her arms like a stuffed toy in a battery commercial. Helen was wearing a long mink coat like I hadn't seen anyone wear before. It was shiny, like it had been freshly oiled or whatever they do to make mink shine, and black as shark's eyes.

At Helen's side stood a tall, manly-looking businesswoman. Her hair was short and silvering at the temples, and her face was cold and tight, as if cracking a smile wouldn't so much warm up her face as tear it. She wore a dark pin-striped suit over her thin, masculine figure, and her briefcase was more of a boxy attaché case than a lady's business satchel. When Ben noticed the two women had emerged from backstage, he climbed the temporary house stairs to greet them.

"I think you're wanted backstage," I heard someone say, and turned to see Mark Blane going over every detail of his stage design. The sleeves of his white shirt were folded to his elbows, and he glanced at me for a second before returning his stare to the set.

"Thanks."

I moved to the front of the theater and climbed onto the stage to search the greenroom for Tabby. I overheard some of Helen's and Ben's conversation as I passed by.

"Ben, you know my agent, Maureen Burns," Helen said. I shot my eyes in their direction just long enough to see Ben, dressed in blue jeans and tan L. L. Bean jacket, take hold of the woman's skeletal hand to shake it as if she were royalty.

I expected the greenroom to be chaotic, but it was dead calm. Even Tabby treated the cast as if she were only there to serve … well, *direct* and serve. I waved to her, a casual check-in that seemed all that was required of me. According to my contract, I was obligated to stay backstage in costume until the start of the second act, then I was free to go. On opening night, of course, there was no way I was leaving.

Beneath the calm, there was an electricity buzzing between cast and crew members as they shared rumors about who would be in the audience. Critics from every New York paper; Sean Connery, who was in town; and maybe even the mayor.

I walked to the makeup room at the end of the hallway where our makeup artist, Laura, was working on Avril. A second artist, Tina, arranged her three-tiered makeup case while waiting for her first actor. A long mirror covered the length of the wall in front of them, encased in warm, bright makeup lights. Avril closed her eyes while Laura sprayed eye shadow on with an air compression applicator.

"I'm glad you made it," I said.

"Was there ever any doubt?" Avril's grin was half obstructed by Laura's arm.

"Good evening, girls. Are you ready to put on a show?" Helen asked as she entered the room, sans the dog, the mink coat, or Maureen Burns. She sat in Tina's chair. Avril, who loved show business, was ready.

"Why, Ms. Payne, we're ready to put on a double feature: *Apartment 19* and *West Side Story* as an encore."

"You know, girls, I was in the original Broadway production of *West Side Story.*"

"You're kidding," Avril said, coming to life in the makeup chair, entering Ms. Payne's domain with ease. Tina swiveled Helen's chair into position in front of the mirror. Helen's dark eyes focused forward until it was obvious she could see only herself as she spoke.

"Oh yes, Winter Garden Theatre 1957. I was a dancer in the chorus. It was an unbelievable show. Jerome Robbins was absolutely brilliant, a true genius. Every actor in New York wanted a shot at that production. I got a call from my agent that they were looking for dancers and I waited in line almost four hours for a chance to audition. They'd rush us onstage in groups of thirty and teach us the dances to see who could learn them fast and do them right the first time. I never wanted anything so bad in my life as a part in that play, and when auditions were over I left Philadelphia in shambles—that's where they held auditions. I was angry with myself for not having done a better job, but the next day they called me."

"Helen, you've done it all," Avril said, getting up from her makeup chair, brushing away the smallest flecks of powder.

"Not yet, I haven't," Helen said, her voice steely with determination. "There's plenty more I have in mind to do. You just watch me."

Avril's dark brown wig made her look barely old enough to drive. Above Avril's eyes, Laura had applied a shade of sky blue eye shadow so thick even the back row would notice she was new to town, or presumably new to applying make up.

Laura joked, "You were really beautiful, Avril, before I started working on you."

"Sounds like something Hollywood would say," Avril retorted. Laura unsnapped the apron from Avril's neck, revealing her costume. I shook my head, marveling at the look of her. Brown hair, thick blue eye shadow, New-York-City-here-I-come wardrobe. She was a completely different person.

"Is that you?" I asked, standing in the doorway.

"It's all me. Like the wig?"

Avril went into her worried and bewildered character, Roxy Dupree.

"I didn't mean to break the vase, Miss Bradford! Honestly, I was only trying to help!"

She broke character and smiled at me, trying out her Roxy look in the mirror one more time.

"I love this character," she said. Avril and I left the makeup room and walked down the hallway, on our way back to the greenroom.

"Is Jon coming to the opening tonight?"

Avril bit her lip. "I still haven't told him about the show."

"Avril …"

"I know, I know, I will soon. It's just that things are going so well. It's a small thing. It's silly, I know, but I've waited for so long to tell him that it's really starting to feel like a secret I'm keeping."

"But you *are* keeping a secret from him."

Avril stopped in the hallway, looking pouty as her Roxy Dupree.

"Oh, I know, and it's not a big deal, but every time I've tried telling him about my career, I worry he'll say, 'Why didn't you just trust me enough to tell me this?' and for that I don't have an answer."

Helen's dressing room door had been opened, every lamp and overhead light switched on bright. Bouquets of red roses were lined up in crystal vases across the counter, doubling in the mirror's reflection. I saw Helen's mink coat dangling from a special hanger on the tall wardrobe rack as we passed by, and then the face of Maureen Burns appeared in the doorway, larger than life, and even scarier up close. She locked eyes with me, never moving a muscle in her cold pale face. Her unexpected emergence imprinted an image of the woman in my mind, like the lingering ghost of a flashbulb.

"In the beginning I didn't know him well enough," Avril continued. "Now too much time has passed. That perfect moment to be up front with Jon about who I really am came and went without my even noticing it."

"You need to just fess up and take your lumps," I said. "After meeting Jon today, I think he'll understand. You can't keep your work a secret forever. Besides, he'll probably be delighted to learn he's dating a TV star, and he'll understand why you were so hesitant to tell him."

My role in the show that night was to be little more than a fly on the wall, so once in the greenroom with the others, I gave Avril the space she'd need to be ready to perform. I stood instead near Harriet, who was breathing in and out like a woman in labor. She and I made eye contact.

"I always get nervous before a show," she told me.

One of the tech assistants came back to place an almost-undetectable performance microphone on Avril's ear and weave its thin cord inside her costume while Phyllis knelt behind her tucking the audio battery pack into the folds of her costume.

"Well, she's here," Ben announced, entering the greenroom.

"Who?" Tabby asked.

"Elisa Mouldain. She'd hinted that she *might* attend our premiere, but I thought it was just a courtesy comment," Ben said. He looked nervous, and for the first time, I felt anxious too. Having nothing to do only added to my anxiety.

"If Elisa Mouldain's out there, Ben, we'll give her the *best show* in New York."

Everyone looked up to see Helen Payne step into the greenroom, decked out in her costume—beige leggings, traditional skirt and vest, royal blue, and her hair bound up in pins and spray.

Helen's Audrey Bradford gave off the impression she'd never felt an emotion she hadn't crushed, but the confidence exuding from the real Helen Payne said there was no battle she couldn't win. She wasn't going to allow the presence of the Pulitzer-winning playwright's daughter to be anything more than a subplot to her performance, seldom-seen recluse from London or not.

"Helen, you look fantastic," Ben said. She leaned in, inviting him to offer a faux stage kiss near her cheek.

"Oh, thank you, Ben. I just wanted to come in for a moment and say to all my fellow actors, *this is the night* we bring Mouldain's masterpiece back to American theater where it belongs."

The circle of cast members cheered. I hadn't seen this motivational side of Helen before.

"New York has a well-deserved reputation for producing some of the finest theater in all the world. Broadway! Mark my words, you will remember this night for as long as you live. The night you were a part of the electricity that lit up the Great White Way. Now, all of you, *break a leg*, and make a *great* show."

Helen turned and left the room. I expected to see a royal cape flowing behind her. "That's why you hire a 'Helen Payne,'" I said to Harriet.

"Worth every penny."

"To that," Ben said, "let me only add it's a full house tonight, a totally sold–out show. We were about one hundred tickets shy of that yesterday, but with walk-ups, there's not an empty seat in the Carney."

More cheers.

Tabby waited until she saw Ben had finished. The microphone of her headset curved against her right cheek, and she listened to the technical chatter coming from the front of the house.

"Okay, I need everyone in their places for Scene one," Tabby said. "Five minutes until showtime."

Avril gave me a hug and said, "Wish me luck," then left for her entrance on stage right. I followed her, wandering behind the curtain, careful to stay out of everyone's way. Three minutes before curtain. A moment later Avril suddenly rushed toward me, away from her spot designated for Scene 1, and I realized she wasn't wearing any shoes.

"I can't find my shoes!" she shout-whispered to me.

I ran back into the dressing room.

"Avril's shoes," I said to Phyllis. We scoured the room in a flurry of costume wrap, wire hangers, and paper cups. Phyllis, ever organized, got down on her hands and knees, digging through paper, shoe boxes, plastic from garment bags, and costume debris. She reached in and found the shoes for Scene 1 still in their box. Phyllis lifted the lid and dashed past me to the backstage area. She knelt before Avril, who lifted her foot and pointed her toe for a fitting. In a scene from the pages of Cinderella, the shoe was a perfect fit, and with less than sixty seconds before curtain, Avril dashed away to the wings.

I gravitated to the other side, stage left, and peeked out at the audience, a sophisticated-looking lot dressed in New York City chic. Aisles of black against crimson. The lights from the grand chandelier above them reflected in eyeglasses like fiery sparks until Richard began to dim the houselights.

"Ten seconds," Tabby said, her hand cupping her microphone. I heard the powerful whirling hum of the thick, red velvet curtain being pulled open on its steel cable. This was it. The spotlights pointing from special platforms on the balcony shined so brightly that the light flooded underneath the black curtain backstage, lighting up Phyllis's shoes.

There was no music in the show, but we had the best sound effects. The opening scene was accompanied by the sounds of a busy, downtown Manhattan of yesteryear.

Roxy Dupree opens the scene. She's so thrilled to be in the Big Apple. She's left her small-town pond where she was the big fish, and she's set her sights on making a name for herself in Manhattan. She knows no one in town; she has just one connection—a distant relative everyone back home said she should call. Roxy wouldn't dream of asking to live with her; she was too polite. She just knows, however distant the relative, that visiting was the right thing to do, and who knew, maybe Audrey Bradford knew a lonely older lady with a room for rent.

I'd never worked with a star of Helen's stature before, and wondered if the audience would applaud her entrance, the way they did on all those old TV sitcoms when a door unexpectedly opens and the star walks in.

When the lights went down on Scene 1, the grips rolled everything off the stage, raising the first backdrop and revealing Audrey Bradford's apartment in the dark. Once every prop and fixture was in place, the lights came up, bathing the luxurious but prim apartment in a yellowy wash. Helen stood in the middle of the set, her back to the audience, yellow cleaning gloves pulled over both hands. A lime-green feather duster whisked away in one as she attacked dust particles on the fireplace mantel.

Audrey doesn't speak right away. She doesn't turn to acknowledge the audience. She cleans and whips the feather duster, snapping it between the silver candlesticks and the photo of her late husband, Charles.

Then the doorbell rings. She knows who it is, of course. It's her kin blood, distant, but family nonetheless. It rings a second time, and Audrey Bradford sets down the feather duster, giving it one good shake into the open fireplace.

Helen hasn't delivered one line in the scene yet. The audience is uncomfortable. She stops and turns to look out over the audience as if she's heard them thinking, and gives them an unsavory, disapproving grimace. The look says she doesn't see anyone out there, but if she did, she wouldn't like it. Not one bit.

Audrey Bradford pulls off the yellow gloves with a snap and, with her work apron draped over her arm, hoists a cheery smile up with one quick pull from somewhere in the dark cellar of the soul. It rises to the lower part of her face, but no higher. It hangs there fixed in position on hooks beneath eyes that are always Audrey, and she opens one of the tall doors, narrow as an ignorant mind, with a twist of the handle. They are beautiful, ornate, clean, and so attractive on the outside like many things are. Roxy Dupree enters Apartment 19.

"Good afternoon. Mrs. Bradford, I presume?" the politely formal Roxy utters as she steps into Audrey's living room.

"Ms.," she replies—a line Helen Payne had used once in rehearsals, only to be told the word wasn't in the script and couldn't be included onstage.

"But why, Ben?" Helen whined. "It's *exactly* what the moment demands."

"It's not Mouldain's word," Ben told her. "No one even used that word when this play was written. It wasn't in the syntax."

But here on opening night, Helen breaks the rules and tells Roxy, *"It's Ms."*

"Oh," Avril says, ad-libbing because Helen has thrown her a curve. Avril's a talented, natural actress but totally lost in the world of improvisation. She knows what she's supposed to say next only when Helen says exactly what she's supposed to say first. The audience doesn't notice, but from across the stage, I do and so does Ben Hughes. I hear him moan something into the curve of his hand resting against his lips. Avril is off for a second, but Helen isn't finished. She adds the line she was supposed to speak in the first place.

"You've called for an interview. Won't you come in?"

And Roxy Dupree steps into a world she cannot possibly imagine—a world that runs according to the whims, rules, timetables, and logic of the psychotic Audrey Bradford.

Harriet fidgeted backstage during intermission. She'd already walked on during the first half of the show, but that first entrance was minor. Her most important scenes were in the second act.

"Don't worry. You'll do great, Harriet," I told her.

"I can't believe how nervous I get before going on. When Helen opened that door onstage and looked at me, I almost forgot my line. That woman scares the spit out of me."

"You're just excited. You'll calm down once you get out there."

"Easy for you to say. You don't have to go onstage," Harriet said, joking while she bordered on the edge of a panic attack. "Harper, would you pray for me?"

Harriet's request surprised me, but I nodded that I would and stepped closer, taking both of Harriet's hands in mine, the way Bella used to pray for me. I pulled in closer, feeling the starch of her hair spray rough against my cheek, and prayed for a calm spirit, for protection and covering for her son, Darius, and that she'd use the gift God had given her to entertain the audience. I prayed that Harriet would feel God's presence with her onstage and that she wouldn't be afraid.

I said "Amen" and saw Harriet wipe at her eye.

"Thank you. I feel better," Harriet said, giving me a hug before going off to wait for her cue.

After that, the night began to gallop like a dark horse over covered bridges. All the actors hit their marks and delivered lines with the force of hoofbeats on wooden planks.

Second act picks up quickly as the tension between Audrey and Roxy builds to a fever. The landlord and the neighbor become involved. Finally, the police are called in, and Audrey is brought before a New York City judge. She's unrepentant, and he's not impressed.

When Audrey finally goes too far and threatens him, the case solves itself. She tells the judge it's he who is wrong—the laws in the state of New York are wrong, and the whole world is wrong. Only Audrey Bradford is right.

Audrey is cuffed by the bailiff and taken into custody. Struggling, she vows revenge as the judge bangs down his gavel and she's dragged screaming from the courtroom.

The judge asks if there's anything he can do for Roxy, and she says, "Forgive her, your honor. She doesn't know any better."

The next day Roxy and her friend Bill are moving her into a new apartment in the light of a new day.

"It must be quite a relief for you, moving into a new place on your own," Bill says.

"What will happen to her, Bill?" Roxy asks, concerned for the woman who's made her life a prison.

"The judge said six months," he tells her. *"But I don't know that you'll ever see her again. Audrey's not the type that mixes well with others."*

He leaves, and a moment later there is a knock on her door. Roxy opens it to find a wild, crazy-eyed Audrey Bradford standing in the doorway, somehow freed from custody. It's a reversal of how the two first met, only Audrey blames Roxy for everything. Audrey swipes a knife at Roxy, misses, and fatally stabs herself.

Audrey struggles to speak, to condemn one last time, but collapses onto the ledge of the fire escape with only her legs hanging inside the window.

The stage lights went dark, and the audience at the Carney abruptly seemed uncomfortably silent.

The applause came like the opening of a shaken soda can, a sudden, instantaneous roar pent up until the spellbinding end. When the stage lights came back on, I watched from the wings as each cast member returned to the stage, taking their bows. The audience was on its feet, all 702 ticket holders unable to contain their enthusiasm. As each major cast member came out—Harriet, Melissa, Marshall— the expectation of the audience grew. When Helen stepped onto the Carney Theatre stage for her ovation, it was as if she owned all of Broadway. She had given them the performance of a lifetime. Now Helen fed on their appreciation. This was New York—Broadway, not St. Louis, Kansas City, or Seattle. A packed house filled with theater critics, guild members, wealthy patrons of the arts, and even Mouldain's own daughter.

Helen stood at center stage and absorbed their applause, their recoronation of her as the Queen of the Great White Way.

Finally, Ben Hughes stepped onstage with another two dozen roses for Helen, who graciously accepted them. Ecstatic cast members disappeared through the wings while Helen stayed onstage until the very last scream, waving to the crowd, shaking a few hands of the standing fans fortunate enough to be in the front row. Then she blew them all a kiss and exited stage left.

A festive party broke out in the greenroom. Someone had brought bottles of expensive French champagne and set it to chill on ice in stainless-steel buckets. Marshall wasted no time popping the first cork. I listened as reporters interviewed Avril, who sat in a chair, sparkle makeup still glittering underneath her eyes, about what it felt like to be her at that moment.

Ben's production partners joined the elated cast. One of the investment bankers held a half-filled glass in one hand, waving the other around with excitement as he brought Helen the news.

"You should hear what they're saying about you in the front lobby, Helen," he said. "They're saying it's the role of a lifetime. You were magnificent! Everyone is going to be talking about this show tomorrow."

Helen smiled, always happy for a grateful public.

The rumors proved true about Elisa Mouldain. I saw the demure woman backstage, shaking Ben's hand and telling him how pleased she was. His gamble had paid off. Ben gave his speech of gratitude to the cast and crew, and in thirty minutes, all hangers-on were gone, or taking off to another venue.

Theater life is surreal because everyone believes in the magic. Even adults, who know we're just pretending, believe that somewhere, somehow the story must be true. They don't accept that there's no Apartment 19, no Audrey Bradford, and no Roxy Dupree.

No attempted murder, no death by knife wound.

It's all just a show.

~ Twelve ~

The *New York Times* Theater section featured one, and only one story—*Apartment 19*. A single, shocking headline stamped across the front page staggered Avril and me, zapping us like static electricity every time our eyes flashed on it:

A HIT!

We'd ventured out that cold morning to the neighborhood newsstand to buy all the city papers we could carry. Every superlative printed in black and white by the New York reviewers burned like fuel to warm us.

The show was "mesmerizing" … "original" … "a triumph." Helen's portrayal of Audrey Bradford was "stunning," they said. It marked her return to Broadway, and was "more than a little scary."

Reviewers raved about Avril, the skinny blonde girl from "that California TV show" who, they discovered, could actually act.

In the bottom right corner, the *Times* ran a small black-and-white illustration of Mouldain. It showed the playwright looking out from beneath his trademark white Panama hat, wearing his Teddy Roosevelt glasses, smoke flowing into the frame from some unseen rolled cigar. Mouldain seemed to look back from beyond, ready to accept his much-deserved accolades from modern critics.

The sidebar told of Mouldain's work, its mysterious departure from American theater and decline in popularity, and Ben Hughes's Herculean campaign to bring *Apartment 19* back to Broadway.

Avril and I sat on the carpeted living room floor, newspapers spread out around us as if we were training a new puppy. We lounged away the morning in our pajamas, giddy with the reviews and the prospect of having the day off. From then on, the cast and crew would come together only at night for performances and on Saturday for a matinee.

A short electronic beep sounded in the kitchen, followed by a woman's voice on the speakerphone. Avril had an eccentric habit of shutting off the phone's ringer so the first thing you heard when people called was the sound of their voice.

"Avril? Harper? It's me, Sydney. Would you please pick up?"

At 7 a.m. Pacific time, our beloved theatrical agent, Sydney Bloom, telephoned us from her offices in Los Angeles. I pictured Sydney sitting at her sunny California desk in the bungalow not a five-minute drive from Paramount Studios. I could see the potted palm trees in the reception area and the brown Spanish tiles that had always felt cool on my bare feet but warm in the sunbeams.

"Avril, your stock is rising," Sydney forecast. I perched on a bar stool at the black marble island, watching Avril lean in on the other side.

"Since the run for the play is an insanely short forty-two shows, we should pick out a day next week and conference on what you want to do next. Every production company in Hollywood starts the day reading the trades, and this morning they'll be reading your reviews. You know who I'm talking about. I'll tell you right now, I think you should come back to LA and do film because that's where the money is. We're going to double what we've been asking for you."

Avril smiled from across the island.

"And as for you, Harper—even though you're not onstage, the fact that you're a part of this Mouldain revival paints a smiley face on your portfolio. Have you girls seen the trades posted online this morning?"

"No, we've just been basking in the reviews."

"Well, allow me to share some good news. Variety is reporting that half the shows for *Apartment 19* have already sold out, and ticket sales remain brisk. I wouldn't be surprised if the whole run sold out."

Sydney gave us the latest Hollywood news and speculated about what it might mean for our careers, but soon the conversation shifted exclusively to Avril. When she lifted the phone off the charger, disengaging the speakerphone, I wandered back to my bedroom.

The apartment felt cozy, warmed by good news while a light snow fell on New York outside my bedroom window.

I lay down on my bed to pray, thanking God for blessing the show with success. The contrast between my old life in Chicago and my new one in New York wasn't going unnoticed either.

A rare sense of peace made my spirit feel healthy, as if some phase of a program had been completed. I still couldn't answer Katie's question about what role I played in the show, but I was confident God was at work in my life, even if I didn't know exactly what He was doing.

Hearing Avril still on the phone, I slipped into the computer alcove, set my half-empty coffee mug on the coaster, and booted up Avril's computer. Once the Mac was up and running, I clicked back onto LoveSetMatch.com.

A colorful new company logo welcomed me—a beautiful daisy with open petals bloomed behind the LoveSetMatch name, its green stem looping through the logo like a vine. But the daisy wasn't all that was new. Seven additional matches had come in overnight. I closed out six of them without batting an eye, and the seventh I closed after batting it only once. Of the twenty-three matches I'd received so far, only two remained active. It wasn't the quality of people so much that made me close them out; there was just something about shopping for a best friend and life partner online that didn't agree with me. I thought about canceling my subscription and scrolled along the bar at the top of the screen looking for help to do just that. LoveSetMatch.com had upgraded their site, making navigation easier, even if the search for a soul mate was as much an enigma as ever. A new tab appeared overnight, a light blue clickable button that caught my attention with a word and a number: "Messages (2)."

I clicked, opening my in-box and saw a message from James, the architect and father of two in San Diego. I read his email titled "Greetings from San Diego!"

> Hi Harper! It's nice to meet you. I read your profile and even though it says you live far away in NYC, I thought I'd say hello. I'm the father of two young boys, both busy with soccer and private school. Don't know if you'd read my story of how we all got here, but the boys lost their mother just over two years ago, very suddenly. We have held on through of our faith in Jesus Christ, and slowly, we are trying to pick up the pieces again. If you feel so led, write back. I'd enjoy hearing about your life in The Big Apple.
>
> –James

Is there any reasonable way to explain attraction? How is it we know when we're drawn to one person and not another? There was something about his simple story that compelled me. Acting on impulse, I clicked to reply.

> Hi James, thank you for your message. I'm new to LoveSetMatch.com, so I haven't figured out what it is I'm doing here yet. I was moved by your family's story of loss, though, and can't imagine how difficult it must be for you and the boys. I'm sure you don't need me telling you that. I just wanted to send you a message to say I'm praying for you.
>
> –Harper

I pushed Send and watched the message I'd written vanish into the screen.

Avril's phone call with Sydney had ended, and she'd slipped back to her bedroom, passing me in the computer alcove, and closing her door. I thought she'd glance over my shoulder and ask about my matches, but she didn't. I didn't really have anything to say, anyway.

I clicked on the other message, this one from the flying lumberjack in Alaska. A time stamp in the corner told me his message had been sent within the hour.

> Hey Harper,
>
> Greetings from the wilderness of Alaska. I almost closed our match when it first came in because of the distance between us, but I'm glad I didn't. I think you're very beautiful, and after reading your profile, I just wanted to at least reach out and say hey.

I wish everybody could see the view from where I work. I spent
yesterday on a bulldozer clearing an acre of timberland, a
preventive step we take to stop forest fires. The sky is the brightest
blue here, and there are miles and miles of pine trees as far as
the eye can see. I'm not sure if you'll reply or not, but I thought I'd
extend my hand anyway. Have a good one.

–Luke

I hadn't taken time to look at Luke's photos or his profile the
day of our match, disenchantment ruling the day and all. There
were three photos on Luke's page. I'd seen his profile picture the first
night—Luke on a snowy mountaintop somewhere, wearing a blue
ski parka and dark mountaineer's glasses.

The next showed Luke standing on the front porch of a rustic cabin,
its timber showing the marks of the hand tools that cut it, a stack of fire-
wood behind him. The third photo was an action shot snapped as Luke
boarded a small airplane for takeoff. He was giving the thumbs-up sign,
and the plane's door was open so the cockpit controls were visible over
Luke's shoulder. The plane itself looked like it might carry four people at
most. I imagined it buffeted by winds at 18,000 feet and started to feel
a little green just from the thought. I clicked on Luke's message to reply.

Hi Luke, Alaska sounds beautiful, but maybe a little chilly. I like your
photographs, and wanted to say thanks for the compliment. I'm
responding just to say I'm not really interested in a long-distance
relationship. Sorry, that sounds pretty cold written out like that. :)
But I don't know another way to say it. I won't be at all surprised if
the next time I sign on, I find you've closed out this match. A friend

of mine encouraged me to try this, but I think I'll focus on matches here in the NYC. Take care!

–Harper

Poor guy. I was sure life in the Alaskan wilderness could get lonely, which would explain why he joined an online dating community. I pushed Send, then glided the mouse pointer down to close out my match with Luke. I paused, the blinking arrow pulsed over the Close button. Maybe I'd just let him close me out. My message hadn't been very friendly.

I shut down the computer, aware of its fan whirling and humming until the monitor screen went dark. I decided the online dating world of LoveSetMatch.com was odd, awkward, and just not for me. I'd cancel my membership and try to get a refund. Like that was going to happen.

♫🖱

The marquee lights of the Carney Theatre were as radiant on the second night as they'd been at the premiere. They seemed to be saying something new, however—that *Apartment 19* had proved itself worthy of attention all over again.

I walked in through the front lobby and through the open theater doors into the vacant house. I half expected to see Richard adjusting lights as he'd done the night before, or George behind the control console fidgeting with knobs and sliders, but the room was dark and quiet.

Tabby had telephoned late in the afternoon saying that Ben wanted to see me. Could I come into the theater an hour earlier?

I didn't think to ask why. Anything trivial, Ben could have just told me over the phone, and anything general, he'd relay to the entire cast. So why had Ben asked the stage production director to call me? Had something happened to Helen?

The temporary stairs the cast used during rehearsals were gone, rolled away by stage grips and hauled out of sight. I used a service entrance to go backstage and watched carefully where I stepped in the dusky jumble of props, cables, and clutter.

The narrow service hallway let out behind the curtain. I walked in dimmest light past the costumes and the greenroom. Eventually the route took me past the star's dressing room before reaching Ben's office. Helen's door was open, her lights on, and I was startled to see her sitting alone backstage in what looked to be a new, cushioned makeup chair. She looked up as I passed by.

"Harper, will you come in here for a moment, please?"

Helen was wearing a bright red silk kimono with small golden dragons embroidered in a delicate pattern. Her hair was piled high, held up in a clip as she applied cold cream to her face. She exuded a calm power sitting in that tall chair with padded armrests, seat, and back. She stroked on skin cream, watching herself in the mirror. I could tell she was all business.

"Sit down," she said. I sat in one of two white canvas director's chairs against the wall. "And close the door, will you?"

I stood again, hiked over to the door, closed it, and returned to the closest of the two uncomfortable chairs.

"It must be killing you, not being more a part of this production," Helen said, glancing my direction between swipes of cold cream. "I know it would me.

"I like you, Harper," she continued. "You've put up with a lot of crap in the time you've been here. You've come into a difficult situation and you've worked hard, and for that I admire you. No one would think any less of you for wanting to have what I have. To stand on that stage tonight before an expectant Broadway audience and give them the performance of a lifetime. It's every young actress's dream ..." She halted her soliloquy to turn and face me.

"But Ben and I had a meeting earlier today, and I want you to know there's no way that's ever going to happen. I wish you no ill will, because that's bad luck in the theater, but I won't have you shadowing me around in costume every night hoping that I somehow fall off the stage and break my neck so you can go on in my place. Is that clear?" Her voice rose slightly in pitch and volume.

"What are you talking about?" I asked, confused by Helen's suspicions, the boiling paranoia now seeping through her fractured thinking.

Helen turned back to face her reflection in the mirror, dabbing on powder, and I thought of a wicked queen in a Disney fairy tale who looked to the mirror's image to tell her future.

"Helen, I've never once wished you any ill will. I'm *your* understudy. It's my job to be here for you just in case ..."

"I know all about why you're here," she said, turning her half-powdered face in my direction, snapping at me like Audrey Bradford. "Don't waste my time with your explanations. I've already discussed it with Ben, and it's decided. From now on, I'd like you to be where I can't see you, preferably not in costume, and definitely not backstage. Don't you have a cell phone or something? I don't know why you couldn't be outside the theater entirely. Why not sit in a coffee shop across the street? You can be wherever Ben wants to place you, but for the good of this show, you can't be where I don't want you."

She turned one more time to face me, peering out of the tops of her eyes as if staring over the rim of bifocals. I stood up, since I couldn't think of a reason to stay any longer. This woman was nuts. She was a lioness killing off any competition who threatened her.

"Unbelievable," I said, dumbstruck. I moved toward the door to leave.

"Now, don't pout about it. Being understudy for me in this show is the biggest break in your career. We're all called upon in life, and especially in the theater, to do things for the good of the show. I'm sure you will have your day in the sun, but this is mine. And *this* is how it has to be."

Helen shifted gears on a dime, going from demanding diva to sweet as a grandmother.

"There, there, I hope you don't think me too harsh. I do like you, Harper, but I must put my performance and this show above all else. You do understand that, don't you? Good."

I closed Helen's dressing room door behind me and stood there, stunned. I felt a presence watching me from down the hallway, and I turned to see Ben standing outside his office.

"Please don't tell me Helen just had a word with you?" he said, though it had to be obvious by the look on my face. He stepped closer, placing his hands on my shoulders, then held me, his compassionate face inches away and bathed in backstage lighting.

"I specifically told her I would be the one to talk to you about this," he said with a measured tone.

Ben escorted me to the office, shutting the door behind us. He wore a haggard expression I didn't expect to see on a Broadway director with a hit play. He gestured for me to take a seat and took his on the corner of the desk.

"Helen called me this morning and told me she didn't want you around the production any longer. I asked her why, and she told me you were bad luck, which doesn't make sense, but that was her reasoning."

Ben blew out his frustration and anger.

"I think this is all about jealousy," he continued. "She had a fit when she saw there were different Audrey Bradford costumes for the two of you. She demanded I explain why her understudy should have a better wardrobe than the star. Then her agent-slash-pit-bull, Maureen Burns, read me the riot act for twenty minutes over the phone asking why I would want to *purposely* aggravate the star of the show."

Ben closed his eyes, massaging his eyebrows with his thumb and forefinger. "Helen is a legendary actress, but she's also one royal pain in the backside."

Ben stood. "I've been working on this show every day for a year and half. Suddenly, we have an overnight hit on Broadway. We just got word that *all* the tickets have sold out, but I've got a leading lady who knows she's a star and she wants to push it as far as she can."

"It's all right, Ben. I understand."

"This isn't even the show I intended to direct. But we had to have a 'Helen Payne' if we hoped to make any money, and we had to stay inside the box creatively and do things old school."

Ben continued talking, and I realized he wasn't consoling me anymore, but popping the cork on something that had been bottled up inside him for months.

"She also called Tabby this morning demanding a new makeup stool be installed in her dressing room before tonight's performance. The other chair hurt her back. Then that Burns woman called to tell me *I agreed* to pay Helen a percentage of the box office receipts should the play sell out. She said that's a standard part of all of Helen's agreements. Funny how I hadn't heard about this until now."

"It's a wonderful play, Ben. I'm sorry it can't all be about the acting and the story the way it used to be."

Ben stopped pacing and sat in the chair next to me, placing his hands on mine, searching my eyes for an answer or perhaps a simple peace. "I'm the one who should be sorry. I don't mean to burden you with all this. It's just a little insight into the magical world of theater production. Seems like the longer I do this, the less it's about art and the more it's about the business."

He looked at me without speaking for a moment. "It *was* all easier then, wasn't it? The rush was bigger, the egos were smaller. It all made sense. *Love* made sense."

"We were young and romantic, all of us were, Ben. We studied acting, lived it, breathed it. The passion poured over into everything we did."

He was quiet.

"Do you remember?" he asked.

"Yes."

"What happened to us?"

I snorted. "You know what happened. You went to London to work in the National Theatre. It was the opportunity of a lifetime."

"Indeed, it was. I got a chance to direct for money, and never looked back. Maybe that's my problem, Harper. I never look back, and I lose focus on what really matters."

Neither of us spoke. His words resounded in the room, impossible to ignore. I felt angry, hurt, and wanted to quit. To escape someplace where life was easier, but I couldn't imagine anywhere fitting that description.

"Which sadly leads me back to Helen's third demand of the day." Ben shook his head, exasperated. "I hate doing this, Harper. It goes against everything I stand for, and you know I hate the politics. But I'm going to be honest enough with you to say this to your face. I am going to do what Helen wants because I've got two business partners who backed me on a risky venture and I owe them my loyalty, and because there are only forty-one shows, but I won't do it without apologizing to you. Professionally, you're a talented actress. Personally, well …"

"I understand. I can't say I like it even a little bit, but your hands are tied. I'm not sure what my role is here anymore."

We stood and embraced in another awkward silence. It was a lingering hold on each other that reminded me of the Ben Hughes I knew at Northwestern, when we were both acting students and starry-eyed boyfriend and girlfriend.

"Harper, you've always been a genuine person," he said, his mouth next to my ear. "It's your heart, I guess. You seem even more real to me now."

We stepped apart, not knowing what it meant.

"So, as much as it pains me, it would probably be best for you to just find a seat with George and Perry at the soundboard. Tabby or I will let you know from night to night what's going on."

Ben's tone was beleaguered, defeated. He'd never treated actors this way.

"It's okay. Looks like I'm going from understudy to undercover."

That brought a smile to Ben's lips, but it soon faded along with any remaining hope I had of rediscovering my career as an actress.

On the night of the second performance, I sat in the sound booth with George and Perry. I didn't see Ben again that night, or Helen, or even Avril, except for watching them perform Act 1 under the bright lights onstage. At the beginning of Act 2, Tabby sent a text message to my phone that read:

You can leave now.

I stood up from my seat, grabbed my leather jacket from the back of the chair, and left quietly. Except for ushers and a man leaving the restroom, the lobby was empty.

I let myself out through the front door.

~ THIRTEEN ~

Back in the quiet apartment I took a long, hot shower. The tears didn't come until after I'd slipped into my pj's and curled up in bed with the lights off, my comforter pulled up to my chin. I must have cried for half an hour, wiping away tears of confusion and rejection with tissues I found in the bathroom. I set the box within easy reach on the nightstand.

An hour later, I went into the kitchen in stocking feet, poured a bowl of Cheerios, and carried it to the alcove. I pulled the tasseled chain on the desk lamp and felt its heat instantly warming the back of my hand.

I logged onto LoveSetMatch.com to search for life in cyberspace. There were two new messages, each bearing its own intriguing title.

LIFE IN CALIFORNIA

LEAVING TOMORROW

I opened "Life in California" first, from James.

Dear Harper,

I'm glad you wrote back. I'm not sure what I'm doing in an online dating service either. Some people are able to pick up the pieces and move on more easily, I guess, but for us, it's been very slow going. My friends worry that after two years, I'm just not getting back on the relationship horse fast enough, so to speak. So, at their well-intentioned urging, I'm finally interacting with the opposite sex. Believe me when I say, I'm fine with you being in New York City. That's as close as I can possibly handle.

–James

I shifted in the chair, lifting my foot to the pillow on the seat and resting my heel there. I didn't know what to write, but I wanted to say something.

Dear James,

I know what you mean about enjoying the distance. What I've gone through this year doesn't compare with your loss—not by a long shot, but it's given me a new compassion for people facing adversity. Just a short note to say I'll be praying for you, for peace in your life, as well as healing. I won't pray for the dating and marriage stuff. That's all too crazy anyway.

–Harper

Seeing that Luke hadn't taken my hint and closed our match, I opened his message hoping for something to cheer my mood.

Hey Harper,

Close us out? No way! :) This is my main line of communication when I'm clearing land in the Northeast Territory. It's my social network when I come back to the cabin after work and cook dinner. Tonight's menu? Canned stew and dinner rolls.

My ten days is almost up here, then it's back to civilization: Wasilla, Alaska, population 9,000. I'll have to tell you about my other job sometime—bush pilot and delivery guy. I fly supplies to missionaries in remote regions.

So, I'm not planning on closing our match, at least not until I get to Wasilla. :)

–Luke

Our lives couldn't be more different. Not only was Luke three thousand miles away, he lived in wilderness. He had to drive for days to see another living soul. I had to take the train to Central Park just to see trees.

My cell phone rang. I slid back the desk chair and dashed to the bedroom to answer it.

"Harper? It's Avril. The show's over, and I just now heard what happened to you. I can't tell you how disgusted I am with you-know-who. I about lost it with Tabby when she told me." The crowd noise behind her made it difficult to hear. "The whole cast knows, and they aren't too crazy about it either."

"They're not angry with Ben, are they?"

"Go higher up the food chain. I love actors. They're totally self-focused half the time, but some things will definitely pull them together. The star kicking out the understudy is one of those things. It's ticked off a lot of people."

"Like who?" I asked, covering my ear to better hear her.

"Well, Tabby's not real thrilled. Marshall wants to file a grievance with Actor's Equity. My gosh, Harriet said—and this is an exact quote—she said, 'I'm gonna go in there and strangle that woman.' She was obviously joking, but I think you get the picture."

"I knew I liked Harriet."

"Oh, Harper, this whole thing stinks. How about I bring you some of those Chinese egg noodles you love?"

"And maybe some hot and sour soup?"

"Yes, definitely. I'm super pumped from the show, so I hope you aren't planning on going to bed anytime soon. We can stay up all night talking, eat Chinese food, and I'll fill you in word for word on what everyone said tonight. It probably won't change things, but it might make you feel better."

Avril was right; talking wouldn't change my situation, but her call did make me feel better.

I closed the cell phone and set it on the desk. Luke's message stared at me from the computer screen. For a second time, I thought about shutting down our online match because of the distance, and yet a part of me agreed with his line of reasoning. What harm was there in just having fun with it? I'd paid for the membership.

Luke,

Life in New York couldn't be more different from where you live. The only trees here grow in Central Park, and I'm fairly certain even the governor can't cut them down.

You'll have to tell me more about piloting goods to missionaries, unless Wasilla proves too great a distraction for you.

–Harper

By 10 p.m., Avril had returned home bearing gifts: Chinese carry-out boxes, one with curry chicken, another with brown rice, and an extra-tall container of hot and sour soup. I peeled open the lid with my thumb and inhaled the comforting aroma.

"Fill me in on everything that happened tonight," I said, getting two soup bowls from the cabinet behind the island.

"No one likes seeing a member of the cast mistreated, even if that someone is the new understudy," she began. "You don't know Marshall very well, do you? He's a by-the-book kind of guy when it comes to this stuff. Actor's Equity union member. If anyone does something wrong to a fellow actor, Marshall's right there. Tabby's like that too, but you have to know Helen hasn't exactly been kind to Tabby either."

"She hasn't?"

"Are you kidding? Helen will only talk directly to Ben about things, even small matters. She considers Tabby to be of no impor-tance; she won't even acknowledge her. Harriet's just on your side. I don't know what's gotten into her, but she made that very clear in her own outspoken way.

"And I spoke with Ben after Tabby told me what happened, and he's just down. He should be basking in the show's success, but it's only made Helen harder to work with. To make matters worse, Ben told me Helen's agent, Maureen Burns—whoa, is she one scary broad—insisted on dinner with him and Helen after the show, which Ben was looking forward to like a root canal."

"Poor guy."

"It's a ruckus, but you know how the winds can shift with a cast. They can be standoffish about accepting a newcomer, but you were definitely getting some good vibes backstage tonight."

"I'll take what I can get. There's been such a rivalry hanging over this cast. Helen's against Tabby, Tabby's hostile to me, Helen and her agent are going after Ben. There's such a spirit of acrimony. It's not right."

Avril took a bite of noodles dangling from chopsticks. "I don't know why it's that way, but yes, I've definitely noticed. As for the show, the audience absolutely loved it. People are so excited to be in the theater because every other Broadway show runs until ticket sales dry up, but with *Apartment 19*, there are only forty shows left, baby, and we're out."

"Thirty thousand tickets on an island of eight million."

"There were actually scalpers outside the theater tonight. Oh, and get this, when I walked out onstage in the first act, I could literally feel the excitement in the theater like it was a rock show. It's crazy, so crazy I'm actually thinking of inviting Jon to come see me in the play." Avril smiled at me, her own problem resolved. "Tabby told the cast there are a few Annie Oakleys reserved for us to invite friends."

"Have you told him yet?"

Avril sighed. "No, and he hasn't mentioned anything. All the advertisements just mention Helen, not me, and he's too busy to sit around reading theater reviews. So, it will be a surprise."

I was tempted to give Avril my disapproving face, but just kept it to myself.

"I was going to tell him yesterday, but it was a timing thing. I mean, I really don't think it's that big a deal. So what, I haven't told him I'm actually a *working* actress. There's probably things he hasn't told me, but now that the show's a hit, I'm sort of excited to tell him."

"You'd let him know before you walked onstage?"

"Absolutely. I think some fair warning is in order. I'll just say, 'Would you like to come see a show I'm in?' and he'll say, 'Of course! What off-off-off Broadway theater are you performing at?' and I'll say 'Brace yourself, Jon. I'm starring at the Carney Theatre in *Apartment 19,* and I'll leave a ticket for you at the Will Call window.'"

I smiled. "You know, he may actually go for that."

Avril set her chopsticks across the dinner plate. "It always works out, Harper. You just have to learn to go with the flow."

At 1:43 a.m. I was awakened by the sound of someone talking in our apartment. A woman's voice, raspy and low, was coming from the kitchen. Startled, I raised up on one elbow to listen.

I tossed off my covers and jammed my arm into the sleeve of my robe, yanking open the door to find a sleepy-eyed Avril emerging from her bedroom across the alcove and looking like a mirror's refection of myself. We'd both heard it, the amplified breathing and the woman's voice.

"Hello?"

The apartment was dark but for the whisper of yellow light coming from a night light next to the sink, and a pinprick ruby dot the answering machine displayed.

"Harper, this is your agent, Sydney Bloom. Will you please pick up the phone? Harper, I realize it's late, but I have to talk to you. Please call me as soon as you get this message."

We both charged into the kitchen and pushed the button for the speakerphone.

"Hey, we're here. What's going on?" I said, my voice rough with sleep, edgy from the rush of adrenaline.

"Good. I caught you. For a minute I thought you might be out somewhere. I tried reaching your cell phone, but it goes directly to the message. Anyway, that's not important. Harper, are you sitting down?"

"No, I'm standing in the kitchen with Avril. Sydney, what's going on?"

"Here's what's going on, Ben Hughes has fired Helen from the show. Apparently, her agent requested a business dinner right after the show tonight, or last night, whatever. Anyway, Maureen Burns has been Helen's agent forever and has a reputation for giving directors migraines. Maureen told Ben they had a right to some of the box office for Helen's performances. After going back and forth for an hour, Maureen wouldn't budge, and Ben told Helen she could clear out. He agreed to pay Helen for Sunday and Monday night, but said she wouldn't be performing on Tuesday. So guess who is?"

"Are you kidding? Ben fired Helen from the show?" I said.

Avril looked at me with an exaggerated look of shock.

"Sydney, this is incredible. But how could Ben do that?"

"Ben had already spoken to his business partners. Apparently, she'd brought this up to him before, and they agreed it wasn't in her contract. It's a money issue pure and simple, and I guess Helen's been making some other demands that haven't gone over well, and this was the last straw. As for the tickets, the producers are willing to risk that the interest in the show far outweighs the number of ticket holders who will demand a refund. Ben just telephoned me to write up a contract. You're moving from understudy to lead role. Harper, you walk onstage tonight at the Carney in *Apartment 19*."

"I'm in a state of shock."

"All of Broadway's going to be in shock tomorrow morning when word of this breaks out. Helen is a legend in New York, and she's just received the best reviews of her career. But Ben's young enough, and brash enough, that he wasn't going to bend over backward to acquiesce to the star's demands.

"Helen and Maureen must have wagered that a sellout meant she was indispensable," Sydney said. "In fact, just the opposite proved to be true. It's new school meets old school, but you can bet every New York theater critic will be back out to the Carney tonight to scrutinize your every move."

"Okay, now I think I'll sit down," I said. "Yesterday I was told to become invisible."

"Take a deep breath, Harper, and try to get a good night's sleep—if that's at all possible. I'd expect a phone call from either Ben or Tabby first thing in the morning."

~ FOURTEEN ~

Avril and I were drinking coffee when Tabby called from the back of a taxi, somewhere on the upper East Side, if I overheard her giving directions to the cabbie correctly.

"Good morning, Harper. By now you've heard the news, Helen's out and you're in. Ben and I met for breakfast early this morning to hammer out how we're going to make this transition. Can you and Avril make a lunch meeting today at noon? We'll need to go over a few things with you."

"Sure, of course."

"Good. Midtown Deli is on Fifty-seventh Street. Ben and I will meet you there. The theater press are going to absolutely have a field day with this."

I cleaned up the kitchen, rinsing off our breakfast cups and plates while Avril took a shower. She came out of her bedroom thirty minutes later dressed and ready to leave.

"I'm just going to meet Jon for a quick coffee at Cafés. It's right near his office, not far from Midtown Deli. Do you want to come along?"

"No," I told her. "I need some quiet time to get ready for tonight."

Avril came close, a look of optimism and reassurance brushing her cheeks. "Harper, don't worry. You're going to be fine."

"I just want to be prepared," I said, not mentioning the butterflies gathering in my stomach.

"You will be," she assured me. "See you at Midtown Deli."

Avril closed the door behind her, and the apartment fell silent. I spent the next forty-five minutes drinking coffee, reading my Bible in one of the living room's comfy chairs, and lapsing into still moments of prayer whenever a passage plucked a chord. There was so much for me to be grateful for. Every time I said "thank You," my soul overflowed like a cup of coffee poured past the brim and onto the saucer. I had endured entire days in Chicago when I didn't leave my apartment, lying in bed in melancholy silence. I spoke to no one except God and heard no sound other than the ticking clock until … the phone call. *Understudy.* Like Lazarus, I felt called out from a tomb.

How much stillness is really possible when you're whirling on the Potter's wheel? I closed my eyes again, attempting to settle the vertigo of accelerating events. I finally gave up and returned to the alcove. I flicked on the computer before heading to the bathroom to brush my teeth, tired of the taste of coffee. When I returned, I pushed the Bookmark button for LoveSetMatch.com and saw one new message awaiting me in my in-box.

PHOTOS FROM ALASKA

I clicked to see three new pictures, beautiful landscapes of Alaska's wilderness. Five caribou listening at a riverbank, a snowy mountainside behind them. The fog on a lake in the early morning, a lone canoeist paddling across the water. A close-up image of a single yellow wildflower. Inexplicably, the pictures made me feel at peace. A slice of simple life. I scrolled down further.

Hey Harper,

I took these shots with the camera I use to document my work. Maybe you can stick them up on the fridge if you get tired of looking at skyscrapers. :)

–Luke

There was a "PS" at the bottom.

Hey, just a thought. If you ever want to instant message me, my handle is Forestry4B.

A new and sudden rush came over me, like when you stand on a high dive for the first time, staring down into the blue pool from a great height, and realize you're going to jump. I glided the cursor to LoveSetMatch.com's main tab page to find the IM button—a green oval the color of sour apple candy. I felt nervous and excited, all my emotions that morning a pulse of high spikes, and clicked on the button. An address window appeared and I entered Luke's ID, *Forestry4B*, typed *Hello?* and pushed Send.

And then … nothing.

I stared at the computer screen for a few minutes, waiting. When nothing happened, I figured Luke just wasn't around. Then a communications box appeared in the center of the screen.

Is that you, New York?

I stared at Luke's message, momentarily confused—as if he'd only been a figment of my overactive imagination until now.

Harper: *Yes, it's me.*

Luke: *I see you got my last message.*

Harper: *I was just reading it, enjoying the beautiful pictures you sent me. Thank you.*

Luke: *I keep a camera with me in the Jeep. Yesterday, it was unbelievably beautiful up here, I had to share it with somebody.*

Harper: *It was nice of you to pick me.*

There was a pause. What do you say to someone you've never met, and can't see sitting in front of you?

Luke: *I didn't know if you'd IM me or not. I thought it would be nice to talk to you. I mean, the emails have been great, but IM makes Manhattan feel a little closer.*

Harper: *I didn't know there was an IM feature until a day ago. This whole LoveSetMatch phenomenon is still new to me. How long have you been subscribing to it?*

Luke: *I signed up for three months. This is somewhere in month three for me.*

Harper: *Sorry for the cliché, but meet any interesting people?*

He hesitated before answering, and I couldn't tell if I thrown him a tough question or if he'd left the computer to go refill his coffee.

Luke: *Some. Most are nice, and almost all live in the lower forty-eight. Friendly, but no love connection so far. How about you?*

Harper: *I'm not sure I'm LoveSetMatch material. I prefer to be in the same room with the person I'm falling in love with.*

Luke: *Do people still do that? LOL. One day we all woke up to a world that texts, twitters, and emails. I'm not sure it's progress.*

Harper: *Tell me about Alaska. There must be a few real flesh-and-blood people up there who still talk face-to-face.*

Luke: *There are folks up here like that. I see them at the coffee counter where I have my breakfast most mornings, when I'm not out in the Northeast Territory. My family's in the logging industry and tree-planting business. I work for my uncle Don, as a surveyor, environmentalist, fire preventionalist (yeah, I just made up that word), and tree farmer.*

Harper: *And also a pilot?*

Luke: *That's my side job, ministry, my leisure pursuit. There are communities scattered across Alaska with fewer than two hundred residents. Depending on the season, I fly supplies to missionaries serving in remote regions, who are either snowed in or just have cabin fever. You'd be surprised what a few almost-hot Papa John's pizzas and copies of the latest* People *magazines can do for the morale of families serving in the tundra.*

Harper: *I'll bet you make a lot of friends that way.*

Luke: *Let's just say when the skis of my plane land on a snowfield in a small Alaskan village, I'm a very popular guy. :) What about you? Your profile says you're some kind of entertainer, a singer or something?*

Harper: *I'm an actress.*

Luke: *An actress in New York. Sounds very glamorous. Have you met anyone famous yet—Kirk Cameron?*

Harper: *Sorry, I haven't met Kirk yet. When I do, I'll tell him you said hello.*

This time it was me who paused. I'd discovered when reading James's story how quickly I'd been tugged into someone's life, something I hadn't expected. Now IM'ing back and forth with Luke, I felt almost the same sensation. Was he stranger or friend? Or more?

Harper: *Until yesterday I was the understudy in a Broadway play that hasn't been performed in thirty years. Today, I got word I'm now playing the lead in the production, so it's a day of elation and nail biting.*

Luke: *The lead in a Broadway play. I don't know a thing about show business, but that sounds like a big deal.*

Harper: *Maybe. It's part of a bigger story God's telling in my life. Sometimes I feel as much a spectator as a participant. Maybe acting is my sideline, my leisure pursuit. Sometimes I wonder if it might even be a ministry. Today it feels like I'm about to go over Niagara Falls in a barrel, so I'm a little distracted.*

Luke: *Let's call it a day then, shall we? Thanks for IM'ing me. Should I look for you again sometime?*

I didn't know what to tell him. I had no answers and was fairly sure I didn't even have questions.

Harper: *Let's just play it by ear, okay?*

There was another pause. This time Luke waited so long to reply I thought our Internet service might have failed.

Luke: *Sure, I understand. I'm flying to a settlement near the Canadian border tomorrow anyway, so I'll be out of touch. But, Harper. I enjoyed talking with you. Truly.*

I wrote a line or two of good-byes, polite words like *nice talking to you* and *have a safe flight*, but when I pushed Send this message appeared on the screen:

Luke is no longer online.

It had been a sweet conversation, a respite in my day of jangly nerves, but as Luke and I said good-bye, I questioned whether or not I'd handled it well. How long had it been since I was in a relationship? Or on a date? Or in love?

A year, a year, and maybe never.

$$\wp$$

I crossed midtown Manhattan by taxicab, a jostling terror ride dodging crater-sized potholes, crisscrossing lanes, and blazing through red lights en route to Midtown Deli. When I wasn't fearing for my life, I was checking my cell phone for a text message from Avril, hoping to read a simple "On my way!"—but each time I looked my data screen was blank.

When I arrived, Ben and Tabby were already seated in a large dark wood booth inside Midtown Deli. It was the first time I'd seen Ben since he'd fired Helen. He looked disheveled, edgy, like a patient whose doctor has just delivered bad news. Tabby sat across the table from him, bent forward and stage-managing the crisis with animated gestures and movement. Two mugs of steaming coffee sat between them. I slid in next to Ben.

"Hello."

"Hello," Ben said. "A lot has changed since our talk backstage yesterday, Harper. I want you to know I hadn't decided anything up to that point. It would have been easier to keep Helen in the show, obviously, but hour by hour that got harder to do."

"It was a bold decision," I said. "But I've never known you to be anything but rational in the directions you make."

Ben's breathing was labored. He clasped his hands tightly in front of him on the table. I wondered if he'd slept the night before.

"I'm going to confess to you something I told Tabby earlier. My stress levels are through the roof, but it's not all because of this Helen stuff. I'm going through a tough divorce right now. I'm not sure I've done the right thing, and I ping-pong back and forth about it, but we're not going back."

"I'm sorry, Ben. I didn't know."

"One crisis at a time," he said, holding up his hand.

I shifted my gaze toward the front door, watching for Avril. I didn't think she'd miss our meeting, but there was no sign of her, just a heavy, closed door festooned with random event posters and fliers.

"What do you think about this, Tabby?" I asked. Tabby leaned against the high back wall of the booth. A hanging table lamp tossed its light on her face in a way that reminded me of the first time I'd seen her at the Carney.

"Helen had to go. You made the right call, Ben. Ultimately, all that matters now is whether or not the production will survive without her."

"And the cast?"

"I spoke to Marshall and Melissa after last night's show, before Ben made his decision, and they were open to the possibility then, although no one thought it was likely to happen."

"Who all knows about this?"

"Everyone in the cast knows now. Helen and Maureen, obviously, and it wouldn't surprise me if they were contacting everyone they can to try and spin the story their way."

"Ben already received a call this morning from a *Post* reporter asking for a statement, so it's out there."

The front door of Midtown Deli opened, and Avril entered, unhurried and haloed in a splash of sunlight. I signaled to her with a friendly wave, and she waved back, dropping her cell phone away in her shoulder bag and joining us in the open seat next to Tabby.

"Sorry I'm late. Did I miss anything?" Avril said, unruffled by the conspicuously solemn mood.

"We're talking about the fallout."

"I think it's best thing that could have happened to the show. I'll never say Helen wasn't a great actress, but there's been this *tension* in the cast since day one. I think we've all been trying to dance around it," Avril said. "But with Harper playing the lead, that's not a problem anymore. It's a whole new ball game."

"Exactly right," Ben said, refreshed by Avril's point of view. "I've been feeding this fantasy of doing a more modern production. Well, here's our chance. Honestly, it's the only part of what's going on that really excites me. I've been dying to bust out of the conventional wisdom of *Apartment 19*. I've got Mark working on a slightly hipper variation on our apartment set, and Harper's demonstrated she can step outside the lines we've chalked for blocking. So, are we all in agreement?"

Avril said, "Heck, yeah. This is going to be the real premiere."

"Tabby?"

"It will certainly be an adventure."

I looked into Ben's eyes when he turned to me. He was no longer just a boy from Northwestern with dreams of shaking up the theater world. He was the Broadway director making a run for it.

"Harper, normally when an understudy goes on, the play has been running for months and months, and everyone knows how the whole thing works. Nobody knows what tonight is going to look or feel like, because there isn't time to rehearse with the cast. Are you ready?"

I thought about how Tabby's taskmaster approach, so unpleasant at the time, had accelerated my readiness to perform. It couldn't have happened any other way. "I've been through the show three times, Ben. I'm ready."

"Harper, it might be good for you and Avril to walk through the play once—at least selected scenes," Ben said. "Let Avril get a feel for where you're taking Audrey. Could you do that?"

"Sure," I said. Avril nodded in agreement.

"And, Harper … I want you to trust your instincts tonight. Do what they tell you."

Ben shook his head like even he couldn't believe we were doing this. "I once thought it'd be nice if Helen took a night off so we could experiment and test this direction for the show. I guess we don't have to wonder about that anymore."

~ FIFTEEN ~

At 6 p.m., Tabby greeted me at the foot of the Carney stage, clipboard checklist close at hand. It was a moment of calm before the storm of the coming performance. I saw something in Tabby I'd missed before, something that can only be revealed through crisis. *She was good at this stuff,* wired for emergencies. In the hours since our lunch meeting, fear had coiled its sinewy vines around from my feet up to my head, threatening to choke the confidence out of me. Tabby expected her back to be against the wall, and she channeled her pragmatism into a practical plan.

The dim houselighting quieted the large, empty room, transforming it into a tranquil world, serene until the evening's performance when the audience was seated and the actors used their gifts to bring a mirage to life.

"Are you ready for tonight?" she asked.

"I think so. Are we the only ones here so far?"

"Ben's in his office. Phyllis is here. She wants to make sure all your costume changes are ready. Can I show you to your dressing room?"

We hiked up the loading ramp through the exit door at the left of the stage, fondly referred to as "The Tunnel" by actors, to the backstage level, past two lighting fixtures upended on the floor and old show posters autographed by leading actors and pinned up on the walls. I read the titles and gawked at the names of Broadway and Hollywood stars who had dazzled Carney Theatre audiences decades before us.

Tabby stopped at Helen's dressing room door.

"I think you'll be comfortable in here."

She stepped into Dressing Room 1, flipping on the overhead lights as I trailed in behind her. In a single day, Helen's dressing room had been swept clean of every remnant belonging to her. Among the missing were Helen's ergonomic makeup chair, the full-length wardrobe rack that lined the back wall, her cosmetics and personal photos, and the vases of red roses.

In their place, a modest chair with armrests, two Monet prints displayed on opposing walls, a fake ficus tree that I liked for some reason, and a new Bose stereo, factory fresh from its box.

"Ben said you liked music."

"It's wonderful, Tabby. Did you do all this today?"

"Most of the items were already here, but Helen had replaced them."

"Right."

Tabby moved toward the door, clutching the knob in one hand and supporting herself against the jamb with the other.

"I'm going down the hall to the office. Reporters have been ringing the phone off the hook. Nothing for you to worry about. Be sure to check in with Phyllis right away, in case she needs to alter anything. And, Harper, if you need anything for tonight's performance or have any questions, just ask."

"I will."

Tabby showed her smile to me for the first time; it was a sad but sweet smile. Then she left, pulling the door closed behind her.

A funky floor lamp stood next to the chair. I pulled the dangling chain cord, upsetting the tassels hanging along the bottom of the colorful orange and red shade, which was hand stitched with sunsets, globes, and horizons. A single red rose in an etched crystal vase smiled at me from the makeup counter.

Leaning against the vase, there was a card in a pink envelope, which I assumed was from Ben. The front of the card showed an aerial photograph of a snow-covered mountain. A female climber carrying a hiker's pack stood atop the summit, beholding its magnificent view. The note inside read:

Climb every mountain.

Love, Avril

Who said God didn't have a sense of humor? Or the power to move mountains when His timing was right?

I closed my eyes to meditate and pray, letting the room burn away until there was nothing left of it in my concentration but the floor beneath my shoes. God built me a bridge to New York, blew away the smoke of Tabby's rebuff, and snuffed out the heat from Helen Payne's fire. I didn't have the words to express gratitude equal to what He'd done for me, but I could at least be still in His presence.

Lord Jesus, I know this is Your doing, and not my own. Help me play my role well, onstage and in life.

I wanted to speak more eloquently, but the words didn't come. On the other side of the door, I could hear the muffled sounds of other cast members milling through the hall on their way to makeup and wardrobe.

There were two short knocks at my dressing room door, then Avril showed her sparkling, sunny face.

"Are you ready for tonight?" she asked, as if all life's best moments should be this surreal. I didn't have words for Avril either. I only held out my arms, and she entered, her own outstretched. We held each other in an embrace, reminding me of scenes we'd shared on the stage at Northwestern, almost ten years earlier.

She spoke in my ear. "I've always believed in you, Harper. You break a leg out there tonight."

Avril exited, and I left to find Phyllis. Harriet was in the wardrobe room, already in her costume, the dandy-man suit she wore that gave her landlord character. Phyllis looked up from her work.

"Harper, I was planning to come after you if I didn't see you here in the next minute."

"Sorry, I came in early, but time is flying by."

Phyllis ran a sticky lint roller over Marshall's detective sport coat. His expression was serious—it rarely was anything else. My Audrey clothes were hanging from the rack, face out and dangling over every pair of shoes I'd slip on or kick off during fast costume changes. Belts, jewelry, hats, and a pricey watch were laid out across Phyllis's alterations table. She made one final pass on Marshall's coat before coming over to dress me.

"Here, put this one on. I'm normally not the harried type backstage, but we really should have had you in here an hour ago."

"I'm sorry. Avril and I were rehearsing in the apartment this afternoon and …"

Phyllis smacked at her forehead with the palm of her hand. "Oh, I just realized you probably don't know the dressing assignments! For tonight, you'll just have to watch for Tabby's instruction as you come offstage. Between the two of us, we'll make sure you get in and out of the right costumes."

I nodded, trying to keep track of last-minute backstage directions while I tested myself on two hours of memorized dialogue Avril and I had rehearsed.

Marshall left the room for makeup, and I stepped behind a Japanese rice-paper screen to slip into my first costume. How quickly the mood backstage had morphed from "empty and quiet" to circus-like. But instead of the excitement present on opening night with Helen, I saw uncertainty on the faces of the actors and even some of the crew. Our championship team had lost its star player. Reality was sinking in. Helen Payne was a legend. I was a nobody.

"All right, let me take a look."

I stepped out from behind the screen, and Phyllis spun me around, tugging at my hems, swiping lint off my sleeves, grooming my costume to perfection.

"After makeup, come back down here so I can go over this one more time. And remember, watch Tabby and me for changing cues."

I responded with a nod of my head before stumbling down the hallway to the makeup room, breaking in a new pair of heels and more than a little concerned about tripping. I looked at the back-stage clock. It was already six forty-five. The curtain would go up at seven thirty, ready or not. I could already hear voices out front. It was too early to open doors for audience members, but maybe Ben and Tabby had allowed critics in. I imagined them discussing among themselves how we had ruined a perfectly good show. Other negative voices inside my head were talking too, and I just turned each irritant over to God, yet another pinch of wisdom I'd learned from Bella.

It was seven fifteen when I opened my eyes in front of the makeup mirror to see the new, sophisticated Audrey Bradford staring back at me in lighted reflection.

Laura whisked off the trimmer's apron, and I slid off the barber's stool to see my character for the first time in full wardrobe. Slightly spiky hair, dark red lipstick, and penetrating eye shadow to complement the exquisite dress, Laura had somehow pulled off making me look like a fashion model. I was about to say something when Tabby's voice rang out in the hall.

"Come on, Harper. We need you down front."

I followed Tabby's voice down the long production hallway. My hands were sweaty and shaking, my heart drumming so loud I was sure everyone could hear it beating. I could only think about the next step. My legs felt numb and weightless. Turning the corner for the greenroom, I caught a glimpse of the packed house through a gap in the side curtain, the faces of those who would judge my performance. I tried to shake off the mental image and focus on remembering my first line of dialogue, but failed.

Ten minutes before curtain, the quiet cast gathered outside the door of my dressing room. Ben and Tabby offered last-minute instructions and reassurance that the show's magic hadn't exited the theater along with Helen Payne.

"Okay, five minutes before curtain," Tabby said.

Then words spilled out of my mouth before I had a chance to consider them.

"Could we all just join hands and pray for the show?" I asked, lousy at hiding how nervous I was.

I expected eye rolling or disappointed sighs, but the actors gathered backstage at the Carney grabbed hold of each other's hands and formed a circle. Ben invited those in the crew to stop what they were doing and join us, like we did back at Northwestern when the show was about and included everybody. The circle grew larger to accommodate the crew. Avril squeezed my hand on the left side, and I noticed a smile from Harriet, my protector, supporting me on the right.

"Dear Lord, we love You for the work You've called us to, and the talents You've given every member of this team. Help us tonight to make use of these gifts and to bring glory to Your name. Amen."

We broke, and Harriet said, "Helen Payne never did nothing like that."

Immediately, the backstage lights dimmed.

"Shhh ..." Tabby silenced the cast.

The reality that I'd walk onstage in mere minutes fell upon me like a sticky web of fear and heat. I heard Tabby whisper into her headset microphone, "We just finished cast prayer, and we're running one minute behind."

Avril said, "Break a leg," and disappeared stage right for her entrance. A man's voice came over the house PA.

"Ladies and gentleman. For tonight's performance of *Apartment 19,* the part of Audrey Bradford will be played by Miss Harper Gray."

An audible groan of disappointment rose from the Carney Theatre, jeers of dissatisfaction from the balcony, booing from the lower seats.

A rush of fear rippled through my body, making me sick to my stomach. A tear flooded my eye, and a sudden, overpowering grip of panic seized my nervous system. My adrenaline pulsed, my breathing constricted. I couldn't remember a single word in the script! Phyllis took a tissue from her pocket and dabbed my eye with it, careful to not smear Laura's makeup.

I closed my eyes and repeated to myself over and over again, "Get a grip, get a grip." I heard the whirring sound of the rotor opening the stage curtain. The full lights came up, and I realized Avril had already stepped onstage. She was no longer my friend, but Roxy Dupree, my other roommate. Audrey Bradford's roommate.

I closed my eyes. *Fix this, fix this. Please, fix this!* Prickly sweat rolled down my back, and I worried about what my costumes would look like after an hour of sweating like this onstage.

When my eyes opened again, I was staring into the face of a concerned Tabby Walker, the woman who told Ben Hughes there were twenty other actors who could walk in off the street and nail the role I was about to play. She took hold of me by the shoulders and looked me in the eyes.

"Harper, get a grip," she said sharply, but without anger. "You are going to succeed tonight. Listen to me. I can't do it, but you can. You are a great actress. You're going to go out there tonight and make this role your own. So let out what God has put inside you."

Tabby stepped behind me. She laid her hands on my shoulders and literally pushed me toward the wings at stage left.

The stage went dark at the end of the first scene, and in pitch blackness, the grips rolled out the props and scenery for Scene 2. Backdrop number one rose high into the ceiling, coming to rest against the railing of the catwalk. Tabby poked me gently in the back with her finger, and I stepped onstage in costume.

Anyone could ask God for a favor in a prayer circle, but only a real God could answer back. I took my mark at the fireplace, the set decor obscure in near, total darkness. The audience couldn't see me.

Transform me, Lord. Make me into another person.

Isn't that what He'd done all year? The spotlights and ceiling cans flooded me from above and behind. I could feel their heat on my body. The eyes of the audience were watching me now.

I was onstage. I had to *do* something.

In front of me, I saw that the mantelpiece was dusty. I was sure the grips had wiped it down prior to opening night, but stored backstage, it had gotten dusty all over again. A cleaning rag and green feather duster were lying on the stage to the right of me, so I reached down and picked up the cloth, running it through the crevices, stripping off dust particles and watching them somersault through the beams of the bright stage lights.

Why is it things can never stay clean? There was a knock on the door. What was her name? I could scarcely remember that woman who had called an hour before wanting to see me with some excuse. She would probably try to sell me something, or ask for a handout. They always do. She'd already interrupted my cleaning. I walked to the door of my apartment, opened it, and that woman, Roxy Dupree, or some such thing, stepped in—without even being so much as asked!

Avril delivered her first line, and I found that place of inspiration and muse. I uttered my line, surprised to hear the inflection coming out on pitch, strong and round. She spoke again and I knew what I would say next. No pallor tinted my face or voice. The rehearsals, the acting, and the instincts all kicked in. I could *feel* how to move onstage, stepping into the apartment as comfortably as if it were my own. I knew how to speak each line, the words snapped in rhythm as if they were taps on the soles of a dancer's shoes.

The story felt fresh and alive to me. One part of me acted, as another watched, aware that the audience was watching us too.

I heard the words in my ears like I was somebody else. It was a dance, an unexpected ballet, and Avril was stepping up the intensity of her performance. Whatever she'd held back in scenes with Helen was surfacing now.

Avril walked to the front of the stage and turned back to look at me, swallowed up by bright stage light behind her, eclipsed from my view.

"Do you expect me to believe you?" Roxy asked, her brown hairdo piled high on her head.

"Oh, Roxy," Audrey pleaded with her, moving closer to the center of the stage. "I expect you to *trust* me."

The night flew by in a blur, an exquisite silver blur, a dream where everything is lovely, and rings with perfect meaning. When the dream was finally over, the lights went dark onstage, and I left the window where Audrey lay dead, killed by her own knife, and wiggled out onto a safety mat on the backstage floor. One of the grips met me with a small flashlight and escorted me over to the wings. I heard applause. Then I saw Tabby. I looked past her and saw the audience for the first time. They were on their feet. Ben appeared behind me, wrapped his arms around me, squeezing the life out of me.

"I knew you could do it," he shouted in my ear over the raucous noise in the Carney. I nodded like I knew what he meant, or even knew what I was doing. Tabby rushed forward.

"You're on, get onstage," she said, moving the headset mic away from her lips, shooing me forward.

I walked out from the beyond the curtains, my fellow actors waiting at center stage, clapping their hands, their faces owning a secret to which I was still ignorant. Avril held a bouquet of yellow roses. When I stepped into view, the flashbulbs went off. The houselights were full up, and I could see everyone standing in front of their seats.

Harriet and Marshall made a place for me in the middle, where I joined them, waving to the crowds. A lady in the front row stepped up to the stage and presented me with a bouquet of red roses. I knelt and said "Thank you," my voice drowned out by the clamor.

Harriet and Avril took my hands and raised them as we all bowed to the audience. I felt like we were the privileged few. We all bowed again.

Still in a daze, I followed Avril back to the wings. She threaded her arm through mine, the nerves returning, shouting as she'd done in Times Square on New Year's Eve.

"That was amazing!" she said.

Tabby and Ben were standing backstage clapping their hands as though they were simply spectators. The cast hugged, and Harriet leaned in, whispered to me.

"I knew you could do it," she said.

The actors didn't want to scatter after our performance, so I opened the door of my dressing room and switched on the bright overhead lights and the stereo.

"Everybody, come in here," I called to them, and the small room filled with actors in their costumes, stage grips, our producers, Phyllis, Tabby, and Ben.

"What just happened out there?" I asked them. "Did you feel what I felt?"

Ben spoke. "That was one of the most incredible productions I've ever seen," he said. "You all took a play that hasn't been performed in *thirty years*, and opened it two nights ago—to rave reviews I might add. Tonight, this same cast—with one notable exception," Ben said, gesturing toward me, "*reinvented* Mouldain's classic drama as a modern theater piece."

The cast exploded in good cheer.

"There were times I literally didn't know what was going to happen next," he continued. "Avril, you were electrifying out there. Roxy never stood up for herself like that before. Every cast member brought their performance to new heights tonight, but Harper ..." Ben looked at me, temporarily speechless, or perhaps holding the moment for effect. "The old *Apartment 19* was black and white. You brought Technicolor to the stage. The tension was palpable. When the audience realized the rumors were true and they weren't going to see Helen, they didn't want to like you. That only made their reaction to Audrey Bradford that much more uncontrollable. They were beside themselves, but by the end of the first act, they loved it. Now we just have to hire a new understudy for you."

"Yeah, they came here expecting a comfortable ride in a classic Cadillac," Tabby said. "You gave them a spin at one-twenty in a brand-new Ferrari."

~ Sixteen ~

The Little Play that Could

By Eric Starns

New York Times/Theatre

Three nights ago director Ben Hughes demonstrated that Broadway can reinvent itself by dipping into the musty files of long-forgotten playwrights and plucking out a cherry. Mouldain's *Apartment 19* premiered Sunday evening in triumph, mostly due to Helen Payne, whose spot-on performance only reinforced her status as Queen Diva of The Great White Way.

But alas, this is Broadway, and dreams go up like Roman candles, dazzling us one minute, only to fall back to earth the next. Fortunately for those who love theater, Ben Hughes has a full bag of fireworks and a pocketful of matchsticks with which to light them. Hughes must have known his bench was deep with talent to allow a legend like Helen Payne to pack up and walk away, leaving not shoes to fill, but footprints carved deep in the Carney's historic stage. For Payne's replacement, Hughes tapped unknown actress Harper Gray, but the Carney Theatre doesn't care who impersonates Mouldain's eccentric psychopath. It knows but one word this season: revival. From its multi-million-dollar renovation, to the resuscitation of Mouldain's masterpiece, to the stunned reactions of theatergoers blessed enough to possess one of the show's limited thirty thousand golden tickets. New York theater has a new neighbor in *Apartment 19.* Unpredictable, stunning, and shockingly good, Ben Hughes's new production is breathtaking in the razor sharp risks it takes both onstage and off. It satisfies an audience's appetite for remarkable theater while leaving you hungry for what exists nowhere else.

Harper Gray doesn't steal the show, as Helen Payne did in her brief turn as the nut job Audrey Bradford. Instead, she draws electricity out of thin air like a lightning rod, then directs it back into audiences, shocking old emotions they've long since

forgotten and zapping new ones they never
knew they had.

$\wp$

After a wonderfully long night, I rewarded myself with the luxury
of sleeping in on Thursday morning. I awoke just after 9 a.m. to a
quiet apartment following my first two performances of *Apartment
19*, good reviews from New York theater critics, and a late dinner
with Avril and Ben.

There were no sounds of coffee brewing coming from the kitchen
or of shower water hitting tile in the bathroom. I felt content to just
lie in bed and dream.

The sun flickered through the curtains, reflecting off passing
buses. A spurt of nervous energy before my Tuesday-night debut
resulted in an extra-tidy bedroom. One more sign that things were
falling into place.

As I lay in bed, it dawned on me I'd missed the Wednesday night
service at Fellowship Community Church. I thought about Luke
and whether or not he'd returned from his arctic pizza delivery, and
wondered if it was dangerous to fly over miles of ice and snow in a
small plane.

I thought of James and his boys, and said a small prayer, remembering something my dad once told me—that people are usually
happy in their careers or in their home life, but seldom is a person
successful at both. James had both and lost one. I wondered if he felt
like God had suddenly realized He'd dealt him too many blessing
cards and decided to take one back.

Finally, my thoughts turned to finances. My modest share of Avril's three-thousand-dollar-a-month apartment was six hundred dollars. In one overpriced week of living on the island of Manhattan, I'd managed to shell out almost three hundred dollars in food, trains, and taxis. Asking Ben for an advance on my first week's salary would be humbling but critical if I intended to keep feeding and sheltering myself.

By ten o'clock, I'd showered and brewed a full pot of coffee. Avril finally came out from her dark chamber of sleep looking seriously drowsy. She passed me on her way to the bathroom, and a moment later I heard the shower come on.

I carried the cordless phone into the sunny living room and dialed Katie's cell. While the signal searched for connection, I studied her lilac-colored card, noting all the ways there were to stay connected with her and David. Two cell phone numbers, a church Web site, a daily blog, Twitter, and their IM addresses. She answered on the second ring.

"Hello?"

"Hey Katie, it's Harper. I just wanted to call to say I was sorry I missed seeing you and David at church last night. Something's come up."

"No worries. People always think we keep attendance at church, but that's not the case, Harper," she said. "I've been praying for you this week."

I pulled my feet up underneath me in the chair, slouching into its warm cushions. "I think God may have answered your prayers."

"Why? Has something happened?"

"Yes. I'd really love to catch up with you. Is that offer to have lunch still open?"

We set a lunch date for the next day.

After my call to Katie, I went back into the kitchen to grab a peach yogurt from the fridge, along with a napkin and spoon. Tearing off the orange-yellow foil, I tasted the tart, creamy breakfast and tossed the lid in the trash.

I arranged my coffee and yogurt on the desk and scooted the chair underneath me. The shades in the front windows were open, casting sunbeams on my bare feet. The LoveSetMatch.com homepage greeted me, this time featuring a photo of a different happily matched real-life couple. They wore casual clothes and seemed to be on perpetual vacation, their faces beaming with smiles of utter bliss.

I clicked through to my personal page to discover that LoveSetMatch had added yet another new feature. *A signal*, a tiny orange and red flame that glowed beside the names of matches whenever one was online. The little flame flickered beside Luke's name.

I wanted to share my good mood with someone, so I fired off an instant message.

Hey, are you online?

Luke didn't answer. I waited for a minute, imagining a whistling teakettle, a doorbell, or the call of nature had pulled him away from his screen. Nothing.

I refreshed my screen, and when the page finished uploading, Luke's flame was gone. The moment didn't warrant disappointment, but that is exactly what I felt. The little flame was there one second, and gone the next, and with it too my chance to say "hello." I returned to my personal page. The tab bar read:

New Messages (1)

I clicked. It was a new message from James.

Dear Harper,

I appreciate your prayers. They mean a lot to me. Despite our family's loss, I remain thankful that my architectural firm is doing well. I enjoy my work, and I'm grateful for my boys each and every day.

We live in a house overlooking the ocean, and for me, few things in life are as peaceful as living near water. You'll have to tell me more about your acting and the theatrical world. I know nothing about entertainment, having only stepped onstage once in college, and even then it was only to keep up the back end of a horse costume. So please, don't ask for career advice. BTW—you didn't mention whether you're dating. Is that too personal a question? Keep in touch!

–James.

I hit the Reply button and opened a new message window.

James,

I'm still adjusting to this brave new world of communicating with people online. It takes some getting used to, no? I'm glad to hear business is good, and an architect's home on the coast sounds absolutely breathtaking. I love the ocean, and have found few things that are as restorative.

Life for an actress in New York? Hmm, it's memorizing lines, wearing funny costumes, and pretending to be someone else.

And, I'm finding lately it's also an area God chooses to bless me through. This presents its own special stresses, needs, and feelings of inadequacy. Maybe that's a pressure not limited to theater people.

Thanks for your messages, I enjoy them. As for dating, I seem to know less about it the more time that passes. Keep me in your prayers, and I'll keep your family in mine. God is our architect, our Designer, and I have to trust that He's building something out of so much rubble. Although, it's not always easy being a project under construction! :)

–Harper

I signed off LoveSetMatch and noticed I'd brought Katie's card with me from the living room. *Two cell phone numbers, a church Web site, a daily blog, Twitter.* I typed in the address for David and Katie's ministry blog. A blurred image of the church's front door served as the site's background, and in the foreground were photos of Fellowship's worship services, a young women's Bible study with Katie teaching, and a group photo of ten or so people eating Chinese food at a long table, waving to the camera.

I could almost hear Katie's voice narrating as I read the bio page. It was obvious she'd written it. The page told the story of how she and David had come from Oklahoma City to the Big Apple, drawn by the belief that God wanted them to plant a church. She shared their heartache of a miscarriage, something she hadn't mentioned in person, and yet here was their deeply personal story posted online for all the world to read.

It struck me how in a city the size of New York, those I was getting to know best I was connecting with through a computer screen. Sure, I'd met Katie face-to-face on New Year's Day, the night we shook hands, but the most private things I knew about her, I was learning online.

My cell phone began to vibrate on the glass coffee table in the living room, its rattle making the call seem urgent. I flitted across the apartment and picked it up. The name *Sydney Bloom* appeared illuminated in neon blue in the caller ID window, and I flipped open the lid to answer.

"Good morning, Harper. Do you know how rare a thing it is to say something's *never been done* on Broadway? Critics are flipping out over Ben's replacement of Helen with you as a younger Audrey Bradford. They're casting him as some sort of rebel genius who dared to shake up Broadway."

"It looks so different from the inside. Ben would have been happy to just keep Helen, but she made that impossible."

"Be that as it may, in one week *Apartment 19* has flip-flopped everything the experts thought would and would not work on Broadway. It's all been geared toward big musicals for so long, but from the online reviews to the conversations I'm having with other agents, everyone is talking about it. They still hadn't gotten over Mouldain's revival on Broadway, and now they've got the firing of Helen Payne to chin-wag."

"We're feeling some of that same excitement inside the theater, Sydney. Scalpers have been selling tickets out front before the show; we've been getting standing ovations. People come up to the stage afterward and want to shake our hands."

"This is what I've always dreamed for you, Harper," Sydney said, reminding me of the night she gave me her business card outside the Lookingglass Theatre. "I've always believed in your abilities, but no one knew what you were capable of, until now. You're becoming a star on Broadway, do you realize that?"

"Only if 'star' means broke. This move from understudy to lead actress does include a bump in salary, right?"

"Didn't you get the contract I emailed you?"

"No," I said. "When did you send it?"

"Wednesday afternoon. Ben and I agreed it was fine for you to go ahead with just a verbal okay for the first performances, with everything moving so fast. Now that you're the official lead, a new agreement had to be put in writing."

"So, that doesn't answer my question."

Sydney laughed. "Harper, I think you should just print out the agreement I sent you, read it over, and sign it. It's fairly straightforward, and I'm sure will answer all your questions."

"Sydney," I said, slightly put out by her coyness.

"We'll talk in a few days. Gotta run!"

I shut my cell phone and went to the computer. Closing David and Katie's Web site for now, I checked my email. Sydney's message was third in a stack of eleven emails—junk mail, mostly, and congratulations from a couple friends back home. The contract was an attachment, and I began reading it online while printing off a hard copy to sign.

It was four pages of legal jargon, requirements, expectations, and duties that outlined everything from the number of performances I was to *render*, to how I couldn't do anything so dangerous as to be life threatening, and how I could get myself canned for moral failings.

Then on page three under a section called "Payment for Services" I saw for the first time what I would be earning, not as understudy but for playing the lead role in *Apartment 19*.

$19,585.33—per week.

By the time Avril presented herself it was almost eleven thirty. She'd dressed in one of my favorite outfits of hers, a peasant skirt with patterns of turquoise, pekoe brown, and simple white. The look was very California and completely disregarded all the New York rules about fashion she'd given me my first night in the city.

"You're looking colorful this morning."

"I had to. It's a bad biorhythm day, and I'm trying to overcome the gloomies with a big dose of LA."

I followed Avril into the kitchen where she got out the orange juice from the fridge and poured a glass. She took down several bottles of vitamins from the cupboard over the coffeemaker and began taking them with the juice.

"What's got you so down?"

She shook her head, still swallowing a vitamin, then answered. "I couldn't get a hold of Jon on the phone this morning. I think he's mad at me."

"Why?"

Avril leaned against the counter, a pill in her left hand, the glass of juice in her right. "I finally tried telling him about the show yesterday, and he didn't take it very well," she said, her brow furrowed with worry. "I don't understand it."

"How did you tell him?"

"I just told him about some of the things I've done, and he seemed fine at first, excited about it. But when I mentioned I was performing in *Apartment 19*, he just froze. He started getting mad and asked me why I hadn't told him about it before. I tried to explain it was just a question of timing. Maybe I hadn't spoken up when I should, but I *was* telling him."

Avril looked hurt. She put down her juice glass, and I gave her a hug.

"Did he seem upset that you weren't more up front about everything?" I asked, parting again.

"He accused me of keeping secrets." Avril started crying. "And I just said I was sorry, that I didn't mean to hurt him, but he was so upset with me."

I looked around the kitchen for a box of tissues, but remembered they were still in my bedroom from a few nights ago.

"I thought you should have said something earlier, but I didn't think he'd take it like this. Have you spoken to him since?"

Avril shook her head. "I tried calling him last night, and texting him this morning, but nothing."

Avril let out a long, trembling breath. She moved toward the paper-towel roll and swiped off a large square to dab puffy eyes. She took the last vitamin, placed it on her tongue, and washed it down with juice.

"I *know* how important it is to be honest, but I don't feel like I was keeping a secret."

I took hold of her hand, trying to comfort her. "Avril, he'll come around. You guys have been seeing each other for two months. He probably just feels like you should have trusted him more."

"I know," she said.

"What are your plans for today? Do you want to go by the theater with me and maybe grab lunch?"

"No, I wouldn't be good company. I thought I'd run by Cafés on Fifty-second Street and see if Jon's there. I just don't feel like I can do anything until we talk and I can explain everything."

~ Seventeen ~

After calling Ben and explaining my money situation, he agreed to meet me in the Carney's office. I carried the signed contract with me, feeling it represented my half of the exchange and finalized the nuts and bolts of Sydney's business dealings.

It was Tabby, however, not Ben who met me outside the Carney. She let us in through the side stage door with her ring of keys and led us back to the office.

"Looks like someone's going shopping," Tabby said, tearing the long pale blue check from the ledger book and handing it to me like a parent hands money to a child for the movies. But instead of five dollars for a matinee, I was given an advance of five thousand dollars.

"Tabby, I meant to thank you for the other night, for what you said to me before I went onstage."

She blew it off. "It's no big deal. You'd be surprised how many nervous actors I've had to prod onstage. It's all part of the job."

Tabby got up from the desk, a signal that meant our conversation was over.

"You said 'I can't do it.'"

"What?"

"When you helped prod me on. You said 'I can't do it.' What did you mean?"

For the first time since I'd met her, Tabby seemed at a loss for words, flustered. She finally turned to face me, crossing her arms against her body, constricting herself.

"Acting, I suppose."

"Were you ever an actor?"

"Once, very briefly," Tabby confessed. "Until I realized I lack the natural ability to be free spirited, to forget myself and become someone else. But I recognized I was good at organization, something most actors stink at. So, instead of becoming the worst actor in New York, I decided I'd become the best producer. Any more questions?"

"No, I just appreciate what you did. It seemed kinder than someone just doing her job. Maybe I'm wrong about that, but I still wanted to thank you."

I opened a checking account at First Bank of New York on Broadway, depositing the advance Tabby had handed to me, and left the FBNY equipped with a modest stack of starter checks and a wallet filled with cash.

In an afternoon shopping splurge, I purchased two sacks of groceries, meats, fruits, and veggies. I tucked a few hundred-dollar bills into an envelope to repay Avril for the clothes she'd thoughtfully purchased for me and to catch up on rent. The windfall also seemed like the perfect opportunity to buy myself something nice. The single purchase item topping my fantasy list? I didn't even have to think twice about it. An Apple MacBook. Some people see themselves behind the wheel of a brand-new cherry-red convertible, cruising the countryside, zipping down the highway with the wind in their hair. I pictured myself reclined in one of the oversized lime-green chairs at Vibe, the coffee shop across the street from our apartment building. I could see myself indulging in a venti cappuccino with my feet up on a square block coffee table, and reading the latest message from James or Luke on LoveSetMatch.com without a worry in the world.

I also wrote out a check for five hundred dollars, ten percent of my advance, not to put too sharp a point on it, but the number fit so I stuck it in an envelope. When I decided I couldn't wait until Sunday to deliver it, I bought a card for David and Katie and stuffed the folded starter check inside, pushing the sealed envelope through the letter box in the church's Roman arch door.

After my visit to the computer store and Fellowship Community Church, I stopped at Vibe to live out my fantasy. There I popped the lid off a steaming cup of tea and kicked my feet up on a small table against an exposed brick wall. As promised in the ad, my new laptop was up and running in minutes. I logged on to LoveSetMatch.com to check for updates and saw the flame was on again next to Luke's ID. Then his message appeared on-screen.

Luke: *Hey, Harper. Are you online?*
Harper: *Yes. Hi. Are you back from your pizza delivery?*
Luke: *Just barely. I busted a ski on impact while landing. The pizzas were fine though, no pepperoni were lost in the mishap.*
Harper: *I thought I saw you online this morning.*

Luke: *I was, but only for a minute. My uncle Don called. There was a small problem at the plant, and now that I'm back in Wasilla, he wanted to talk to me. What's new on your busy island?*

Harper: *A few things worth mentioning. I'm writing from behind a new Apple MacBook, and my work has changed considerably since we last IM'd. Giants are in the playoffs.*

Luke: *A new computer? That's very interesting. Does that lend itself to seeing more messages from you in the future?*

Harper: *Possibly ... would you like to see more messages from me?*

Luke: *Yes, especially if they're accompanied by more photos. You just have one posted, you know.*

Harper: *I can probably handle that, but as long as we're on the subject, I've missed seeing a message from you.*

Luke: *That means you like talking with me. Good. I wasn't sure.*

Harper: *I'm sure. Your absence over the past few days made me sure. This isn't exactly talking though. It's more like typing.*

There was a pause, the kind of moment when you know instinctively what the other person is thinking. At least, I felt that way with Luke.

Luke: *I have a cell phone number, if you'd ever like to call me. Some people communicate this way, I hear.*

Now I was the one on pause. He'd introduced a new level of communication, but I didn't know if I was ready for that. Avril would be. Who was I kidding, almost everybody would be.

Harper: *Okay, sure. I don't know when I'll call, but it might be nice to have your number if ever the mood strikes.*

Truth be told, I was scared to call. *I was bluffing.* Pretending to be cool, completely comfortable about dating, *Internet dating*, as if I did this sort of thing all the time.

Luke: *Okay, here's my number. Remember, I always carry my cell with me. So, if you ever want to talk to me, and I'm awake, I'll answer it.*

I copied the number Luke sent and pasted it in a Notepad program on my MacBook.

Harper: *Thanks, Luke. For some reason I like having your number. It kind of makes my day.*
Luke: *Well then, my good deed is done. I took the day off to work on my plane so I'd better get to it.*
Harper: *Right, I didn't mean to keep you.*
Luke: *You didn't keep me, Harper. You just gave me some things to think about while I'm working. Talk to you later.*

I closed out our instant message session, his words "you didn't keep me" oddly hanging in the air. I wondered if Luke, but for the distance, wasn't the kind of man a woman tried hanging on to. I noticed it was getting late and wondered how Avril was doing, if she'd caught up with Jon and worked things out. I hoped so.

I stuffed the MacBook back into my canvas shoulder bag, an olive-green carrier with a distinctive Brazilian stitching along the flap, and exited Vibe heading back across the street to the apartment.

I rattled my key into the lock outside and turned open our door. The sound of a frail whimper coming from the living room was my first clue something was wrong.

"Avril?" I called out.

I closed the door and crept deeper into the apartment, following the moaning, and found Avril curled up in a ball on the living room floor. She was sobbing. Her limbs were rigid like those of a victim who's fallen from a great height. Her face was twisted into a vacuous, lifeless stare, and her eyes were drenched with tears, as pink as cotton candy.

"What's the matter?" I asked, rushing to her side. I knelt down and picked up her hand. It was as cold and as lifeless as a rag doll's. Avril shuddered. She didn't answer me.

"Avril, honey, what's the matter? Are you hurt?"

"Jon and I broke up," she said. Her lips were dry, cracking, and pale, and the lower one trembled as she lay there.

My heart broke at the sight of her, even as my head was thinking, *No, no, you didn't do this over Avril not telling you she was an actress.* I ran my hand over Avril's forehead, brushing away perspiration and strands of wet hair. Her petite body heaved in and out, swallowing tiny gulps of air.

"What happened?" I asked.

Avril pinched her eyes closed, and when she did, two droplets streamed from each and ran in jagged lines across her scarlet face. She'd fastened her eyelids down with so much intensity, I wondered if they'd ever open again. And when she finally spoke, I understood the reason.

"He's married."

The two words collapsed Avril's mouth into a strained frown, an uncanny likeness to tragedy's mask, and a sound escaped from a heart so broken it seemed to have come from a wounded child.

"How do you know? I mean, could there be a mistake?"

"I saw them together," Avril said. "Jon and his wife, and their son. *They have a child.*"

Avril's chest heaved again like she was trying to blow out a fire, but couldn't draw enough oxygen to dowse the flames. Her chin dropped against her chest in defeat, and she covered her face with both hands.

"They … they were eating breakfast in the front window of Cafés in midtown. I was standing, across the street, waiting to cross … and I saw them. They were smiling and laughing together."

"Did he see you?" I asked, trying to get the basic facts. "Did he know you were there?"

Avril stared off into blackness, replaying the scene in her mind.

"Not at first, but he looked up, and then he *saw me.*"

"He saw you? How? What did he do?"

"That's just it," she said. "He didn't do *anything.*" Avril was numb with shock and grief. "He didn't react at all. He just stared back at me, standing there on the other side of Fifty-second Street, like he knew he was caught but he didn't care."

"Did you go in and talk to him?"

"I couldn't," she said. "I wouldn't know what to say. They were just having a normal breakfast. A *family* breakfast."

Avril sat up, shaking her head and wiping away tears with the back of her hands.

"I was so stupid. All the classic signs were there. He'd never take me to his place, he never gave me his home or work number, only his cell. He used his work as a cover. Such a cliché."

Avril stood up, looking a bit lost and unsteady on her feet.

"They're in my room, Avril," I said, reading her mind.

She came back from my bedroom, a tissue box pinched under her right arm, wiping her nose with a tissue in her left.

"He just made up a persona online, and I bought it. He was running a con game," she said in disbelief. "All the things he said to me, all lies, all fake. Every time he said he loved me … "

"Do you know this for certain? That it was all fake?"

"What does it matter? He's married," she said.

"You're right, I guess it doesn't matter."

She sat in her favorite easy chair, plopping the box of pink tissues down in her lap, shaking her head.

"Why can't anybody love me?" Avril whispered to no one. She looked down at the new computer slipping out from my satchel.

"Avril, what Jon did to you is so wrong, but don't think it says anything about you. He lied. How could you have known?"

For almost an hour I stayed beside Avril smoothing her, telling her everything would be okay. At 5 p.m., she took a shower and some aspirin and got ready for the theater.

"Are you sure you can go on?" I asked.

"No, but I'm a pro. I'll do what I have to."

Avril brushed her hair in the bathroom mirror. I watched her from a bar stool at the black granite island. She didn't deserve to be hurt like this; no one did. How could anyone be so selfish? So cruel? She stepped out from the bathroom, ready to go to the Carney. I wondered how she could leave the apartment, let alone act onstage. Every emotion in her soul had been cauterized.

"What if I see him again?" she asked me from the back of a taxi near Times Square. "What should I say?"

"New York's a big city. I doubt you will. But if you do, just tell him whatever comes to mind. I'm sure you'll think of something."

~ Eighteen ~

Over the next four weeks of winter in New York, Avril, the rest of the cast, and I performed to packed houses almost thirty times. Every night felt a little different, but the audience reaction was always the same. They gasped at Arthur Mouldain's sinister suspense, laughed at the play's subtle humor, cried at its unrelenting sadness, and cheered for its persevering spirit. They gave each performance a standing ovation when one woman's bravery overcame tremendous adversity.

As the days turned into weeks, the cast polished their spot-on performances, adding twists, refining gestures, teasing new subtleties out of Mouldain's brilliant script. *Apartment 19* was music, each actor onstage a musician.

We performed the show over and over again, until one Tuesday night in February when the walls came crashing down.

The opening scene rolled just fine. "People love the *bam* of it," Avril always said, meaning the opening sound effects, street noise, and the hustle of recreating 1950s Manhattan.

Even Scene 2, where Audrey and Roxy meet for the first time, started out well, the two of us volleying our lines back and forth, faster than those first weeks. We were playing off each other, catching the audience's responses with the sensitivity of a butterfly's wing.

In theater, you get used to the rhythm of the performance, even if each night is a little different. That's how I knew things were wrong even before they all fell apart. The cadence broke down in Roxy's pattern of speech, her intensity fell. Roxy didn't sound like Roxy anymore. She sounded like Avril. Onstage, standing in front of a packed house, Avril began to speak her lines directly to the audience, at a time when she usually projected them directly to me. Then suddenly, they weren't even Roxy's lines anymore.

"I can't believe you would do this to me, Audrey. You played a game with me when I trusted you. I loved you, but you were just lying to me!"

I glanced into the wings where Tabby was standing, and we locked eyes. Trying to remain in character, I looked to the front of the stage to see what was going on, but the stage lights were too bright. I couldn't find Avril. I only knew we weren't in *Apartment 19* anymore.

I left the stage chair Audrey was suppose to be sitting in and walked to the front of the stage in character, a confident saunter. Meanwhile, Avril continued speaking in a monologue she wrote as she went along.

"Does she know? Does your wife even know about us? About all our dinners, and our walks in Central Park? Does she know you said you loved me? Does she know?"'

As I approached the front of the stage I could make out Avril clearly, blue eye shadow streaming down her cheeks. I scanned the first few rows of the audience, unable to see any farther, but I saw him. Angry, red-faced Jon, sitting cross-armed in his seat on the aisle, and next to him, his lovely, and very humiliated, wife. Avril pointed directly at him so there was no mistaking whom she was talking to, no longer projecting any visage of Roxy Dupree.

"*I believed you,*" she cried, her microphone headset dangling from her ear, shaken off in the emotion of her soliloquy.

Even without amplification, everyone in the audience heard Avril's cry. Her emotions as raw and inflamed as a friction burn. Members of the audience looked on in shock. Some stood, wondering if this were all some elaborate new Ben Hughes twist to the show. The room was in turmoil. The houselights remained down, but I could clearly make out the expression on the woman's face as she got up from her seat and ran quickly up the center aisle and out of the theater, her husband, Jon from LoveSetMatch.com, following close behind.

Avril stood at the front of the stage, blue makeup running from her eyes, her body heaving and drained of emotion. She sobbed, and I put my arm around her shoulders, turned her away from seven hundred confused faces, and walked her off the stage. Her body shuddered under my arm, her breath sawing in and out like a dull blade cutting a tree. I caught Tabby's expression as we exited stage left. She was ticked off. We'd blown it. We were done for the night, and maybe for good.

Backstage, I held Avril tight.

"Things will be okay," I told her.

Harriet joined us, throwing a coat from wardrobe around Avril's shoulders since her arms looked goose-bumped from the chill. More of the cast soon gathered, and Ben joined our huddle, all of us just holding on to one another, no one knowing exactly what to do next.

"Harper, is Avril all right?" Ben asked.

"I don't know," I said. She looked like her body was in a state of shock.

"I'm going to make an announcement to the audience," Ben said. "The show's over for tonight. If they want, they can have their money back."

Ben walked out to center stage and introduced himself. The audience, many still standing, quieted down to listen.

"Ladies and gentlemen, if I can have your attention for a moment, I have an announcement," Ben said, without benefit of a microphone.

"Tonight's show is canceled, but we will try to add another performance to the schedule."

Half the audience returned to their feet in protest. Loud objections, boos, and even a few catcalls boomed toward the stage. Ben raised his hands to quiet the crowd.

"On behalf of the entire cast, I want to apologize for the cancelation of tonight's performance ..."

The audience, most of whom could no longer hear him over the noise, groaned with disappointment. Avril reacted to their dissatisfied shouts and excused herself to the bathroom. When she fled down the hallway, I found myself drawn back onstage, joining Ben where he struggled to calm the audience.

Some in the crowd cheered when I stepped back onstage and took Ben's arm to lend moral support. When he seemed at a loss for words, I cued George and Perry at the soundboard to switch my microphone back on.

"It's rare that I have a chance to come out and speak to you not as Audrey Bradford, but as myself, Harper Gray. This is an excellent time to tell you all how wonderful it's been for us to perform for you over the last few weeks. We have only twelve more performances, and then this production will close for good."

The crowd began booing again, only this time it was because they were used to Broadway shows that ran forever, and for years unto infinity.

"My dearest friends in the whole world are here tonight. Ben Hughes, our favorite director, and the man responsible for bringing Mouldain's classic play back to Broadway where it belongs."

The audience clapped, recognizing Ben's accomplishment. Some of the standing audience returned to their seats, the tension in the room calming.

"My very best friend, Avril LaCorria, who you met earlier as Roxy Dupree."

They applauded again, perhaps realizing it hadn't been Avril's best night.

"And all of you who give us far more during every performance than we could ever possibly give back in return."

I saw a couple of men and women in the back of the room stand up and applaud. A few others followed, but this time they were standing in a show of support, not out of frustration or disappointment.

I sensed someone else at my side. Avril, dabbing mascara from her puffy pink eyes, was putting her earpiece back in position.

"I want to apologize," she said, and the crowd, which had become festive and forgiving, hushed to listen to her words. "I don't know if this is allowed," she continued, turning to Ben for approval. "But would it be possible just to start the whole thing over again and try it one more time?"

The room exploded with thunderous applause. All the actors poured out from the wings and met in a group on center stage, hugging like it was closing night. The audience was on their feet and cheering. Avril was still crying, but I had a hopeful feeling that the worst might be behind her.

For the next two hours, the cast of *Apartment* 19 gave New York the best show of our lives. We blew them out of their seats. Avril became unleashed, acting with enough raw emotion and drama that the crowd jumped, hooted, and cheered.

After the show, all of us greeted the audience in the lobby, signing autographs and sharing well wishes until well past midnight.

The following day, it wasn't a review that ran in the papers, but a full column in the gossip page about the incident that set things off with an "unidentified man and woman" and ended with "the most enjoyable night I've ever spent in the theater." New York was buzzing once again about *Apartment 19* and starting the countdown until we would all say good-bye to Arthur Mouldain's masterpiece forever.

Scalpers sold tickets for one thousand dollars a pair, and before it was all over, we'd shake hands with the mayor of New York, Hollywood actors, cabbies and street cleaners, shopkeepers, bartenders, Wall Street bankers, and even a U.S. senator.

♫

Sydney called my cell phone one morning as I sat at Vibe drinking coffee.

"Harper," Sydney said, "when the play finishes next week, I want you to think about coming back out to Los Angeles. It's time we reintroduce you to Hollywood."

When Sydney invited me to California, my first thought wasn't about the next chapter of my career, but rather about a phone number stashed away on my computer for safekeeping. I hadn't called Luke yet. We'd spent the last four weeks talking through the instant messaging service, compliments of LoveSetMatch.com. My morning routine usually centered on drinking coffee at Vibe while typing away on the MacBook in conversation with Luke. We passed emails back and forth, but I often wondered what it would be like to hear his voice.

"I'd love to come back to LA, Sydney."

"Good. You can plan on staying at my bungalow. I'll set up a few meetings with the people who've asked. I'll be in touch."

Before I left Vibe, I opened the lid of my MacBook and double-clicked on the Notepad icon. It opened, a yellow square on the screen, and in the upper-left corner was Luke's name and cell number. I sent a text message to his cell phone.

isn't it time we talked?

Back at the apartment, I knocked on Avril's door, opening it a crack to peek inside. Avril was wrapped in her fluffy strawberry bedspread, looking listless and dull-eyed.

"Do you want to come out to the kitchen? I'll make you lunch."

Avril's bedroom was decorated like a teenager's with touches of pink and fuzzy throw pillows. I stepped inside and sat on the edge of her bed.

"Tell me what's going on."

"I want to change this room," she said. "It's too childish."

"Change is good. I'm all for change," I said, still holding her hand, waiting in the silence until she felt like talking again. I held her hand, wondering if she'd allow me to straighten up her room. Her vanity was uncharacteristically jumbled, a playbill from the show obscuring her makeup and perfume, things she normally put away. Her laundry basket overflowing with inside-out shirts and jeans, and one of her closet doors was open.

"I didn't see it coming, Harper. I didn't even think it was possible for me to get burned like that."

"Jon's behavior was totally wrong. How could you or anybody know?"

I helped Avril sit up in bed, arranging her pillows against her sturdy white headboard. Her lips were chapped, so I took out a bottle of water from my leather satchel and held it up for her to drink.

"I'm not talking about him, I'm talking about me. How shallow am I? The idea that someone could use me that way had never even crossed my mind."

"I don't think that's the right lesson to take away from this …"

"Life is hard, that's the lesson. I've been dancing on a high wire all my life, and never dreamed I could fall. I was naive, seriously."

"Scoot over."

I joined Avril on top of the blankets, leaning my back against the headboard. I kicked off my shoes, resting the soles of my feet on the comforter. "So where do you go from here?"

Avril leaned the weight of her head on my shoulder. "I'm lost, Harper. I don't know what to do."

"Your confidence will come back. Meanwhile, I'm here for you, Avril. I'll always be here for you. You can stay in bed as long as you like. I'm going to make you lunch."

Avril drank the bottle of water but didn't eat the grilled cheese sandwich, only a few of the grapes I'd brought her in a cereal bowl. An hour later, she'd fallen asleep.

I closed Avril's bedroom door quietly and returned to the living room for the MacBook. The sun felt warm as I sat cross-legged on the floor between two stripes of sunlight.

Every active tab on my LoveSetMatch homepage was lit up with color. A red light alerted the presence of three new messages. Little orange flames twinkled next to both James and Luke's names. An instant message from Luke popped up on-screen as soon as I'd logged on.

Ready when you are.

I rummaged through my satchel searching for the phone. Frustrated and impatient, I turned the bag upside down and dumped out all of its contents on the floor.

I found Luke's number in the Notepad program and entered the ten digits into my cell, then pressed the Send button. My skin felt electric, and I worried for a moment that I wouldn't be able to speak or control my breathing well enough to keep my voice from cracking.

The signal looped from cell tower to satellite. Somewhere in a small Alaskan town, a cell phone rang. I listened to a popping noise, and then a man's voice on the other end of the line.

"Hello?"

"Hi, it's Harper," I said, nervous and trying to hide it. I stuck my tongue between my teeth to keep them from chattering.

"I wondered if you'd call." Luke's baritone voice sounded clear and strong, certain when he spoke.

"I just … felt it was time," I said, standing up to pace around the living room, fiddle with the window sheers, and stare down at traffic in Greenwich Village.

"I'm glad you did," he said. "It's been nice getting to know you these past five weeks. I wondered if we'd ever talk."

"Me, too. What are you doing right now?" I asked, wanting this conversation to feel normal, when it sounded anything but normal.

"I'm at the office in Wasilla. I've got a crew out in the field today. I was just going over a few survey maps before heading out to join them."

"Is this a bad time to talk?"

"No, I'm walking outside to my Jeep, and driving is a perfect time to talk. There are no distractions."

I tried to picture Alaska's wilderness, the pine trees framing every vista, the timber-built houses and cabins with their chimneys billowing smoke, calm fishing lakes, the boats against overcast skies.

"I thought we should talk. I have news to share with you. The show I'm in wraps up next week, after that, it looks like I'll be spending time in Los Angeles."

"LA's a lot closer than New York."

"That's what I was thinking."

"Let me check on a couple things, okay? Maybe I can arrange something, if you would like to meet."

"You mean there's a chance you'd fly down?"

"Well, yeah, Harper. The thought of meeting you in person has crossed my mind. I was just waiting for you to be ready."

"It's crossed my mind too," I said, still pacing the room. "This is so weird. We don't even know each other. Just photos on a Web site, instant messages, emails."

"I've actually been a real person for a lot longer than I've been a photo on LoveSetMatch.com. I mean, be as cautious as you need to be, but I'm a guy who's lived in the same small town his whole life, worked the same job for the same company. I signed up to online dating because I wondered if there might be more beyond the world I live in."

"So, are we beyond typing to each other?" I asked.

"Man, I hope so," he said. "I think I've developed carpel tunnel with all the messages I've sent you." A laugh escaped my mouth, and I heard a chuckle on the other end of the phone.

"Okay, well, this is still strange, new territory for me, but maybe we'll meet in LA," I said.

"Harper?"

"Yes?"

"I hope so."

"Yeah, me, too."

~ Nineteen ~

A reporter from *Variety* magazine interviewed Harriet backstage as Avril and I walked in to wardrobe. It was the first tangible sign that our days of performing *Apartment 19* were coming to an end. I overheard the reporter asking Harriet what was behind the success of Ben Hughes's revival.

"All the actors have a stake in the show. We are truly a family who prays together, understands that we need each other, and you'll never read this in any review, but I believe that bond translates to audiences who come see the show."

When Harriet noticed Avril and I watching, she left the *Variety* reporter in midquestion, holding open her arms to embrace us. The mood felt like those last days of high school's senior year when everything you do is for the last time. The reporter moved closer to our circle with her microphone.

"Harper, people are talking about awards for you and Avril for your performances in *Apartment 19.* How would you explain the show's success?"

"People want to credit its acting, its direction, or its playwright, but after watching audiences these last six weeks, I've come to the conclusion there were a lot of people in New York who needed something special, and somehow an unexpected play became that for them. It's just that simple."

Closing night arrived like the last pages of a book you hope will never end.

Ben had a bouquet of red roses delivered to my dressing room, something he hadn't done on previous nights because the act reeked so much of what he'd gone through with Helen Payne.

At the closing curtain, the entire cast joined hands at center stage. Ben waved on the backstage crew, and together we all took our last bow.

The applause thundered in my ears, and I closed my eyes, burning the moment into memory.

At the cast party in Ben's apartment, Tabby approached me, appearing stress free with nothing left to manage but a glass of red wine.

"You did good, Harper," she told me in the kitchen when the two of us were alone. "You should be proud of yourself."

In the living room I heard Marshall banging away at the piano, running through a medley of Rodgers and Hammerstein songs while the cast belted out what words they knew, making up the rest. Outside the apartment, the Manhattan skyline pulsed with the lights from a million windows.

"I'd rather be your friend than proud," I said, since the night felt like a time for saying things. They were the last confrontational words I'd ever speak to her. "Is that even possible?"

"Why is that important to you?"

"Because I hate thinking the only thing we've accomplished over the past seven weeks is entertainment. There's meaning in everything if you look for it, and I can't think of a single reason why we shouldn't be friends."

"I think this cast *has* accomplished more," Tabby said. "But I don't know what you're looking for. You and I couldn't be more different. I don't see you coming with me to the next scotch tasting party, and I'm not planning to go to church with you on Sunday."

Marshall's piano music quieted in the other room. I recognized the opening strains of "If I Loved You," the ballad from *Carousel*, and the dedicated few still singing knew all the words.

"Maybe not, but for me this production was about things coming together. I guess I'm looking for some kind of closure. I don't want to leave things unsaid."

Tabby's cell phone lit up on her belt clip. She glanced down, tilting its face at an angle so she could read the caller's name, and decided uncharacteristically to ignore it.

"Life's not that simple, Harper. Things don't always resolve themselves like a half-hour sitcom. You see the world in black and white, but I see gradations. You want everything to tie up neatly with a bow, but I think that's just painting a happy face on things. I just came in to say 'a job well done,' and nothing more. This doesn't have to be a bonding moment."

"Maybe it doesn't, but one of the advantages of living in a world of absolutes is always knowing where you stand. I want to be someone who reaches out. I think it has its own rewards, and it's the right thing to do."

Tabby sipped her wine, saving her rejoinder until after she finished her swallow. "That's very noble, just as long as you can accept that not everyone is going to reach back."

Harriet appeared from around the corner. "I'm reaching out, friend. In fact, I'm taking you home with me," she said.

I felt Harriet's arms wrap me up in another of her world-class hugs. She held and rocked me like a baby she'd never let go.

"You say that like you're getting ready to leave," I said.

"I am. This is later than I typically stay out. I have got to get back home and see my Darius," Harriet said, breaking off our embrace, nodding good-bye to Tabby.

"I'm sorry I never got the chance to meet him," I told her. "I would have loved to watch Animal Planet with the both of you."

"You will, you will," Harriet said. "As long as you can find Brooklyn, and like to eat microwave popcorn, you're welcome anytime."

Harriet gestured for me to follow her to the front door. "Come walk me out. I want to tell you something."

I followed Harriet out of Ben's stainless-steel kitchen, glancing back at Tabby one more time before we abandoned her. She'd taken out her cell phone and was reading her text message. I hoped it was from someone who loved her.

Harriet made her way through the crowd, handing out a second round of good-byes. She lifted her coat off the rack by the door and hurried herself into it.

"God brought you here, and you brought God here with you," she said, once our conversation could be more private. "You weren't ashamed of Him, you were bold for Him, and see what He did for you? That made it easier for me, being here," Harriet continued, tears welling up in her eyes. "I have to earn money, and this is what I do, but this is *not* my crowd. You lifted Him up, and now He's lifted you up."

Despite our promises to never part company, Harriet and I hugged once more, and she left to hail a taxi back to Brooklyn.

I followed the music back to where Marshall and George sat on the piano bench singing a duet of "Edelweiss." Ben approached me, opening his arms, loose with wine and song.

"Harper, I feel like we've packed a year's worth of life into the last six weeks together. I'm not sure I want it to be over."

He ran his hand through his hair, a familiar nervous gesture. "I hope the flowers I left in your dressing room conveyed the right message—a great big thank-you for all you did. No matter what was going on in my private life, I could always come in to the theater and escape. You helped make that possible for me."

"What's next for you, Ben?"

"I told my business partners I had to take some time off. I called Denise to say I was willing to try. We fly to the south of France this weekend to give it a month together and just see how it goes. Wish us luck."

"Do you mind if I pray for you both?"

"No, I don't mind at all," Ben said and embraced me again.

"Then I'll be praying for you and Denise. Give my regards to Paris."

The audience had gone home, the critics were writing their final reviews, and the cast party was breaking up for good. Like a wonderful dream, *Apartment 19* was over. The masks and the stages, the make-believe and props all put away. The characters we portrayed went back in some hidden box for safekeeping, and the emotions we acted out vanished into thin air.

Avril and I fell into a cab on the Upper East Side and I asked the driver to take us down West Forty-fourth Street on our way back to the Village. I leaned back and peered out the window as the taxi drove past the Carney Theatre one last time. The ghosts of our memories clowned beneath the brightly lit marquee that read:

Apartment 19

Final night

Lights fell on Broadway like stars from the heavens. Our cab merged into traffic, and I watched the bright theater marquee grow smaller and dimmer until the title was a blurry line surrounded by a nostalgic moon. Then the buses, cabs, and cars hustled by us until even that was swept away from my vision.

~ TWENTY ~

The New York Theater Society threw a gala fund-raising dinner in Ben Hughes's honor the night after *Apartment 19* closed. Traditionalists at heart, the Society relished the opportunity to boast the play's success as an example of the classics still having the power to pack out a theater, if given the creative juice and financial backing they deserved.

It was rumored that Helen Payne, still the beloved diva of Broadway and longtime member of the Society, would be there, but it turned out to be nothing more than a rumor.

Under a grand chandelier in the red-draped ballroom at the LaPierre Hotel, the cast was treated like royalty by the upper stratum of Broadway luminaries. Directors, actors, producers, entertainment reporters and theater critics, choreographers, dancers, and cherished guild members gathered to raise money for the Society and to shake our hands.

It was the New York Theater Society director Miriam LoRosh who introduced me to Joseph Hagen, the famed Hollywood director. He looked as dashing in real life as he did in his photos. A man in his mid-sixties, he had a Californian's sun-tanned face and sapphire eyes.

"Harper, I have someone here I'd like to introduce you to," Ms. LoRosh said, guiding the director toward me and handling formal introductions.

"Harper Gray, meet Mr. Joseph Hagen. I'm sure you both must have heard *of* each other but haven't had the pleasure of meeting face-to-face. Joseph has won so many awards it's rumored he keeps his Oscars on the west wing of his house, and his Tonys on the east, closest to Broadway."

Joseph Hagen bent his head toward me in a bow.

"Joseph was just telling me he's seen *Apartment 19* twice in the past two weeks, so I'm sure the two of you will have plenty to talk about," Miriam said before gliding off to her next introductory duty, something she did rather well.

"Miss Gray, I don't say this often, but I fell in love with your portrayal of Audrey Bradford. I had the privilege of meeting Arthur Mouldain in London when I was a young actor. That chance encounter had a profound effect on my life and is responsible in part for my becoming a director."

"He must have possessed an extraordinary charisma."

"Mouldain was the sort of playwright who couldn't *squeeze* enough ideas into his plays. He was like a classical composer. Once he had a main story line, he wove layer upon layer of subplots and themes into it. I think he would very much appreciate what this cast has done with his play."

"Thank you, Mr. Hagen. That's very kind of you to say. I believe Ben Hughes deserves much of the credit for the production's vision."

"Yes, I agree, but there are some things a director can't do. Mouldain would say your performance 'fiddles at the edge of his fingers,' meaning he could half picture it, but he left the last pieces of his work to be completed by the ensemble."

"I'm flattered, Mr. Hagen. Your commentary on our work is a high compliment indeed."

"Well deserved, Ms. Gray. Tell me, where do you go after this? What project are you working on next?"

"A trip to LA is the only thing on my calendar. I'll spend a week or so with my agent in Malibu. Sydney Bloom, do you know her?"

"No, I do not. Does she represent you in her own agency?"

"Sydney Bloom Talent," I replied, the name unexpectedly sounding like a mom-and-pop charm school in the presence of Joseph Hagen.

He nodded. "Well, I hope that we shall meet again sometime, Miss Gray. It is Miss Gray, isn't it?"

"Yes," I answered, thinking, *For thirty-one consecutive years.*

"I wanted to meet and tell you how much I sincerely enjoyed your performance."

"The honor's all mine."

Joseph Hagen walked away, bringing to mind all those old black-and-white movies with fancy Hollywood cocktail parties and debonair movie moguls in ascots who always spoke in clever one-liners and were perpetually on the verge of breaking out in a dance routine on polished floor or wall. Some part of me expected Lauren Bacall and Humphrey Bogart to walk in next.

But it wasn't Bogey who entered my sight line at the far end of the ballroom. It was Avril. She wore a baby blue gown looking like a battered Cinderella at the ball. Matured by love's betrayal, she had fallen down private rabbit holes, and I feared she might fall down one in front of everyone.

"Are you all right?" I asked, meeting her in the center of the ballroom. She practically floated to me. "Avril, honey, you look so *frail.*"

"I feel *light*," she said, striking a smile that chimed with a hollow cheeriness.

"Let's go home, Avril, and make some pasta. This gossamer world isn't a place for us."

Avril closed her eyes and opened her mouth to let out a roar of laughter, but nothing came out. There was no genuine humor inside her.

I poured Avril into a taxi that transported us back to the Village. Once we'd climbed three flights of stairs, I helped Avril inside the apartment and put her to bed. She was in no condition to be left alone, a matter that weighed heavily on me that night as I confirmed my ticket online to Los Angeles.

I'd need most of the next day to pack and ship my belongings. It wasn't like I was moving West, but when I tried to picture my future, I couldn't see myself coming back to New York.

I needed to say good-bye to Katie and David, and more than anything I wanted to have a long conversation with Luke.

Avril awoke around 11 p.m., and I coaxed her into eating some veggies and cottage cheese with me on the living room floor.

"Avril, I want you to come to California with me. You're due some beach time. It will do you good."

"I'm too tired to fly. It's so far away."

"We can both stay with Sydney. You don't have your next acting gig lined up, which is a blessing because you need a vacation."

"I'm slipping away, Harper," Avril told me. It was the first time I considered that that might actually be true.

"In New York, yes. But when you come back home to California you'll feel strong again."

"What if I never come back, Harper? What if there isn't any me to come back to?"

"I never told you this, except for what you heard that night at church, but last year my life fell out from under me. Sam left, I was out of work, out of money, and I was so down I even thought of taking my life. But there was this girl, a friend named Bella, who invited me to go to a church with her. You know, I was never that way, religious, churchgoer, whatever. But I believed the message the pastor told, and I prayed for God to rescue me, and He did."

"I can't go on like this," she whispered, raising her knees to her chest.

"I know. I'm trying to get you to take one small step. Just come with me to California for a couple of weeks. You'll see. It will do you a world of good."

~ Twenty-one ~

The next morning I didn't feel like going through the usual routine, coffee at Vibe, chatting with Luke online, especially since we'd moved on to cell phones. Call it nervous energy, but my head was spinning with things to do on my last day in New York before flying to the West Coast.

I ate breakfast at the island, sketching out a preflight to-do checklist and wrote out a check for next month's rent, tucking it into the wicker organizer Avril dutifully kept on the granite counter. After taking care of my dishes, I packed up everything I owned into travel bags and took a quick shower.

I left the brownstone before Avril had roused, fighting my propensity to worry over her situation and weight loss. Instead, I walked down Bleecker Street to the nearest FBNY bank branch and closed my checking account, wiring the balance to my main bank in Anaheim, California.

What a difference in my financial picture. After coming to New York with nothing more than a maxed-out credit card, I now had almost eighty thousand dollars.

I called Katie's cell number to see if she could meet me that afternoon for coffee. We'd seen each other at church every Sunday morning for the past six weeks, but I wanted to talk to her before leaving New York. She didn't pick up, so when the system bumped me over to voice mail, I left a message.

"Hey Katie, it's Harper. I'm flying to Los Angeles tomorrow, maybe for good, and just wanted to know if you had time today for coffee. Give me a call."

At the newsstand, I stopped to browse, thinking I'd pick up a magazine or paperback to read on the plane. I heard the muted ringing of my cell phone stuffed into my pocket and pulled it out to look at the number. It was local, but it wasn't Avril or Katie. I placed the phone against my ear, turning away from the street noise to answer.

"Hello?"

"Harper Gray?" It was a woman's voice.

"Yes? Who is this?"

"This is Maureen Burns, I work for Helen Payne. Perhaps you've heard of me."

I'd never been introduced to the steely woman, but I remembered the cold shadows she'd cast on the night she'd visited the Carney. "Yes, I've heard of you."

"I expect you have. First, let me say congratulations, Harper, on your performance. Few actresses achieve that pinnacle of success in a lifetime. I'm sure it's like having a crown placed on your head, isn't it? Helen wanted you to know she has *no hard feelings* toward you for what happened. You were just doing what you were contracted to do."

Talking to Maureen Burns felt like being questioned on a witness stand. I'd been on the phone with the woman less than a minute, and already I had a creepy feeling I'd regret it.

"How can I help you, Ms. Burns?"

"Cutting straight to the point. I like that. You understand time is money, so I'll get to my point without wasting any of our time. Helen Payne would like to see you. She asked me as her agent and friend if I could get in contact with you."

"Why does Helen want to see me?"

"I think that's a private matter between the two of you. I'm sure I don't know. Would you be free this evening?"

Maureen Burns had a slithery way of making an invitation to a social call sound like a trap was being set.

"Tonight? No, I can't meet with Helen tonight. I'm leaving town tomorrow morning."

"Harper, Helen is a kind and munificent woman. She would never say this, but I think you owe her somewhat for where you are today. You'd never have gotten this far without Helen dropping out of the show. If it were up to me, there would have been a lawsuit."

The wind turned cold on Bleecker Street, and I moved to the other side of the newsstand. A city bus passed, belching fumes and smoke, making it impossible to hear Maureen.

"A lawsuit? For what?"

"All sorts of things, breach of contract, the tarnishing of a beloved actor's reputation, but that's neither here nor there. Helen would never injure an institution she loves as dearly as the theater. I just thought you'd want to know how generous she's been, and I don't think it's asking too much of you to honor her request and see her tonight."

"For coffee?"

"Coffee it is. Helen lives in Trump Tower. I'll tell her you're available. Around seven thirty?"

"I'll be there," I said, wishing I'd had a better reason to say no.

"Good. And Harper, why don't we agree to keep this meeting a secret among the three of us for now?"

♫◊

A yellow cab let me out in front of Trump Tower on Fifth Avenue. I entered the glass-tiered building through the grand lobby and looked for the elevators. It was my first time in the renowned building, a splashy display of gold and mirrors, shops, escalators, and a walking bridge.

"Harper!"

I turned to see Maureen Burns coming toward me. She was dressed in a tweed business suit like the one I'd seen her wearing at the Carney. Her skin was ashen, saved from the ravages of the sun by never wandering out into it. She lived in office buildings, courtrooms, and under florescent lighting. She held out her hand to me as if she could be trusted, and I reached over to shake it.

"I'm glad I bumped into you. I was just walking out for the night," she said. "Helen and I only this minute finished our regular business meeting."

She guided my elbow like a rudder toward the elevators and pushed the button. The timing of our bumping into one another was too convenient. The elevator doors opened and I stepped inside.

"Seventeenth floor," she said, handing me a card with Helen's address printed across it. "Just ring the bell. Her housekeeper, Bonnet, will let you in."

Bonnet? The elevators doors closed like metal theater curtains, and I couldn't help feeling I'd been invited to coffee much the way a turkey is invited to Thanksgiving.

Bonnet opened the door after just one ring of the bell. She was a plain middle-aged woman with robin's nest hair, and she was wearing just what I'd expected: a maid's uniform, looking like a Bleak House servant from the nineteenth century.

"Ms. Payne asks that you wait in the den," she told me without making eye contact.

I seated myself in the next room on a long cream-colored sofa with bamboo framing. The den was immaculate, like Audrey Bradford's. The furniture looked expensive and rare, as though it had just arrived in crates, shipped from Asia by slow freighter. There were two birds, parakeets I guessed, locked in a brass cage suspended on a hook, each facing a different direction. The carpeting smelled like it had been professionally cleaned, a chemical odor lingering in the air. Twenty or so framed photographs decorated the lid of a closed baby grand piano. I stuck my nose closer in to read the autograph inscription on a picture of Robert Mitchum.

Helen surprised me, appearing suddenly through one of three entrances in the large apartment.

"Harper, I'm so glad to see you again." Helen greeted me with a friendly embrace, squeezing both my hands in hers.

"Sit down. I've been looking forward to having a chance to talk to you."

We sat across from one another.

"Maureen Burns said you wanted to see me?"

"I do. I wanted to congratulate you on all you've accomplished. You surprised a lot of people, Harper, including me. I was just talking to Maureen about your talents as an actress and how I think they'll serve you well over a long and prosperous career."

Helen's face took on a conflicted look. "She's also my attorney and has strongly suggested I file a lawsuit against Ben and the producers of *Apartment 19*, but I won't do it. That's not why I asked you here, Harper."

"Why did you ask me here?"

Helen stood. "I don't want to sue Ben. That's not why I got into this business. If I'd wanted to spend my time in a courtroom I would have become a judge. However, that doesn't excuse Ben for what he did. He humiliated me in front of New York's theater community. Ben Hughes represents all that is wrong with the current generation of producers and directors. They don't have the *respect* for the art form, or the deference required to work with an actress who was starring on Broadway before he was out of his diapers."

"Helen, listen, I don't want to get into why things happened the way they did …"

"You're not married, are you, Harper?"

"No, I … what does that have to do with …" I began.

"Good, keep it that way. You've got a bright future. Don't spoil it by running off and surrendering your life to some man. They're really good for very little when it comes right down to it."

"I would disagree. My dad's been there for me, and I know another man who risks his life for people he hardly knows."

"Risks his life?" she asked. "What is he, a fireman?"

"He's a pilot in the arctic."

Helen made a face like she smelled day-old fish. It was the face of Audrey Bradford. I recognized it from all those rehearsals at the Carney, and I was sitting in her apartment, a real life Roxy Dupree.

"Do you live in the arctic?"

"No."

"Then you don't know him, do you? I wanted to see you because I want to give you some good advice, Harper. You've got real talent. I'd give anything to be young again, like you. But you … you have the world on a string right now. You can do anything you want as long as you don't let anyone get in your way. Stay focused on the prize, Harper, and someday if you're lucky, you'll be just like me."

~ TWENTY-TWO ~

"Hello, Katie? Hi! No, it's not too late to be calling me back, unless you're hoping to grab coffee. I just landed in Los Angeles. Yes, I'm walking to baggage claim right now to pick up my luggage."

I pulled my carry-on down the concourse. It was warm and sunny throughout LAX. The Muzak system piped in an old song by Fleetwood Mac, and I could smell California Pizza Kitchen from the food court.

"I don't know how long I'll be out here. I have business with my agent, Sydney Bloom, and I can hardly believe I'm saying this, but I'm driving to northern California this weekend to finally meet Luke."

"You're going to meet your flying lumberjack?" Katie asked.

"Yes, finally. He's flying down to Seattle, and so we decided to meet halfway. Avril's still in New York, but I talked her into flying out tomorrow to join me. Today was just too soon. Could you do me a *huge* favor and check up on her?"

Sydney picked me up in front of LAX in a brand-new white Escalade with tinted windows. I saw the temporary tag taped in the back window when I came around to load my luggage.

"Oh, Harper. It's so good to see you." Sydney wrapped her large arms about me, swallowing me up in her welcome. She looked the same as the last time I'd seen her, with the addition of a large floral-pattern beach hat.

"I was just thinking on the way over here, it's been a year since we've seen each other. Isn't that amazing? I can't believe time has gone by that quickly."

Sydney popped the SUV's hatch. I picked up my suitcases and carried them to the back.

"I'll finish loading your suitcases. You climb in front. I have news I can't wait to tell you."

A minute later we were driving away from the airport. I rolled my window down and stuck my hand outside to catch the warm, thick breezes. Palm trees waved on the sides of the road. I was definitely not in New York anymore. Even the yellow taxis looked like they were headed to the beach.

"Harper, you'll never guess who graced me with a phone call this afternoon, asking about your status, about your *professional* availability."

"Who?" I asked, shifting my point of view to watch Sydney as she drove.

"Jos-eph Ha-gen," she said, speaking each syllable with care. "He told me all about your black-tie rendezvous at the Society benefit in New York, and that he'd seen *Apartment 19* twice. I'd actually never spoken with him before. Joseph's one of those A-list directors who doesn't usually associate directly with casting and theatrical agents. Of course, we all know him by reputation as a director with a long and some would say *infamous* history of discovering leading ladies."

Sydney peered over the top of her sunglasses at me.

"He's smitten with you, Harper. I can hear it in his voice. He called to say he has a script he wants you to read—and I don't mean 'just read.' He has a script with a strong female role he wants you and only *you* to play."

"My gosh, are you sure? He didn't mention a word to me when I met him."

"Quite sure. He kept me on the phone for the better part of an hour this morning discussing the project and your availability."

Sydney pulled up to a stoplight, waiting until the last second to brake. She looked over at me with disbelief on her face.

"He also said you'd told him you had nothing lined up. Harper, you're not new at this. That's the last thing in the world you want to tell a successful director like Joseph Hagen, or anyone else for that matter. They'll get the idea no one else wants you."

"I *don't* have anything else going on," I said, looking out the window at a father and two young boys playing catch in a park; the scene stirred with activity, men fishing, seniors walking, kids on skateboards. The light switched to green, and Sydney pressed her lead foot to the pedal, whisking it all from sight.

"Well, you do now. In this situation, it probably worked for the best because his production is steamrolling ahead. Get this. He's been looking for his leading lady for seven months. Can you believe it? They've seen literally hundreds of actresses, and while Joseph was in New York on another matter, he heard and read about *Apartment 19*. You're the actress he's set his sights on, and the last member to fill his cast."

"Where would it shoot?"

I'm not sure why that was the first question to pop into my head. Maybe it had to do with meeting with Helen the night prior, or a meeting I couldn't stop thinking about in northern California.

"Right here in LA, but does it matter? Harper, six months ago you were invisible, now Joseph Hagen has your head shot stuck to his refrigerator door with Oscar magnets. He can film his movie at the North Pole for all we care."

I laughed. "You're right. Tell me about the script."

"It's not a big-budget picture with CGI effects and car chases. That's not Joseph's style. The picture's called *Winter Dreams,* and it's the story of a young woman who feels frozen in her life. Her husband dumps her, and she loses her job, so she moves to Los Angeles to start over. While she's here in LA, she meets a man, a kind of mysterious rugged stranger, who it turns out isn't really a stranger at all, but her guardian angel."

"Her angel?" I said.

"Yes, that's the basic premise. There's more, of course, like the little detail that he falls in love with her. Are you getting the picture?"

"That's called *The Bishop's Wife.*"

"Well, sort of, only it's not a Christmas picture, and it's set in sunny LA, not snowy Vermont or Connecticut, or wherever."

Sydney stopped talking.

"So what happens to this woman?" I asked.

"She learns some heavenly lessons. It's a drama, a life changer, lots of tears and some laughter, a happy ending. Joseph's sending over the script. Why don't you read it and tell me what you think?"

"You said it has a happy ending. Just how happy?" I asked.

"She finds true love. Sure, there's some heartbreak along the way. There always is. The point is, it's Joseph Hagen."

We drove awhile until Sydney pulled up to her beach house in Malibu. She turned the wheels of her Escalade into a parking space at the rear of the house. Over the privacy fence, the Pacific Ocean was a sparkling blue, brush stroked across the horizon. Sydney's rose bushes burst with red blooms, and the tiered levels of her sundeck had been landscaped with driftwood, natural rock, and sea grass.

She turned off the engine and looked directly at me. "So, what do you think about the picture? It's perfect, right?"

"Yes, it's perfect. Completely perfect." I looked out at the sailboats dancing with the wind in the afternoon sun. I wanted to be out there on the water, or at least walking along the beach. "I know there's more to discuss, Sydney, and I'll want to read the script, but I can't imagine not doing the picture."

"What's wrong, kid? You look kind of shocked." Sydney said.

"It's just a bit overwhelming," I confessed. "The story, the long flight, and everything that happened in New York. I guess I am feeling a shock."

Sydney grinned. "That's Hollywood electricity, Harper. The power company switches it on when you're offered the role of a lifetime."

She pulled the handle on her door, stepping out into the sunlight. I followed, instantly revived by the smell of saltwater and the touch of a dry, warm breeze that brushed my hair with gentle, invisible fingers.

"Is it, Sydney?" I asked, pulling out my suitcases. "Is this really the role of a lifetime?"

"Yes," she said. "You're about to appear on the front page of every magazine and entertainment TV show in the country. If

Joseph captures half of what I know you're capable of, you'll see script after script from the top directors in Hollywood for years. But if the movie is a hit, Harper, you'll break through the ceiling for A-listers, and you'll see seven-figure salaries per picture, easy."

"Should I ask what this one's paying?"

"If I knew, I'd tell you. Joseph said he's sending over the script tomorrow, although I wouldn't be surprised to see it sitting in my mailbox right now. If we like it, we'll talk terms."

Sydney showed me to my room. It was filled with bamboo furniture, a matching bed frame, and sunlight. Beach-themed knickknacks littered the wicker bookshelves—shells, white sand in a bottle, photos of Sydney's nieces building sandcastles with lime-green buckets and raspberry-red shovels.

"I'm running back to the office for a couple of hours, but let's plan on having dinner around seven, okay? I know I'm needing Tex-Mex, and if you've never had Mexican food in Southern California, Harper, you're about to fall in love. Oh, and I almost forgot to ask. Do you have an update on Avril?"

"She's flying out here tomorrow. Why?"

"I'm just a little mad at her."

"How come?"

"She's supposed to start work on an independent film in Seattle in two weeks. Well, she called me last week to tell me she wanted to drop out of it."

"Did she tell you why?"

"She just said she needed a break, but she's the one who told me she wanted all the work I could find. It doesn't look good to bail on a film production, although admittedly, all we gave them was a verbal agreement. Still, I thought it was a good match for Avril."

Sydney left, and I decided to take a nap. I fell asleep to the sound of the ocean smoothing the sand and drifted into dreams of an unfrozen life.

Sydney decided to work from home the next morning. We sat on the wooden deck underneath a blue and white umbrella tilted to shelter us from the sun, eating a breakfast of eggs, coffee, and grapefruit. The morning air had a cool, crisp feel to it, and I found watching the surfers navigate the curling water to be the most relaxing thing I'd done in months.

"So did you ever get in touch with Avril?" Sydney asked.

"I'll call her again this morning," I said. "She was still making flight arrangements the last I knew, and she'll probably need a ride from the airport."

Around 10 a.m. the phone rang once, then stopped.

Sydney was working at her laptop at the dining room table. Suddenly the phone rang again as both of us sprang into action.

"It's got to be Joseph," Sydney said, reaching for the phone.

"Caller ID?" I asked.

"Not on this one."

Sydney pushed on the speakerphone.

"This is Sydney Bloom," she said, as we waited for the unmistakable accent of Joseph Hagen.

"Hey, Syd. It's Avril. Guess where I am."

"Hon, I'm not that good at guessing anymore."

Avril laughed. "I decided to take Harper's advice and fly out of New York. I got stuck in Denver last night, but I'm back at the airport, waiting for my flight. It's kind of a screwy schedule, but I should be at LAX in a few hours. Sorry I didn't just come with Harper yesterday, but can I beg you to pick me up this afternoon?"

"Beg us? Honey, you and Harper are my two favorite girls in the whole world. This is turning out to be one of the best weeks for news. Just tell us what time your flight lands, and we'll be there!"

We had a couple of hours to kill. After breakfast, I took a long walk on the beach. I wore light brown shorts and a gauzy yellow summer shirt. The sun and wind warmed and cooled my face as I walked near the waterline, where the sand is wet and firm.

Back at Sydney's I grabbed a bottle of water from the fridge and took it to my bedroom. I lay back in bed and found Luke's number on the speed dial. The bedroom shades were still pulled shut from sleep, so I got out of bed while Luke's phone rang in my ear. I took hold of each side of the thick blue drapes and yanked them apart. Sunlight brought the room to life. I unlatched the door to the terrace and pushed open the sliding glass door. The sounds of the ocean filled the room, as did the smell of coconut suntan oil.

"Are you here?" Luke asked.

"Here as in Los Angeles? Yes. As a matter of fact, I'm looking at the most gorgeous view of the Pacific Ocean I believe I've ever seen. Are you in Seattle?"

"Yes, I'm looking at the biggest drops of rain I think I've ever seen."

"So, we're going to do this, right? Meet up the day after tomorrow somewhere near San Francisco?"

"I'll fly my plane into Monterey, rent a car. What do you say about meeting in Carmel? I think I promised you a date."

"Since you're coming through with your end of the promise, I'll keep up mine. Meet you in Carmel."

~ TWENTY-THREE ~

The drive up the coast to Monterey was long and scenic and brought to mind songs that played in my head as I drove. The Pacific Ocean raged beneath a blanket of intermittent fog, but Avril and I ignored it, singing along with the radio and trying not to speed on the winding coastline highway. It was good to hear her laughter again. Really good. California suited us both.

"Thanks for coming with me," I told her. "We should have thought of a road trip a long time ago."

Avril rolled her head to face me, languid and at peace. She looked the best I'd seen her in weeks, flipping through radio stations searching for hit songs we knew the words to, her bare feet resting on the dashboard. It was barely warm enough to have the top down on the rented VW Cabriolet, but we weren't putting it up for anything.

"I totally agree with you, Harper. This is the greatest idea you've ever come up with, possibly the greatest anyone's ever come up with. I had no idea how much I missed California."

Avril squealed, eyes closed, waving her hands over the top of the windshield as if coming down the first tall hill of a roller coaster. No more work, no more New York City snow. Only freedom, stretched out for miles in sea and sand.

The traffic was light. I slowed and changed lanes to allow an organic produce truck to pass us. Technically, we were both on vacation. Avril was taking a leave of absence from five years of constant work, and I had a day, maybe two, before Sydney called with news from Joseph Hagen. I didn't want to think about anything.

Avril set her feet on the floor of the convertible and turned down the radio.

"Okay, catch me up on Luke. All I know is the two of you met on LoveSetMatch.com—uggh, I can't believe I just said that *word*— and that you've been talking to each other for a couple of months. What else should I know about him?"

"Ah … he's thirty-three, never married, no kids. His family is in the lumber industry. He works out of a base camp in Wasilla, Alaska."

"Perfect. It sounds like the two of you have lots in common," Avril said, sarcasm dripping from each word.

I exhaled. "*Oh, stop.* He's just someone I have this *feeling* about. He's also a licensed pilot who flies in needed supplies to missionaries and doctors in remote places."

"Right, so tomorrow morning you and he—and I, as your very strict chaperone—will meet up to get to know one another. Does he know I'm coming along for the ride?"

"Oh, crud. I forgot to tell him. It's not like we talk every day."

"Well, we'll just see how the boy does with minor adjustments. Now let me ask you the big question. How do you really *feel* about him?"

I paused to think about her big question, the open road ahead of us granting me a kind of early-morning clarity.

"I'm not going that far, not yet anyway. I somehow can't let myself have feelings for someone I've never even met. Can I? Maybe I could. I'm just trying to follow God's lead, which is to say it's all still a mystery."

"So, you really don't care whether he turns out to be 'the one'?"

Funny how one simple question can change the way you feel, or make you suddenly realize how it is that you feel.

"I wouldn't say that exactly. I haven't wanted to say this out loud yet, but there is never a time when I find myself *not* thinking about him. I don't know when that started, but my wait-and-see attitude is in place because I don't want to get my hopes up. And yet, sometimes I catch myself not being able to breathe whenever Luke crosses my mind."

I expected Avril to tease me over how serious my answer sounded, but instead she only leaned against her headrest, exercising a degree of personal reflection, I guessed. A memory of what Avril thought she had in Jon. Her world had been a sunny tangerine dream, but sin had crept into it, a wolf in man's clothing, and she'd learned that some fruit could be poisonous.

Our six-hour drive took roughly eight and a half hours with a short stop for lunch at a little roadside place that served crispy chicken tacos and ice-cold Coke in little bottles. I drove the first stretch, then Avril covered a two-hour shift in the late afternoon. We made a few stops to take photos and managed to somehow still be on the road at dusk. As sunset came and went, I moved the GPS from the floor to the windshield to keep a better eye on unexpected turns in the night.

We had a reservation to spend the evening at a bed and breakfast outside Carmel. I'd also gotten a call from Luke on the road. He was in California, and we agreed to meet the following morning for coffee at a breakfast place called Joe's.

I told him that Avril was coming along for the ride, and he thought that was fine. I had more important thoughts swimming around my head—the white summer dress I was planning to wear, the wide leather headband I'd purchased on the beach in Malibu.

Avril and I drove along an unmarked country road, sometimes paved, sometimes not, until the night turned pitch black. Our headlights, two dissipating beams that lit up only the road before us, flashed on an occasional road sign. The female voice on the GPS informed us we'd arrive at the B and B in one minute, and I saw lights shining from the porch of Horsetail Ranch. I turned the wheel down a long, sloping driveway, past a pond and around the circle drive.

We parked the Cabriolet on the stony gravel driveway and walked up to rustic, wide wooden stairs, pulling our small travel bags behind us. The house at Horsetail Ranch was a cozy-looking two-story cabin, more Yankee colonial than Daniel Boone. Two porch lights were mounted on either side of the door, welcoming us onto the veranda.

Terry Dower, the owner of Horsetail Ranch, must have been working inside when she heard us on the porch, because she emerged wiping wet hands on her apron and opened the screen door for us to come in.

"You must be Harper," she said, extending her mostly dry hand. "I looked for you both earlier. Did you have any trouble finding us?

"No, we just took our time getting here."

"Thank you for making a place for us," Avril said.

"Are you girls up this way on business or pleasure?"

"Definitely pleasure," Avril said, having fun with my rendezvous with Luke.

Terry pulled open the wide drawer in the center of a dark walnut sideboard, an antique gold-leaf mirror hanging above it, and took out guest cards the size of recipe placards my grandmother used to keep in a tin box. I filled out the card in the warming beam of a Tiffany lamp on top of the sideboard.

"Well, you girls will love this part of the country. It's hard to tell at night, but come sunrise, you'll see how beautiful it is here."

I signed the card and handed it back to Terry, wondering if it would be impolite to ask about dinner considering the late hour. It had been hours since our last snack break.

"You'll be staying in Room B upstairs. I hope you like it. Do you know about the rooms here? Each of the rooms is themed and decorated after a classic Hollywood star. B is the Hepburn room. Some of her actual things are in there."

"Katherine or Audrey?" Avril asked.

"Oh, Audrey," Terry said, like there was a world of difference. "I purchased a few things at an estate sale, furniture, some of her personal effects. Do you girls like the movies?"

"Yes," Avril told her, "the good ones anyway."

"Oh, I love the movies. I used to go when I was a little girl. It's hard to believe I saw Charlton Heston in *The Ten Commandments* when it first came out."

"They don't make 'em like that anymore, do they?" Avril said.

"No, they don't, and I don't know why. People would *love* to go see a movie they wouldn't be ashamed of or embarrassed by. Why can't people in Hollywood understand that anymore?"

Avril and I looked at each other and smiled. "I don't know," Avril said, "but if we ever get the chance to make a movie, we'll make sure it's a good one."

Terry smiled like she knew what we meant and led us upstairs. A royal red and gold carpet track ran up the middle of the staircase, pinned down with brass tacks.

When we reached the second floor, she hit a light switch in the upstairs hallway. There was a grandfather clock standing tall against one wall between doors marked B and C. Terry inserted an old-fashioned skeleton key into the lock and twisted it to the right, pushing the door open and turning on another welcoming light.

"Are we the only guests tonight?" I asked.

"No, there's a couple staying the night in C. That's the Jimmy Stewart—I always loved him."

We stepped into the comfy space of Room B. It was small but impeccably clean and tastefully decorated. A tall double bed dominated most of the room, with a dresser on one side and a table with a washbasin on the other. I'd imagined I'd find a movie poster hanging somewhere, but instead a beautifully framed color photo of the star hung on the narrow wall by the bathroom door.

"This is my favorite room," Terry said. "This one and the Jimmy Stewart. There's also a Humphrey Bogart-themed room and a Doris Day. I was going to originally give that one an Alfred Hitchcock theme, but thought that was probably too scary for people to sleep in."

Avril and I laughed.

Terry showed us around the room, pointing out the items belonging to Audrey Hepburn that she'd purchased at the estate sale:

a jewelry box, a comb and brush, a vanity with a short stool and needlepoint seat cushion.

"It's beautiful," Avril told her. "You've really done a wonderful job decorating, and I'm sure we'll enjoy our stay."

"Please do, girls. And if you need anything, just knock on my door downstairs."

With that, Terry left, leaving the door open, a gesture that made us feel like the house was ours to wander around in with the memories of Hollywood past.

"Oh, Harper. Check out this bathtub."

I set my luggage near the foot of the bed and walked to the bathroom. Inside was an antique iron bathtub on feet. The faucet was a silver wheel with spokes. A small display of fragranced salts and scented soaps were arranged on a bamboo floor stand.

Avril and I took turns in the bathtub, enjoying the quiet, relaxing time. Then we started talking and couldn't stop. Around midnight we snuck down to the breakfast table looking for snacks. Terry had set up a minifridge with soda, breakfast bars, and small bags of SunChips.

The next morning I wasn't hungry, so I just sipped green tea at the breakfast table and watched Terry and another woman tend to other guests. When Avril came down, she grabbed a cup of tea to go, and we both wished Terry a good day, leaving the way we'd come in the night before.

The morning was warm enough to drive with the top down. We circled the driveway and pulled out onto the narrow road, on schedule to meet Luke in just under an hour. Avril waved at a farmer riding on a tall tractor; he waved back, and it dawned on me just how rural this area was.

Forty-five minutes later, we parked curbside near a blue metal mailbox on a street landscaped with trees that looked liked they'd been there longer than the city. We left the convertible with the top down and walked to Joe's. We were a little early, so we took our time, sauntering, window shopping, and thinking we'd arrive early enough at the coffee shop to get the lay of the land.

I shouldn't have been taken aback to find Luke already waiting inside Joe's, standing next to his table in the middle of the checkered floor, but I was. He was different from his photographs, I'd expected that, but I knew him instantly, a two-dimensional image moving into the real world. He smiled to me from where he stood, a blue canvas awning behind him giving backdrop to his face. Avril would tell me later he looked like a young Harrison Ford in his best dress shirt and jeans.

Luke stepped forward to greet me like a boy who'd been taught manners that the man couldn't deny. He looked like someone the wilderness had formed over a lifetime of living free, someone who'd broken camp earlier that morning, leaving a fishing pole and canoe outside his tent on the banks of a lake.

"Harper?"

"Hi, Luke," I said, pretending to be calm, in control. In actuality, my insides were caving in like walls of wax inside a hot candle. Instinctively, I held my arms open, wanting, needing more than a firm handshake. Suddenly we were holding one another, like the first, simple touch of a high school slow dance.

"Thanks for coming," I said, a whisper close to his ear. "Carmel is a long way from Alaska."

"Or New York."

"Yes …"

Avril cleared her throat and Luke and I broke apart our embrace.

"Oh, I'm sorry. This is Avril," I said, hiding the excitement I felt at Luke and me suddenly being in the same space together.

Avril reached out and shook Luke's hand. "Hi, Luke. You look just like your photos."

"Nice to meet you, Avril," Luke said, his resonant baritone sounding even more compelling in real life than over the phone. "Would either of you like breakfast? Coffee?"

I looked at Avril, who I knew wouldn't be interested in breakfast yet. "Do you just want to tour around Carmel for a while?" I asked.

"Sure."

The three of us left Joe's as a loud delivery truck ground past. We walked along the street, passing by a café where a waitress wearing a royal blue apron was opening a matching blue umbrella above a white table.

"So, you're an actress too?" Luke asked Avril.

"Yeah, I was in the same play Harper was in on Broadway," Avril said. "Do you ever go to the theater?"

"No, I can't say I've ever been."

"How about movies? Do you like to go to the movies?"

"No, I can't say I get out to the movies much either."

I saw Avril bat an eye to me as the three of us window-shopped, breaking the ice, taking in the open storefronts and cottages in the shopping district along Ocean Avenue.

"TV? You do watch TV, right?"

"Sometimes. Mostly I keep busy with things I'm interested in."

Posted inside a store window display was a vintage black-and-white photograph of two men in hard hats. They each held one end of an eight-foot pull saw in the woods next to a massive fallen tree. They wore thin suspenders buttoned to work pants over long-sleeve shirts. The rugged men stared back from the picture, ready to build America or fight Word War II.

"Is this what you do?" I asked, staring up at the nostalgic photo.

"Not exactly," Luke said. "I don't wear a hard hat."

"How long has your family been in logging?"

"Three generations. My uncle Don is the boss of the operation. He's been logging for, oh I don't know, I guess thirty years, something like that. My grandfather started the business in the 1950s with nothing more than a couple of chain saws and an old Ford truck."

"Are you two getting hungry?" Avril asked.

"What are you hungry for?" Luke asked.

"Picnic," I said.

"That's not a bad idea."

Luke piloted us into a farmer's market grocery store. We leafed through the produce section, tossing green grapes and peaches into brown paper bags. I took a quart of blackberries out of a refrigerated display case just as Avril was reaching for a quart of red raspberries. In the bakery, we picked up sourdough bread, and we purchased sliced roast beef and Swiss cheese in the deli. Luke grabbed two large bottles of Pellegrino, and as we headed to check out, he paused at a beach-themed end cap to collect a double-sized beach towel from the display.

Despite a brief protest from both Avril and me, Luke paid for everything. Even stuffed in plastic shopping bags, our impromptu haul looked like a feast. We stepped out into the warming morning and followed the sound of the ocean to a grassy park that overlooked the surf.

I prayed, asking God to corral my emotions. It felt like I was on a spinning carnival ride. Shopping? Walking? Ocean? Picnic? It wasn't like I hadn't experienced any of these things before, but what was this feeling that accompanied them? Joy? Wonder? Fear? Hope?

Avril kicked off her shoes, saying the grass felt good on her feet, and I did the same as we continued toward the shade of a tall, swaying cypress. I watched Luke as he stopped at the base of the tree. He looked at me and asked, *How about right here?* with the slightest raise of his eyebrows. I nodded. And as he began to spread the beach towel on the grass, I realized what it was I was feeling: home.

~ TWENTY-FOUR ~

The three of us catnapped on a grassy hill under the half shade of the Monterey cypress overlooking the Pacific below. After our picnic lunch, we'd talked about everything and nothing at all for the next hour, taking goofy pictures of each other with our cell phones.

Luke appeared to be sleeping, unresponsive to the ringing of my cell phone when it went off sometime during the bright, sunny afternoon. Avril picked it up, all of us lazy from sleep, answering it in her "I don't care who is on the other line" voice.

"Harper Gray's answering service. Who's calling, please? Oh, hello, Sydney darling, how are you?"

I listened on my back, eyes closed, feeling a gentle afternoon breeze whisper across my face, totally at peace with the world.

"You'd like to speak to Harper, eh? Hold one second, I'll see if she's in."

I felt Avril whack me on the arm with the cell phone as she tried handing it over, apparently with her eyes closed. "Harper, a theatrical agent, Madame Sydney Bloom, is on the line for you."

Disinclined to open my eyes, I felt for the cell and placed it against my ear, rolling my face up to the sky. The brightness of the sun penetrated my eyelids, turning them into translucent pink screens.

"Hey, Sydney."

"Harper, where are you guys? You sound like you're all sniffing laughing gas."

"More or less. What's going on?"

"I just thought you'd like to know we got a contract from Joseph Hagen a few moments ago. According to your wishes, we inked the deal today. You're starring in *Winter Dreams*. Go ahead, pinch yourself, scream at the top of your lungs if you want. A hit on Broadway, and now a major movie. You've just checked all the boxes in the career goals of every A-list actress in Hollywood."

"I'm speechless. Really, I don't know what to say."

"I have other news, you're costarring with Elijah Navarro. Joseph has scheduled rehearsals to start on Monday in LA, so I guess you're a Californian now. Shooting begins in ten days, so stop eating bonbons."

"You should talk."

"*I'm* not a film actress, Harper. You are. You're also on an upward trajectory, so don't be shocked when you start getting photographed coming out of Walgreen's without makeup, carrying a quart of orange juice. When are you coming back to LA?"

"I don't know yet." I paused to take a deep breath. The air tasted like dreams come true. "Avril and I are just lying around."

"Well, that's probably good," Sydney said, surprising me. "You need a vacation. It'll clear your head and prepare you for the tidewater that's coming your way. Honey, I wanted to say I'm very proud of you. Just save me the heart attack and be back here by Saturday, all right? Oh, and in case you're wondering, it pays two hundred fifty thousand dollars, and you'll receive half in about ten days. Don't ask what your costar is getting."

I sat up cross-legged on the beach towel, brushing my hair away from my face. In the distance, a young boy pulled a green kite aloft into the azure sky.

"What's everybody doing?" I asked the two zombies who were still lying horizontal. "I mean, what's our plan here?"

Luke was on his back, his right arm sprawled over his eyes. He spoke without moving. "That depends. How long are you staying in Carmel?"

I looked at Avril. "We were thinking we'd drive back tomorrow. What about you?"

Luke sat up, rubbing sleep from his eyes. "My schedule's more or less open. The plane's in a hanger waiting for me whenever I get back to it."

"I think I should take the rental car and drive back to the B and B," Avril said. "Don't you guys need to spend some time alone?"

I looked at Luke, unsure of how to answer Avril's question, although I was suddenly wide awake.

"So what are we thinking?" I asked, looking at Luke.

"This is kind of a wild thought, but how would you like to see where I work?"

"Wasilla?"

"I was thinking farther south, like the headquarters in Eugene. I know a few places we can get a great hamburger, and there's a landing strip on the property."

"Whoa, whoa, whoa," Avril said. "We don't even know how long you've been a pilot, Luke. I was thinking you guys could just hang out here."

"Twelve years," Luke said. "I've flown the West Coast too many times to count, and Hawaii, Mexico, trips to Australia and the Far East."

"And your uncle Don is up there in Eugene too, right?" I asked.

"Yeah, I think it would be great if you met him. He's a little crusty, but you'll like him."

"Then what are we waiting for?" I said, surprised to hear the words coming out of my mouth. Was it wise to put so much trust in Luke so soon? I offered up a little prayer, asking God to redirect me if this was a bad idea. The smile on Luke's face and the way he looked at me—it was a look of kindness and respect—gave me my answer. I would be fine.

Luke followed us back to the B and B, then loaded up my things in his rental, and we started our road trip to the airfield.

"Call me if you need anything," Avril said, like a protective den mother.

The flight to Eugene took less than two hours. I'd never ridden in the cockpit before, never thought of an airplane as being my personal mode of transportation.

An airstrip on the grounds of the head office served as our airport of destination, a long, flat dirt strip cleared of rocks and debris.

"Is this how you always land?" I asked.

"Trust me, it's fine. I've landed on runways far worse than this one."

The prospect of landing in a small plane ought to have frightened me, but I felt a strange peace about the whole thing. I realized it probably had something to do with trusting the pilot.

The headquarters for McCafferty Logging sat nestled in a forest of white pines on more than twenty acres of timberland. As we made our approach over the trees, I could see a half dozen buildings of various sizes, the tallest a three-story corporate structure made of steel and glass. It stood apart from a long, open warehouse and a water tower that had been painted the color of chestnuts.

Luke's descent and landing were as smooth as a skater on ice. He turned the Cessna around at the end of the airstrip and taxied the aircraft into a hangar.

"Let me call someone," Luke said, after he'd parked the Cessna. "There's supposed to be a golf cart nearby we can take to the main entrance. Someone must be using it."

"I didn't realize the scope of McCafferty Logging. How many people work here?"

"One hundred twenty, or thereabouts."

Luke began unloading my overnight bag as a Club Car golf cart came whizzing in through the open hangar door. The stocky driver wore a baseball cap on his head and was dressed in a white short-sleeved three-button crew shirt underneath a nylon jacket, and tan slacks.

"Luke, glad you're back," he said, parking the cart a foot away from us. "Do you have time to meet with Alan about the permits tomorrow morning?"

"Well, hello to you, too. I'd like you to meet someone. This is Harper Gray, my friend I told you about."

Realizing he'd been remiss in the area of social manners, Don McCafferty slid out from behind the wheel of the Club Car and greeted me with a firm handshake.

"Hi, Harper, nice to meet you. I'm Luke's uncle Don. Sorry if I was a little abrupt there. We always have our plate full with things to do."

"Nice meeting you," I said.

Don turned his attention back to Luke. "I won't keep you, but if you can swing a few minutes with Alan, he's got multiple-choice questions only you can answer. Shouldn't take more than thirty minutes or so. He's in his office right now."

"I'm planning to spend the rest of the day with Harper," Luke said. "I won't have time to meet with Alan. Just call Brody and ask if we can postpone our meeting to early next week. We're in the right on this permit issue, and he knows it. Whether we meet this week or next, it's going to get resolved in our favor."

It was obvious Don was expending tremendous energy holding his tongue. Having just apologized for his social skills, he appeared to have obligated himself. Still, Luke's assessment and reassurance seemed to relax his nervous tension, and he asked, "How was the trip?"

"Carmel is beautiful, Uncle Don. You'd love it. It's right on the ocean, and Clint Eastwood lives there, so it's your kind of place."

Don smiled. "I'll have to check it out sometime. Well, nice meeting you, Harper. Enjoy Eugene."

"I told you Don's a little surly," Luke said as we drove the cart along a well-worn path to the main building. "He's a really good guy, but he's seen some rough stuff in his life."

"Like what?"

"Vietnam POW, divorced by his first wife, lost his kids. He's lived alone for twenty years, but he doesn't like it."

"Poor guy. Are the two of you close?"

"Yeah, I mean, we're family so we hang out in our off hours. He likes to fish, and so do I. He makes the trip to Wasilla more than I get down here, but he's probably my best friend."

Luke took me on a tour of the main office, a folksy blend of corporate America meets laid-back northwesterners. I shook hands and nodded to women in the front office, sales guys, workmen coming in from a logging expedition, and a nephew earning college credit working part time in the firm. After making the rounds, Luke took a set of keys off a hook behind the reception area. "Dinner?"

"I thought you'd never ask."

We exited out the main doors, went down a set of concrete stairs, and made our way to the parking lot. A burgundy-colored Jeep Cherokee was parked near the building. Luke unlocked my door and opened it for me. I popped the lock on his side as he walked around and got in.

"Eugene has some great food," he said. "We've only had a light picnic, so what do you think about a fancy meal somewhere?"

"Would it be possible just to find some place a little more homey? I feel underdressed for fancy."

"I think I know just the place."

We drove twenty minutes to a diner on the outskirts of Eugene called Earl's. A neon sign in the window welcomed us and the approaching calm of dusk. A half-filled parking lot told us the wait for a table wouldn't be long. Local and folksy, Earl's entire dining room featured booth-only seating. A five-foot marlin hung on the back wall, and a Hank Williams song played over the speakers, a selection from the small plastic jukeboxes at each table.

"Somehow I think this place will serve the best fried catfish I've ever tasted," I teased.

"And the best chicken-fried steak, chili, and pecan pie."

A waitress broke through the swinging saloon doors that separated the kitchen from the rest of Earl's. She gave Luke a stop-in-her-Airwalks greeting when she saw him. "Hey Luke. I didn't know you were back in town. How long you here for?"

"Just a day. You doing all right, Ellen?"

"Never better." Ellen pulled two menus from a wooden box behind the cash register and showed us to our booth.

"I get the feeling you know a lot of people," I said.

"I grew up here. Wasilla came later. They're both the same place to me in a way. Same kind of people, honest, hardworking."

Ellen returned and took our dinner orders—catfish, hush puppies, and coleslaw for Luke, chicken salad for me—and then hustled back to the kitchen, leaving us alone. As if drawn by instinct, we reached across the table and held hands, staring into each other's eyes.

"Just in case you're wondering," I said. "I'm trying to reconcile all the things I know about you from a computer screen with the real-life person sitting across from me, and shape them into one."

"That's funny, 'cause I feel like I'm looking down on the two of us from above, seeing us here sitting together at this table. And I'm wondering how an actress from New York City and logger from Alaska found themselves in a diner in Eugene, Oregon, holding hands, staring at each other."

"It is one of those unexpected things, isn't it?"

"Unexpected, and amazing."

"When I look at you, I see the man from LoveSetMatch.com, the one I read about in an online description, the one I emailed and texted and talked to on the phone. You're a pilot who flies what I imagine to be somewhat dangerous missions to help others, and your family owns and operates a large logging enterprise. I'm just trying to shuffle all those cards together and get a composite of who you really are."

"And what about you, Harper Gray? You're the woman with one photo on your personal page, some kind of understudy actress in New York who gets promoted to star and who talks more about God than about acting. So what kind of actress are you, anyway?"

"I'm still trying to find that out myself. In my personal life, I'm playing the role of follower. It's a lifelong role, and if anyone sees that part of me, they pretty much have the whole story. Professionally, I've been mostly unsuccessful until this recent break in New York, and for all I know I'll be unemployed again when I least expect it. I may not always be an actress, but I'll always be me."

Luke squeezed my hand. "I can handle that."

Ellen brought out our food, and Luke said grace over it. Then he said, "Well, since we're talking about who we are, you should probably know that I don't feel like I have a right to myself anymore. I don't call the shots. I may not always be a logger, or a bush pilot, but if you can see the biggest part of me is that I am not my own, then you pretty much have me figured out."

"So, we're both servants. I think He gives us the desires of our hearts. Do you ever feel like the desire of your heart is to be with someone, but it's also to give that dream to God at the same time? Two opposite desires, and they swirl around each other?"

"Harper, I know without a doubt that God has my best interests in mind at all times. I used to live with the tension of my hopes versus God's, but I've seen His care for me too many times to worry about it anymore."

It was cold outside when we left Earl's, a billion stars shimmering in the night sky. The dinner and talk had made us tired, but we didn't want to leave each other's company.

"What do you want to do now?" I asked.

"I can find you a hotel room. Come back and pick you up in the morning. I'll drive you to Portland. There will be lots of flights going into LA."

"I'm not ready to say good-bye to you now and then only see you for an hour in the morning."

Luke tempered his steps as we walked across the gravel parking lot, crunching the stones beneath his feet when he stopped. I watched Luke's pensive eyes, both of us anticipating his next move.

"There's a twenty-four-hour coffee and donut place not far from here," he said, modest and chary. "I want to spend time with you, too. I just think we should stay around people."

"I agree."

The Jeep's two bright headlights unveiled the mysteries of the dark road ahead until they fell upon a neon sign welcoming us to the donut shop. As we parked, I could see inside the coffee shop. A man and his young son ordering donuts at the counter. Two women in a booth, having coffee. Above us, the stars pierced the upper atmosphere like torches, and a shy moon watched over Eugene. Luke invited me to sit closer without words. He'd be fine if I chose to stay on my side of the Jeep Cherokee, but I didn't want to. Instead, I shifted my head so it rested on Luke's shoulder. "You're so good at taking care of people. You go where they are and bring what they need. And then you came to me. You came to my rescue. How did you know I needed you?"

"I needed someone too, Harper. God sent you to me by sending me to you."

We kissed, our first, and the best kiss I'd ever had. Maybe it was the darkness. Or perhaps it was the fact that we both accepted that God ruled our lives and had given us this extraordinary day. But in memory, it was the character of the person. I had discovered something about Luke McCafferty that I could never learn from a computer screen: He was a good man.

I watched him, my eyes adjusting to the moonlight to make out his profile. I wasn't sure why God had been so kind to me, but that night I didn't think I'd ever be alone again, and I marveled at the feeling.

We awoke at sunrise, stiff and sore from sleeping only a few hours sitting up in a Jeep. I dreaded the day. Airports and good-byes and questions about when we'd see each other again. I'd found my soul mate, and everything inside me screamed to stay with him, but there were things to be done. I had to think about finding a new place with Avril, and there was that little movie I was about to start filming.

A painful rush of longing pulsed through my body when the United jet left Portland International Airport behind in a swirling cloud of dust and exhaust. I was living two dreams, both classic Hollywood stories. I was the woman who found true love where she least expected it, and the down-and-out actress on the fast track to success.

Looking at the world from thirty-one thousand feet, I thought about James, living alone in his house by the ocean, the only man I knew who'd also lived two dreams, once.

If only the closing credits could have rolled across the screen of my life, right at that moment. Then my story was guaranteed a happy ending. But life's not like the movies, and the only way we learn the ending is to live it

~ TWENTY-FIVE ~

The studio sent a car to pick me up on the first day of rehearsals. I couldn't help but think of Helen Payne and her daily dozen roses as I sat in the back of a white stretch limousine, reading over the latest script for *Winter Dreams*, which had been couriered over to Sydney's beach house the night before.

We did a read-through around a large table in a conference room at Joseph's production company while a dozen executives looked on, jotting notes or typing away on their laptops. During the lunch break, Joseph's assistant, Marcie, took all my measurements and dozens of photos of my face and figure with a digital camera. I met with a publicist for the film, Emily Long, who conducted an extensive interview with me. Emily wanted information she could "leak" to the entertainment media.

"It's the first step in promoting this film. We want to market you as the 'mystery woman,' Joseph Hagen's newest find."

Joseph also introduced me to the Century Pictures Studio VP, Paul DeAngelo, who greeted me warmly and told me how highly Joseph had spoken of my performances in New York.

"I'm looking forward to seeing good things," he told me, and I took it as an encouragement, thanking him.

"If there's anything the studio can do for you, a bungalow to stay in, a driver to transport you around Los Angeles, just contact me directly."

"That's very generous. I'm actually staying with my agent right now. She lives right near the beach, so it couldn't be better."

"Yes, I can imagine that's ideal. Have you ever spent the night out on the water?" he asked.

"No."

"The studio has a yacht docked at Marina del Rey. If you ever want to take your friends out to relax, call me, and I'll make the arrangements. Here's my card," he said, and I took it like a golden ticket, my connection for getting anything I wanted in Hollywood. "My office and cell numbers are on there. If you need anything at all, don't hesitate to ask."

We rehearsed four more hours after lunch, including a break to test makeup for how my character would look at the beginning, middle, and end of the story.

Marcie asked Joseph if there was a particular look he was going for since the storyboard sketches looked reminiscent of Hitchcock films in the 1950s. Joseph only said, "It will look like Hagen, not Hitchcock."

We wrapped our first rehearsal sharply at six, and the driver picked me up again to take me home to Sydney's.

"How's it going, Miss Movie Star?" she asked when I walked in the door.

"It's fun, exhausting. I met Elijah Navarro, studio people, we did hair and makeup, met with publicity, costume measurements."

"Just like New York, Harper, you're joining a work in progress. Everything was up and running, except the leading lady. Now it's time to move."

That night, the studio called to warn me that the writers were making script revisions. There would be new lines every couple of days for the next week, which kept me on my toes and helped to distract me from missing Luke.

"Harper, your character feels elated, overjoyed, and deeply connected to Angel," Joseph said to me on the third day of rehearsals. "She's lost everything important to her, now she's in California. Life, as we know, is very good here. I want the audience to *feel* what Meredith's feeling. I want you to give them the sense that she'd been under duress for the longest time, but she's coming alive again."

"Right," I said, scribbling notes in the script margin.

"Okay, let's try again from the top of the page. And action!"

Meredith: *Where did you come from, Angel? How did you know I needed you?*

Angel: *Let's just say I had it on good authority.*

Meredith: *I'm serious. When everything was falling apart, you suddenly showed up. It's kind of a miracle.*

Angel: *I go where I'm assigned. You needed someone to bring you in out of the rain. So here I am.*

The script called for Angel to stare at me without saying anymore, but the writers had given Elijah a new line not in my printed version of the script.

Angel: *He sent me to you so I could send you to Him.*

I looked up from my script and into Elijah's eyes. He didn't seem to be acting, but talking to me directly. I couldn't tell if he'd broken character. I glanced down the long conference table to our senior writer, Barbara Ward. She was still buried in her script. I thought Elijah might have been ad-libbing, so I decided to follow in kind, theater training, speaking the words that came naturally to me.

Meredith: *I want to be loved. Is that on anybody's agenda?*

My eyes were fixed on Elijah, his tabloid-familiar face reminding me just a little of Luke. The rebel bad boy, he was content to play hooky with the script and make it up as he went along too.

Elijah: *That's all love ever wants. That's how you know it's love. If you can't live without someone, can't breathe, can't think, can't do anything but be with them, that's when you know you've found the real thing.*

Chills shot up my neck like cold icy fingers.

Joseph looked at us over the top fold of his script, over his senatorial half-lens eyeglasses. He flipped the pages back and forth, looking for our dialogue.

"Where is that? What are the two of you reading from?" he asked. "I don't have these pages."

"It's not there, Joseph," Barbara said. "They were improvising."

"Well, that didn't work for me. Let's keep to the script everybody. Pick it up at 'He sent me to you.'"

Elijah smiled at me. I wondered about his story, if reading these lines about God and His love for mortals gave him chills too.

Meredith: *I don't want to be alone anymore, Angel. I've done that.*

Angel: *Who's saying you have to? Just get it through your head. My role is temporary. I'm here for only one purpose and that's to see you through a dark hour. I'm not here to fall in love with you. When my work on earth is done, you and I will say good-bye.*

I felt my heart jump with fear. What if this story mirrored *my* fate with Luke? I'd joked that he was an angel. What if he were, like the movie script said, only temporary? I lost my focus for a moment. Fortunately, Joseph had seen enough for the day.

"Okay, cut. Next week, we begin shooting, and that's where we'll work out all the blocking," Joseph said, his thick European accent staining his words like varnish. "We're done for today. Nice work, everybody. The script is flowing nicely. I like what I'm hearing. Enjoy your last free weekend."

I didn't stay after rehearsal, but politely waved to my acting partner and left through the conference room door. As I stepped out into the studio back lot, I felt tears threatening my eyes when I considered for the first time the possibility of losing Luke.

I paged my driver and started walking toward the studio gate. Then I called Luke, too. Just wanting to hear his voice.

"Hi, it's me," I said.

"Hi, I wasn't expecting a call from you. What's up?"

"I'm just leaving rehearsal and I felt the urge to call you. You're going to think this is silly, but I miss you, and wish we were together right now."

"I was just thinking about you, too. You sound out of breath. Are you all right?"

"I don't know. I just got worried. Something came over me."

I saw the driver ahead of me, parked as close as he could behind the curb barrier. I realized I'd accidentally come out the wrong side of the building. He opened the passenger door, and I thanked him silently and climbed inside.

"Where are you now?" Luke asked.

"Just leaving the studio. This feeling came over me like *what if* something were to happen to someone I care for very much. That scared me."

"Tell me what you need right now."

"I want to see you. I want to know when that will be."

"How long does it take to shoot a film?"

"Six weeks, six days a week. Sometimes seven."

"You mean we can't see each other for six weeks?"

The thought took the floor out from under me. "I can't wait that long."

Luke paused. "Harper, let me call you in a few minutes, okay?"

We hung up. The limo was caught up in traffic, eight lanes of bumper-to-bumper cars going nowhere on the Los Angeles freeway. I turned to the Lord, prayed, trying to lower my blood pressure. A moment later my phone rang. Luke.

"I'm leaving Eugene within the hour. I'll be in LA by seven tonight. I'm flying commercial; it's faster."

"Are you sure? I mean, I feel so silly. I can help pay for the ticket, I don't want you to …"

Luke laughed.

"What's funny?"

"It just struck me how many times I've flown somewhere to deliver goods to a couple who sounded desperate for a taste of home.

Tacos, cheese and crackers, ribs and sauce. I've never actually been the thing that's being requested before."

"It's kind of a lot to ask you to come down for a visit."

"There's nothing I'd rather do, Harper. No place I'd rather be."

After we hung up, I reached for Paul DeAngelo's business card. Its corners were bent, and I found it easily in the bottom of my bag. I punched in the numbers for his cell phone and waited.

"This is Paul."

"Hi, Paul, this is Harper Gray. Remember when you said I should call you if I needed anything? Well, I have a small favor to ask of you …"

~ Twenty-six ~

The night sky was murky black when the limo rolled smartly to the curb at LAX. I sat in the back seat listening to the sound of a 747 fly overhead, imagining Luke inside. We waited in celebrity parking, a designated area for limousines and VIPs. My driver, who told me his name was Angus, was short, burly, and bearded, the kind you might see in a strongman competition heaving telephone poles and lifting two-ton stones. He was polite and perfectly professional and seemed to really enjoy his job.

At 7:20 p.m., Luke walked out of the main terminal with an army duffel bag slung over his shoulder. He looked down the row of cars. I asked Angus to drive slowly and pull up in front of him.

When Angus stopped the limousine, I opened the back door myself and stepped out. Luke had already seen my no-makeup, jeans-and-pullover look on our picnic, but I wanted this meeting to be different. After the rehearsal, I went back to Sydney's and dressed like it was Oscar night—perfect makeup and hair, heels, and a form-flattering black evening gown.

It's difficult to say whether Luke was stunned by the glamour, or merely by seeing me, but either way, he noticed.

"You look fantastic," Luke said. His mouth remained open as if he had more to say, but no other words fell out. The canvas duffel bag fell, and we came together in an embrace, the starlet and the lumberjack still wearing his work jeans, boots, white shirt, and denim jacket.

We kissed under the yellow glow of the airport lighting.

"I feel a little underdressed," Luke said, brushing away make-believe dirt from his jacket. "I barely had time to pack a bag and get myself to the airport."

"Don't worry. I have tonight all planned. You'll be fine."

Angus popped open the trunk and loaded Luke's duffel bag. I introduced the two, always drawn to the practice of inclusion. A picture of the *Apartment 19* cast flashed in my mind, all of us onstage, hands clasped together, bent low in a bow of humility and thanks to our audience. How we hugged one another backstage, like a family once lost and now reunited.

With images of prom nights and wedding days dancing in my head, Luke and I slid in the stretch limo.

"So this is what Hollywood stardom is all about?"

"I've got connections," I joked, even though that's exactly what it was.

"I was expecting a rental car and heart-to-heart talk in the parking lot of an all-night diner."

"As tempting as that sounds, I hope you won't be disappointed with something else I have in mind."

We rode through the neon sprawl of Los Angeles en route to Marina del Rey. Streetlights brightened and dimmed in the back of the limo. Our hands slid across the leather seat until they found each other. Luke's touch was both gentle and strong.

Angus pulled into the marina and got out to open our door. The breeze blowing in off Santa Monica Bay was surprisingly warm.

Luke and I walked to the boat slip where the *Aloha Freedom* would be waiting for us with a crew of three. The yacht was just as Paul had described it—seventy-feet of luxury with a dining room on the top deck and five cabins below.

"Is this yours?" Luke asked

"Not quite. It belongs to the movie studio. They're giving it to us, with crew, for the night."

Paul DeAngelo had been delighted to hear from me so soon. It was obviously an extraordinary perk, but the studio was expecting big things from Joseph's *Winter Dreams,* and they wanted everyone involved to feel good about making the film.

Captain Charlie Brewer welcomed us aboard with his first mate, Lan, and a woman, Alex Preux, who as it turned out was our personal assistant for the duration of the voyage. After a brief formal greeting and some general information to aid us on our private cruise, Captain Brewer and Lan excused themselves and returned to the bridge. Alex invited Luke and me to stow our things below deck.

"Dinner will be served once we're clear of the marina. The boat is yours to roam and explore. There's a game room and full bar on the main deck; all the cabins are below. Is there anything I can get you?"

Luke and I looked at each other, both of us way out of our league. "I think we're good," I said.

Alex returned to the prepping area on the upper deck, leaving Luke and me alone.

"Okay, *now* you have to tell me … how did you arrange all this?"

"It's a gift from the studio."

Luke strolled around the upper deck, as in awe as I was of our surroundings.

"It's really amazing. I mean, I can't think of anything in my experience that even comes close. Sure, I got to sit in the actual car used in *Starsky and Hutch* once. But this? It's a little overwhelming."

"They did go a bit overboard," I said.

Luke laughed. "I'm not sure it's wise to say 'overboard' on a boat."

I laughed too and closed the space between us.

"Maybe this isn't us, Luke, but it is another piece of evidence that my life has changed. It's *still* changing. I don't know what this new life will look like, but I think it's okay to enjoy the good things that come, even if they're unlike anything either of us has done before."

We walked to the railing and watched the marina shrink in the distance, the vanity lights of Angus's limo looking like a fading party on wheels.

"Harper, all I want is you. I don't need all this," he said. "However … sitting in Starsky and Hutch's car is now only the *second* coolest thing I've ever done."

"I was going for special. I guess I overshot that by a bit," I said. I so wanted things to be right.

"No, it's perfect. Why don't you excuse me while I take a quick shower, and I'll join you here in about ten minutes, okay?"

"Okay," I said. He bent down and kissed me before disappearing below deck.

Music began filtering in like fog from hidden speakers somewhere aboard the ship. Alex appeared from the kitchen carrying glasses and a small bucket of ice.

"What is this music, Alex? It's wonderful."

"It's a CD of songs the studio has placed in movies since the 1930s. Big band dance pieces, love ballads, romantic serenades. It seems to fit the ship somehow. Hope you're hungry. Dinner will be served in about twenty minutes."

I took my overnight bag and stepped carefully down five dark mahogany stairs to the lower deck. Everything about the boat was first-class. The hallway was lit by blown-glass wall sconces, and the walls were decorated with original artwork framed in gold. I could hear water spraying from the shower in the first cabin, so I turned the gold handle on the compartment door across the hallway to store my things.

Spectacular didn't begin to convey the extravagant decor inside my cabin. A king-size bed governed the room, dressed in a jade-green coverlet turned down to reveal the Egyptian cotton sheets beneath. Twin brushed-silver wall lamps extended from just above the dark-stained headboard, their soft light spilling onto the bed, revealing the designer's consideration for bedtime reading. A soft ivory carpet welcomed my bare feet like it had been waiting for me, and every other detail, from faucets to electronics, surpassed anything I'd seen even in a showroom.

After putting my things away, I returned to the main deck. Alex had set the table in a space shielded by three partitions, the fourth side open to the ocean. A formal white cloth covered the square table. She'd lit a candle and covered it with a glass globe, while dishes, silver, and glassware all stood at attention.

Luke made his entrance from below deck, hair still wet from the shower. He'd shaved and changed into dark slacks and a smart-looking shirt so free of wrinkles I assumed he'd found an iron in his room.

"Nice music," he said. "I think this may be the perfect time to ask you to dance."

Taking our lead from the music, we danced in a slow, gentle motion, hands on waist and shoulder, not quite formal, not quite an embrace. Around us the Pacific Ocean was like a private playground, clear and black under the starry sky except for a few deck lights from faraway ships and the distant coast of Catalina Island.

"It's so beautiful here. Warm, perfect," I said into his neck. Ripples caught the bright starlight on the water around us. Above us, the moon glowed as white as bone.

"We always seem to find ourselves in the company of 'perfect.' I think it's following us."

"I haven't dared utter how good God's been to me these last few months. I've just wanted to say 'thank You' and keep as quiet as possible."

"You are living a blessed life, aren't you? Broadway actress, Hollywood film star. What's next? Oh, yeah. Dancing with me on a luxury yacht."

"Would you believe me if I told you I'm really just a simple person at heart?"

"Ordinarily, no," Luke said, tilting my chin up so he could look at my face. "But since I'm just an Alaskan logger who owns only one decent suit, I can't think of anything else that would explain what you're doing with me."

"Maybe I like the way you help people. Or the way you do business. Or maybe I was just captured by those photos of you on the front porch of your cabin. If that doesn't convince you, than maybe knowing how you'd drop everything to come help me would show you why I feel the way I do."

"And how exactly is it that you feel?"

I bought a little time by melting into his arms, and we danced cheek to cheek. I wanted to say the perfect thing, but just then Alex appeared with the first dinner course, and I made a midcourse correction.

"Hungry," I answered.

After a meal of Tuscan chicken, asparagus, and a peach torte, Luke and I walked to the bow of the ship.

"I know this sounds idiotic, but the ocean is absolutely enormous," I said.

"No, no. I think Magellan said something like that."

We stared out at the endless expanse, the moon drawing a streak of white as far as the horizon. Luke pointed off into the distance.

"Just a few thousand miles straight ahead of us is Japan," he said. "And if we sailed in *that direction*"—he pointed his hand further south—"for a few days, we'd be in Hawaii. Have you ever been there?"

"No, but I think I'd love the islands."

"They're beautiful. Everything looks like the day of creation."

Luke squinted one eye as if looking through a telescope. He pointed in a third direction. "If we were to sail that way, we'd end up in a remote area of Southeast Asia where I'll be about this time next week."

"Why are you going to Southeast Asia?"

"Another mission trip, supply run, whatever you want to call it. It's the biggest tour I make all year."

"What will you be doing there?"

"Missionaries are building a hospital. Each year I fly in medical equipment, medicine, supplies. Those kinds of things."

"How long will you be gone?"

"About ten days, a little more with travel."

"Send postcards?"

"I would if there was any way to mail them. Everything gets on and off the island by boat or canoe."

We stood at the front of the ship in silence for a moment, holding tight to one another as the breeze began to cool. I was well past the point of recognizing a love that had eluded me all of my life. This was it. I felt like a newborn fawn trying to stand on her wobbly legs for the first time.

"I'm not sure I want to go on much longer without you in my life," I said, the words coming directly from my heart, bypassing logic and circumstance. "It scares me a little to think of you flying across the Pacific by yourself, but on the other hand, knowing how much I'll miss you tells me how I really feel about us."

"Which is where we were before the dinner interrupted us," said Luke. "So … you're an actress. You're good at reading people, right? What would you guess Harper Gray is feeling right now?"

I tried to smile. "Since this is all so new to her, she probably feels very overwhelmed, carried away by something powerful like ocean waves, something that's not safe, but good. Her mind would be thinking, *There's so much you don't know, slow down,* but her heart would be saying, *The fire you prayed for has been lit and is burning a beautiful, healthy glow. Don't douse it, keep feeding it until it's a passion that will burn forever.*"

"And …?"

"And also, she would say …" I paused, not because I wasn't sure, but because I was so completely sure I wanted the words to stand alone and fill the space around us.

"I love you," I finally whispered, hiding my face in Luke's shoulder. I bit my lip, closing my eyes, afraid of what he might say. The silence that followed lasted a long time.

"Do you want to be loved?" Luke finally said in a quiet, confident voice. My heart and mind fused, joined one another in unity of purpose. I felt harmony in a way that touched on the spiritual, as if all of me had finally come together.

"Only if it means being loved by you."

The ship swayed, and with our eyes closed, we kissed, a different act of surrender. I'd crossed some invisible border from a lifetime of being single to a moment of being loved, and I knew at that very instant I could never go back.

"I love you, Harper."

Luke and I rocked gently in the moonlight, listening to the water, feeling the sea breeze.

"I don't want to live without you," I said. "I don't want you to go back to Alaska."

"We don't have to figure out everything tonight. Let's let love grow a while."

"I just feel like I want to grab on and never let go. I don't want to lose you."

"Who said anything about losing me?"

"Can't we just freeze this moment and stay here?"

"If I ever lost you, I hope I'd be satisfied just remembering how

I once touched you," Luke said. "Thankful that God allowed me to hold you, have you in my arms, and know you loved me."

"I don't know if I could be satisfied with that," I said.

After a long period of silence, we walked to the side-by-side chaise lounges on the top deck and scooted them even closer, lay down next to each other, our backs to the bridge and our feet to the horizon. I pulled a light blanket over us, reached under to hold Luke's hand. We were steadfast in our promise to not sleep together and committed to not spending a moment of the night apart.

I nodded off and awoke later while it was still dark. Luke had covered us with a second blanket. I listened to the sounds of the water, then the sound of breathing, and then to no sound at all. I had only one desire in the world. I wanted to be the same person when I awoke in the morning, when the sun rose over the deck as bright as heaven. I wanted to know I was loved and that I'd never be alone again.

~ Twenty-seven ~

There's no feeling in the world quite like waking up on someone else's luxury super yacht. I stirred before dawn, warm beneath the extra galley blanket.

I could feel the ship pitch ever so lightly, rocking us where we'd fallen asleep on deck chairs pushed together. The smell of salty ocean air awakened my senses, filling my lungs with the newness of day and the thrill of possibilities. I sat up, and a light morning gale caught strands of my hair, blowing it in front of my face. How different this bed was from the one in Chicago.

I whispered to Luke, who was still sleeping, "Do you want to wake and see the sunrise with me?"

He roused, first opening his eyes, then pulling himself up to a sitting position. He was still wearing his dinner clothes from the night before, but the once-pressed dress shirt was a mass of wrinkles that brought a smile to my face.

On the starboard side of the ship, a shimmering golden dome was piercing the skin of the sky. It rose from out of the Pacific Ocean like the birth of a planet.

Before the sun had fully risen, Alex emerged from the ship's galley, dressed in white shorts and a matching sports shirt. She carried two thermal decanters of coffee, regular and decaf, and set them on a foldout table with cups, cream, and sugar.

"Oh, Alex, you're so good to us," I said.

"Thought you guys might be ready for a cup," she said. Her face was beautiful in the morning light, and I wondered if she'd ever worked as an actress, like so many in LA had. "For breakfast I can make omelets. Or if you prefer, we have toast, bagels, fruit?"

"An omelet would be amazing this morning. Ham and cheese?" Luke said.

"I'd love one too," I said. "Same thing."

Luke poured two cups of coffee, steam rising off each like a gentle geyser spa in winter. We stood together at the starboard railing, marveling at the brilliant sunlight of morning. There were no other ships in sight except a lone freighter, miles off in the distance.

"What do you feel like doing in paradise today?"

"Captain Brewer said something about deep-sea fishing last night," Luke said. "What about you?"

"I have a script I should be reading."

"That's like doing homework on vacation. Why don't you come fishing with me?"

"I may. Captain Brewer said he won't take the ship back to Marina del Rey until early tomorrow morning. I may catch some rays. I'll bet I can tan in thirty minutes in this sun."

A half hour after breakfast, Captain Brewer brought out deep-sea fishing poles and tackle from the lower deck. He arranged the three of us in cushioned chairs that faced the open sea and taught us how to cast our lines out into deep water. We fished for the next several hours and listened while Captain Brewer regaled us with stories of the movie stars and studio moguls who'd angled for yellowfin tuna, marlin, and shark from that very spot.

As lunchtime approached, I wanted to make myself more useful and decided to lend Alex a hand as she prepared lunch in the galley for guests and crew.

"I've been meaning to ask you, Alex," I said while the two of us pared melon, fingers sticky from the juice, "have you ever worked in movies?"

"Hasn't everyone who lives and works in LA?" she joked. "I dabbled in it long ago. Was a walk-on in a soap for about two weeks, did some improv with a theater troupe, that's about it."

"Can I ask you a favor? Would you help me run lines after lunch?"

"I'd love to."

Following a delicious lunch aboard the *Aloha Freedom*, I dug out the 120-page script from my suitcase and carried it to the table where the five of us had just finished lunch. Alex wiped the table with a wet cloth; it dried almost instantly in the ocean breeze.

"I'd like your help with a scene that begins on page seventy-six," I said, turning to the page in the spiral-bound manuscript and setting it in front of Alex.

"This is a scene between my character, Meredith, and Angel— he's a guardian angel performing some special work in her life."

"Okay, I think I've got it," Alex said, straightening her posture.

"Ah, let's see—*Meredith, you've been blessed with a gift, to love others. Don't you know what a shame it would be to lose that?*"

I stepped back from the table, distancing myself from the script and the temptation to peek at it.

"*I never intended to become this person,*" I said. "*You trust someone with all your heart and soul, and they leave. You don't see that where you come from, but it's pretty common down here.*"

"*If you won't risk loving someone, then what's the point?*"

I turned to Alex, the way I imagined I'd face Angel in the movie. She kept her eyes transfixed on the script, making sense of it in her mind, picturing how she'd speak her next line. I lowered my voice.

"*My heart's been broken, all the pieces dropped to the bottom of the sea. Nothing beats inside me anymore. I appreciate your efforts, Angel, but it would take an act of God for me to love someone again.*"

"And that's where my part of the scene ends," I said, dropping character.

Alex said, "Oh, there's one last line in the scene. Mind if I read it?"

"No, go ahead. They're always adding new things."

"Okay, say your last part again, and I'll read it in context."

"Okay," I said, raising my fingers to my lips to jog my memory. I paced the deck, out beyond the covering into the hot midday sun and back. "Oh, okay. Meredith says, *I feel like my heart is broken. Nothing is beating anymore. I appreciate your efforts, Angel, but it would take an act of God for me to love someone again.*"

Alex said, "It says Meredith exits the room, and Angel says, *Why do you think I'm here?*"

Surrounded by an ocean of blue water, I felt the power of those words.

"That's really powerful," Alex said, thumbing through the rest of the script before closing it and setting it down. "She's saying only an act of God will change things, and apparently, she's talking to the angel God sent to do just that." I nodded, and we sat in silence a few moments.

"I need a break from the sun," I said. Picking up my sunglasses and the script from the table, I ducked below deck and slipped into cooler quarters. In the light of day streaming through a small round porthole, the walls in my cabin became a dark caramel color, inviting a calm I was beginning to get used to.

I could hear Luke and Captain Brewer talking in muted, barely indistinguishable tones. The cozy bed tempted me to climb in for a nap. As I drifted off to sleep, I thought of the commercial I starred in that kept me financially afloat during the hardest year of my life. God had been there even when things were difficult. He had been in that Drowz-U-Tab commercial with me—and in Chicago when I really couldn't sleep—and I felt His presence here as I curled up in this luxurious bed, knowing I could trust Him no matter what the circumstances.

Luke and I bid a fond farewell to Captain Brewer, Lan, and Alex on Sunday morning, once the *Aloha Freedom* had been berthed in its slip at Marina del Rey. Whatever formality existed in the usual separation between guests and crew broke down entirely on Saturday night when the five of us played cards and told jokes until midnight after an amazing meal of freshly caught, freshly grilled tuna. Luke and I slept in our own stately cabins below deck, overcoming the powerful temptation to share a bed, yet feeling better in the morning for our decision.

We could have called for Angus to pick us up, but given the extraordinary hospitality and generosity of the movie studio and our indulgence in luxury superyacht living, we were determined to find our own ride.

"Here we are again, about to say good-bye," I said. "What time does your plane leave?"

"Three o'clock, but I'll have to get through check-in and security, and before that, fight through traffic."

"So we're saying good-bye in the parking lot in Marina del Rey? I go my way back to Hollywood, you go yours back to Eugene, Oregon."

"Wasilla, Alaska. Remember? I have to go home for a few days before I fly to the islands."

"Every meeting starts out with joy and ends with agony."

We embraced again, contact between us sparking melancholy. Luke removed his cell phone and called for two taxis using the number from a painted sign at the marina.

"When will I see you again?" I asked.

"You know the answer to that question. Don't make me point out to you how full our calendars are. I'll be locked into this trip for the next two weeks; you're off to live the dream of every actress in the country."

I shook my head at the absurdity of contradictory ambitions. For almost ten years I'd chased an acting career that came with one-in-a-million odds. At the same time, I'd longed for, *dreamed of*, finding a soul mate, something that seemed even less likely than the acting dream. But both *had* happened, and in a stroke of cosmic irony, happened at concurrent times, their contradictory trajectories represented by two taxis headed in opposite directions.

"I feel torn apart," I told Luke, closing my eyes. When I opened them again, the first of our taxis was pulling in the entrance to the marina.

"Let's keep our cell phones on," I said, my voice more desperate than I wanted it to be. "Let's just stay in contact as much as possible, okay? I want to be able to reach you anytime I want."

"Harper, it's going to be fine. Just pour your energy into this movie. Make it a great one. Time passes, it always does, and we'll get together as soon as they turn off the cameras and roll away your costumes."

We kissed again. It was the lingering sort of kiss where you pray for magic, pray that when you open your eyes you'll find all your circumstances changed.

"I love you," he said.

"I love you, too."

Luke waved his arm to the taxi. It stopped in the parking area on the other side of a chain-link fence.

"You take this one," Luke said.

"No, you've got a plane to catch. You take it."

"There's no way I'm going to leave you here by yourself."

Luke picked up my overnight bag and walked me to the taxi. He opened the door, like a doorman at a fancy theater in New York, setting my bag on the seat and shutting it after me.

"I hate this," I said through a window that only opened halfway. Luke lowered his face toward the window as I raised mine, and we kissed one last time through the narrow space between us.

~ Twenty-eight ~

"Hi Harper, did you see any of the press running on you this weekend?" It was Emily, the publicity manager. "*Access Hollywood, Entertainment Tonight,* and *Variety* all covered the breaking story about Joseph handpicking you for the picture."

"I didn't see any of it. I was away from media for the weekend."

It was just after 9 a.m., and we had yet to shoot a frame of film due to technical lighting issues and a delicate, misty rain. I guess it *does* rain in Southern California. I sat in one of the canvas chairs, already in makeup and costume, sipping a cup of coffee, nervous on the first day of shooting.

"Anyway, I spoke to your agent," Emily said. "She agreed it would be a good idea for you to do a short follow-up interview with *Entertainment Tonight* about the first day of filming."

"Why are they interested in me?"

"Well, the story we've pitched is essentially about Joseph's choice of you, a relatively unknown Broadway stage actress, as his 'next big thing.' So it's as much about him as it is you. We're planning on teasing viewers with small glimpses of you, building on the whole 'mystery woman' angle, but we need to get your face out there a bit at first—to create the initial interest."

I nodded, appreciating the difference between stage acting and movie making. Since arriving at 6 a.m., I'd gone through makeup, wardrobe, and a preproduction meeting with Elijah, Joseph, and most of the technical crew.

"Here's the deal," Emily said, sitting in the chair next to me. "I spoke with one of the producers for *Entertainment Tonight,* and they've agreed to come out and tape the first interview with you here on the set. Joseph's given us permission to do this at any time when they're not filming, but what I need to know is if you're okay to sit down to a taped interview with *ET.*"

"I don't know why not. When would they do the interview?"

"Well, now," Emily said, laughing.

"They're here now?" I said, suddenly anxious about being in the national spotlight.

"*ET* is currently interviewing Elijah. Once he's done, they'd like to do a sit-down with you."

Emily left to work out the last-minute details. It had only taken a day for me to learn that making a movie is like waiting for something at breakneck speed. I ran over my lines, noting the most recent script changes.

I'd kept my pledge of keeping my cell phone nearby at all times, set on silent mode so it wouldn't be a distraction to others. I glanced to where the phone rested on the arm of the canvas chair. One text and one phone message awaited me. I opened the text.

Harper, didn't want to bug you.

Praying it's a good day to make movies. Luke

Suddenly Luke didn't seem so far away from Hollywood. I put the cell phone against my ear and listened to the voice message. It was from Sydney.

Harper, I have news. You, my dear, are officially red-hot in Hollywood. You may have already heard about the press coverage, so I won't repeat Emily's news, but two calls came in this morning, one from Warner Brothers and another from Paramount. And I got a lunch invitation from Paul Weiss, a friend and action pic director who wants to talk about you. The latest grist for the rumor mill is that William Berken Productions is buying the film rights to Apartment 19. *They've already made a preliminary call regarding your interest in the film version. Get this— if you are willing to audition! Anyway, long message, Harper. I know you've got a busy day. I'll tell you more when I see you, but you're looking at a year and a half to two years of back-to-back film work, easy. That's why they're calling. They want to lock you in now before you're completely booked up. Ciao!*

I wasn't sure how to take the head-spinning news, but I knew exactly what I needed to do next. I tapped a text message to Luke.

Luke, hope it's a good day to chop wood.

:)

A temporary media tent had been assembled on the set; the blue can-vas room was big enough for five or six adults to stand in. Elijah was just finishing his interview—his millionth, no doubt, as evidenced by the ease in which he handled it. Emily prepped me on what to expect and how I should answer. "Just keep it light, and let everyone know how excited you are to be making this movie."

I stepped into the tent just as Elijah's promotion was ending. The woman interviewing him shook his hand. "Thanks, Elijah. That was great. I'm a huge fan of your work."

Elijah nodded. He was energetic and charming on camera, but quickly reverted to his introverted, unconventional personality when off camera. Emily politely tapped the woman on the shoulder. She turned.

"Hi, Benton, this is Harper Gray; she's Elijah's costar on *Winter Dreams*. Harper, this is Benton Stuart, a producer from *ET*. She'll be the one asking questions for your spotlight piece."

"Hi, Harper. I've heard a lot about you," she said, shaking my hand. "If you'll just have a seat, Jeremy will get you miked, and we'll run through a couple of questions. I'm just going to ask you about the movie and about the character you play. If any other questions come to mind, I may shoot you one off the cuff, but otherwise that's all we're looking for."

Over Benton's shoulder I could see Elijah watching Jeremy carefully clip a miniature microphone to my costume. Elijah's trademark scruffy beard and moustache were gone, replaced by smooth skin for his role as Angel. He retained his debonair persona and his almost shoulder-length hair. I was surprised that he didn't just disappear back into his trailer. I said a quick prayer, asking God for wisdom that I might honor Him with my words.

"Okay, looks like we're ready. We have audio, picture," Benton said, and then after a couple beats of silence, she asked her first question. "Harper, you've come a long way in a relatively short period of time. How did it feel learning that you were Joseph Hagen's new leading lady?"

"I was thrilled when I learned Joseph had picked me to play the role of Meredith Bancroft. He and I had met briefly at a party in New York, but I knew nothing about the movie until I arrived in California."

"About the character of Meredith Bancroft, she's someone who's lost it all and really can't go on anymore, until she meets up with Angel, played by Elijah Navarro. Did you do anything in particular to prepare for this role?"

I laughed. "Funny you should ask. I feel like I've spent the last year of my life preparing for this role, and preparing for real life …"

From the corner of my eye, I noticed Emily shaking her head, disapproving my answer. She was monitoring my interview with the sensitivity of an EKG machine. I tried to steer back to a more general reply.

"… I imagine everyone can relate to feeling like they've lost everything and wish they had an angel to help them sort things out."

I looked over at Emily again. She lifted both hands palms up, gently pushing them toward me and mouthing the words, "Go easy."

"In what ways do *you* relate to that?" Benton asked.

"Well, God does show Himself in hard times, and whether that comes in the form of an angel every time ... well, I can't say. But when He showed up in my life to rescue me, He did it by answering my prayers. I'm here today because God rescues the lost."

I saw Emily Long roll her eyes and silently slap her palm to her forehead. This was not how carefully planned interviews were supposed to go. But the Spirit of God wasn't concerned about movie interviews or box-office receipts. He wanted me to tell them about Him.

"So are you saying this can happen in real life?"

"I believe that it's only because God reaches out to help people find Him in real life that a movie like *Winter Dreams* can even exist. It's a good story because it's a true story."

I glanced over to watch Emily step out of the tent, all her work torpedoed by a newbie who couldn't walk in the time-honored footsteps of a thousand other actors who are "thrilled to be working on this picture, the director is a genius, I can't wait for audiences to get a look at what we're doing."

Elijah and I locked eyes again, costar to costar. He raised his paper coffee cup to me in silent salute, a gesture saying, *You've got more guts than I do.*

At one in the afternoon, Elijah and I were finally called to the set for our first scene. Joseph had taken over a real outdoor café, the Montebello, on Santa Monica Boulevard for this scene. It called for rain to sweep through as Angel and Meredith are talking in the café. Since the real rain had been replaced by a natural California sunshine, the production team had constructed a rain machine over the top of the cafe, a high metal rigging with hoses and showerheads that could bring down as many gallons of rain as the script called for, from gentle summer mist to a deluge of biblical proportions.

I felt nervous, fidgeted over my memorized lines while talking through the scene with Elijah. We sat together at our table, while the crew worked around us, waiting for the final cue from Joseph.

"First film, right?"

"Yeah, first film, first day. When you walk out onstage in theater, the butterflies go away in a minute. That's not the case in movies. We've been here almost seven hours, and I still feel like I want to throw up. What number film is this for you?"

"I don't know, twenty-three or something. I don't count things like that anymore. I have people to do it for me."

He smiled, underlining his dry sense of humor. "I enjoyed your interview this morning. It was raw, honest. Don't worry, they won't use most of it at this point in your career. They'll wait until you've been photographed coming out of a nightclub at 2 a.m., or when your fiancé walks out on you, or when the LAPD stops you for driving under the influence."

"I'm not worried," I said. "I never worry about telling the truth. If it's my first and only film? I'm okay with that too."

The tech team had solved their small problem, and everyone was returning to their positions. Elijah lowered his voice.

"You really don't care whether or not you make another film? Congratulations. You're the first actress in Hollywood history to feel that way."

"I'm not sure how I feel; I only know I don't have any control over it."

"Well, there's certainly some truth in that. This business is fickle. You sound just like your character in the film. Maybe you've been typecast," he said.

"That's what I've been thinking since I first read the script. What about you? Are you an angel, or at least heavenly minded?"

"You don't know my reputation, do you? My, you are new around here. No one's ever confused me with an angel before."

"So why'd you take the role?"

"I liked the script. I think it's a positive message. It will go a long way toward rehabilitating my image with the public."

"That's why you're doing this movie? For your image?" I asked, making an involuntary face.

"Do you think I decide which movie I'm going to make solely based on its story?" Elijah asked. "My agent would break my arm if I did. No, I decide which movie I'll make based on fee, location, and notoriety first, story second."

"I'm so naive. I'm only here because it's what I think I'm suppose to be doing."

"That's why they call it your first day."

Joseph approached us wearing a white short-sleeve shirt with a V-neck T-shirt visible underneath. He removed his Louis

Vuitton sunglasses to talk with us both with his words and his
eyes.

"Okay, finally we are to begin shooting this scene. Elijah, you
are complimenting Meredith on her beauty, encouraging her as a
friend, but Angel feels more than that. Harper, you are responding
to his message, but realize you have fallen in love, so there is conflict
in the story."

"She's in love, so there's conflict?" I asked.

"Darling, where there is love there is always conflict. Okay, let's
shoot the scene."

Joseph returned to his seat on a movable camera jib. I'd heard
he was a martinet when it came to filmmaking, that the entire
direction was chiseled in his head on a stone storyboard. I could see
the intensity in Joseph's eyes now. This film was the focus of all his
concentration.

"Action," Joseph yelled.

Angel: *Why so sad? You've succeeded when everything around you
said you'd fail. You have a new life, a new career. I'd say my work here
is done.*

Meredith: *Remind me to never ask an angel if he understands a
woman. If you knew what I know, you wouldn't think everything's so
wrapped up.*

Angel: *What don't I know?*

Meredith: *Do angels have hearts? Can you feel pleasure or pain?
Have you ever longed to be with the object of your affection, knowing
they'll never return your love? I think a better question is, what do you
know?*

Angel: *Angels have hearts, Meredith. I can feel love and hate, compassion and apathy, but I have only one purpose ever present in my mind—carrying out the work I've been entrusted with, which means seeing you revived.*

Meredith: *You're so faithful to your work, you don't see how leaving might destroy rather than revive me.*

Angel: *Meredith, if I should go away, you won't be destroyed, you'll only be made stronger.*

Joseph called for a second take. I shivered as a light spray of mechanical rain fell from the sky. A makeup woman touched up my face and hair, combing the mist from my bangs.

We filmed for two hours, changing camera angles, lighting, and varying the emphasis Elijah and I placed on words in the script. The assistant director called for a half-hour break while the crew changed camera lenses and I tiptoed back to my trailer through an archipelago of small puddles. A crowd of tourists and onlookers had formed, watching us work from behind a barricade across the street. A young boy waved to me, and I waved back.

Then a face appeared from out of the crowd, and out of my past. At first I couldn't place him, seeing him so out of context. But that only lasted a moment. Even after more than a year, a slight weight gain, and a dramatic shift to the California look, I'd know Sam anywhere.

He offered a slow wave to say he wasn't just any onlooker but someone who knew me and knew me well. I stepped to the edge of the production lot, staying inside the security barriers. Sam raised his cell phone, suggesting in pantomime that he needed to talk to me. I raised my hands to say, "No phone." Then he mouthed three words: "I miss you." He smiled, an attempt to reassert his charm, and I thought of all the hurt I'd gone through and what I thought I'd say if I ever saw Sam again. I searched my feelings, raking over my heart with a fine-toothed comb, and found nothing. The pain was gone. I watched as Sam lifted his phone one more time, waving it in his hand like a treat he was tempting me with.

"Sorry," I mouthed back, then turned and walked away.

Once inside the trailer, I kicked off my shoes and ransacked my tote bag looking for my cell phone. There were two new texts, one from Luke.

> Let me know when you're ready for
> another ride in my plane. Luke

And one from Avril.

> Harp, call me. avril

~ TWENTY-NINE ~

I punched Avril's number on the speed dial and held the phone against my ear. It rang four times before switching over to message. I spoke after the tone.

"Hey Avril, it's me. Just calling you back. Want to have dinner tonight? It's a rainy first day of shooting, and I don't think we're scheduled to go that long."

I hung up. After more than nine hours on the set, I was tired and wanted to curl up for a nap on the bed in my trailer. I thought better of it. Instead, I took my phone with me to the catering trailer and asked the friendly ladies working inside for a cup of tea. I sent Luke a text while I waited for it to cool.

> Where could we fly to? Somewhere beautiful
> i hope where we could be alone.
>
> harper

The sun was California perfect, though much of the street was wet from our rain machine. I stepped through the jungle of electrical cords and cables snaking over the street. The *ET* media tent was gone, folded up like a traveling newsstand and off to chase the next day's feature story.

"You must be on a break," Sydney said.

"Yeah, I'm just calling because I got your message. Have you spoken to Avril today?"

"I haven't seen Avril since the two of you moved into your apartment. How's that going?"

"It's beautiful, a place on the beach. Avril's doing so well. No one knew how exhausted she really was. When she's ready to get back to acting, she'll be breathtaking."

"I hope that's soon. People are asking about the both of you. I've never had it so easy."

I let out a sigh of relief. "I feel like I've been going a hundred miles an hour for the past two months. When do I get a break?"

"I know you're kidding when you say that because you'll be going that speed for the next two years. We want you to make three films a year. That means about ninety days per film and a couple of months for publicity, and of course, some time off here and there, for good behavior."

"Yikes, I don't know if I can do that, Sydney."

"If I know you, you can. You're worn out now because it's the first day, but you'll find your rhythm. Movie star is not a bad career choice, Harper. Believe me when I say, no one's ever turned it down."

Maybe not, but I bet more than a few had been chewed up by it.

I saw my phone light up with a new message. It was an understatement to say I was enjoying flirting with Luke.

Too bad you aren't coming on my trip
to a lonely, beautiful island.

Perfect. Luke

∽⊘

Back in my trailer, I opened my MacBook and logged onto
LoveSetMatch.com. Since Luke and I were communicating entirely via
cell phone these days, there was no activity on my personal page, with
the exception of a one new message from James. I clicked to open it.

Dear Harper,

Thanks for your message about being in California. Yes, I'd love to
meet you sometime. Any plans to come to San Diego, or as my six-
year-old calls it, "Sandy Eggo"? Remember I have a large house on
the ocean, five bedrooms, and you'd be a welcomed houseguest.

I'll give you my home number, as my membership to
LoveSetMatch.com expires this week. No love connection!
But I think you know why. After much prayer, and I know you
understand this, I've decided to stay unmarried indefinitely. So if
we ever do meet up, you'll know without a doubt I mean it just as
friends.

Take care of yourself, Harper. I hope your match in Alaska works
out. I pray you find love.

–James

I opened up a reply window and sent a response.

James,

I'm writing down your contact information because I'd really like to meet you and your boys in person. As for LoveSetMatch.com, I'm signing off as of today. It's been the most unexpectedly wonderful experience getting to know you, and Luke, who I've told you about. But I'm so ready to be done with the online dating world.

–Harper

PS, I once told you I wouldn't pray for your romantic life, but I think I may if you wouldn't mind. You're too special (and too young) to live the rest of your life without love, and if the right woman does come along, well, why not?

I pushed Send, jotted down James's telephone number, then closed out his match. I then closed out Luke's profile, taking one last look at his picture. Finally, I canceled my subscription to LoveSetMatch.com. How strange it was saying good-bye to an Internet dating site God had used to change my life.

I shut down my computer, ready to move on. A moment later, there was a knock on my door. They were ready for me on the set. I closed my eyes, drew in a long breath, and blew it out, resolving to work hard at the privileged position I'd been given. Before leaving my cell phone in my trailer, I texted Luke one last time.

You've sold me.

Harper

At six that night, we marked our first twelve-hour day. I really did believe Joseph would wrap up, sending us all home for a good night's rest, but that's not what happened. They added more lights, simulating daylight, and continuing shooting until almost nine. We did at least twenty more takes because of some technical glitches or because the performance wasn't quite right.

Afterward, Joseph asked Elijah and me to come back to watch dailies underneath the tent that served as his shade and production awning. A half circle of us, the crew in jeans and baseball caps, Elijah and me in costume and makeup, stood transfixed on the large production monitor. Joseph wasn't pleased.

"This I like," he said, pointing at the screen and using a voice hoarse from talking most of the day. "But, look at this, Harper. Too much head movement. It's distracting. Listen to what I'm telling you, you must keep still on camera."

He drew imaginary circles on the screen with the end of a capped ink pen. "Elijah, your energy is down in one take and too frenetic in another. I need you to find consistency. We can salvage our shooting today, but we'll save time over the weeks if you both can correct the mistakes."

♫

A different driver brought me home to my new apartment, a short five miles from where we'd been shooting. I entered to find Avril watching cable television and eating a bowl of cherries.

"So how'd it go?" she said, holding a cherry by the stem before biting into it.

I fell on the sofa next to her as if dead. "I have neither the energy or the focus to even attempt summing up my experience today for you. You've done this before so you know."

"Oh, yes, only I think I went out after a day's shoot. You look like you need two night's sleep."

I picked out one of the cherries from the ceramic dish, suddenly hungry. "I have to be back early in the morning. You wanted to talk to me?"

"Yes, it's not urgent, but I felt like it was when I sent you the text. I was just lonely," Avril said. She stared, the bowl of red cherries resting on her chest. The TV made noise in the background, but it was the silence from Avril that told me what she was thinking.

"Thank you," she said, adding nothing more. I nodded, because I understood what she'd been through.

"Sydney wants me to tell you to go back to work," I said, admiring how rested and good she looked. "But I'm not going to do it."

"Good, because I'm enjoying these cherries right now, and tomorrow I'm thinking of buying a mango."

"I'm going to bed," I told her, smiling. "Enjoy your vacation."

"I am, thanks."

Luke sent one last message that first day of shooting. I read it when I got into bed.

> Harper, just thinking of you.
> thought you'd like to know that.
>
> Luke

I plugged the phone in the charger and was asleep in minutes.

~ THIRTY ~

On the second day of shooting we made hay, starting with an emo-tionally easy boardroom scene where Angel joins Meredith at work. On day one, I'd been nervous. On day two, I was all work. Maybe it was the lack of sleep, or missing Luke, or seeing Avril enjoying herself, carefree and happy.

Whatever the reason, I played that first scene with fire, opening up my gut, sensing the talent God had given me and trusting that I knew how to do this.

Joseph got out of his director's chair after a particularly good scene and came over to kiss me on the forehead.

"This is the actress I first saw in New York," he said. "Now keep this woman around for the rest of the production."

Meredith was a character I understood completely, and while I listened to Joseph's ideas, I drew her identity from deep within my creative soul. Her moods and words fit like a well-worn pair of jeans. Elijah and I gelled on camera and bantered comfortably between takes. I prayed every few minutes for God to renew my strength and kept Him in the forefront of all my thoughts.

At lunch, I was feeling really good about the day and checked my cell phone, hoping for a text from Luke to help keep the good vibe going.

Harper, leaving for Hawaii.

hope you are well.

Text me if you can.

miss you, Luke

I felt the pinch of missing someone I loved, but there was another feeling too, the excitement of looking forward to his return. Working on the film would make time race by, and I was *enjoying* this. I hoped Luke wasn't already in the air and sent him a text.

Luke, send me a postcard.

You have my heart.

ps, the yacht was nice too.

Harper

It was the print story in *Variety* that got Hollywood talking, but a thirty-second video clip on *ET* drew hundreds of feedback messages on *ET's* Web site. That same clip was viewed thousands of times once it was posted on YouTube. Much to Emily's shock, *ET* focused on the faith theme for their story. The headline? "Is Hollywood Seeing a Resurgence in Spiritually Themed Movies?"

Sherwood Baptist Church had made substantial inroads in movie making after back-to-back hits with *Facing the Giants* and *Fireproof.* Their movies were unabashedly Christian. Just a few years earlier, *The Passion of the Christ* grossed more than 600 million dollars worldwide. The *ET* story went on to say that *Winter Dreams* was controversial because, in addition to having a spiritual theme, the lead actress was a Christian, and director Joseph Hagen had told a reporter that he shared my belief in God. She had then asked if that meant he was a Christian, and Joseph had answered, "I am a follower of Jesus Christ."

The story shocked Hollywood. And though people like Emily worried the story might kill interest in the movie, the more optimistic backers of *Winter Dreams* were counting on that shock to drive moviegoers to the theater.

The first week of shooting was like one of those old African safari movies: a jungle excursion into long days of physically demanding work, following a great leader into the unknown and facing the occasional wild beast—usually an entertainment reporter.

Luke called once during that busy week, a call I missed since it came while we were filming. I hated imagining my phone locked inside my trailer, ringing away on the kitchenette counter. What made it worse was knowing that once Luke reached his island destination, there would be no more calls for a while.

Chalk it up to wishful thinking, but I still checked my phone every morning and on breaks for messages from Luke. I still sent him daily "I miss you" texts whenever the mood struck me, which was more often than not.

On Tuesday of week two, good news came through that little cell phone, not from Luke, but from his uncle Don. I was in the trailer, doing what I did far more than I ever expected to do on a Hollywood movie set: waiting.

"Harper, this is Don McCafferty. Luke's uncle. We met a few weeks ago up here in Eugene?"

"Hi, Don. Yes, I remember."

"Sorry to bother you while you're at work, but Luke wanted me to get in touch with you to let you know he's coming back early. He's planning to leave Tarajuro today."

"Don, that's wonderful news! When did you speak to him last?"

"About an hour ago. We've kept in pretty close contact while he's been down there. We've got a ham radio here in the office. He just asked me to call and let you know he'll be back stateside in a couple of days."

My brain busied itself, conjuring up all sorts of schemes of how we could see each other over the next four weeks. A planner by nature, I thought of coaxing Luke back to LA once or twice over the last month just to spend Sundays together. Who knows, maybe he could take some time off and stay longer; I'd return the favor as soon as my own schedule freed up.

"Thank you for calling, Don. I can't tell you how much I appreciate this news."

"He's pretty excited about seeing you, young lady. I expect you'll hear from him as soon as he reaches Hawaii, if not sooner. Cell phone service is spotty around the South Pacific. Some places have it, others don't."

We hung up. I turned the latch on the trailer door and stepped down to the street where we were shooting on location. I attempted to calculate when Luke would return, doing the math in my head, time change plus flight distance, adding in layovers and sleep. I estimated with refueling and rest, it would take about twenty-four hours before he landed in Hawaii, thirty-six until his plane landed in the States. If I could keep focused on my work, a day and half would pass quickly.

I saw the publicist, Emily, on the set just once during the second week, whispering to Elijah while he chilled between takes. I didn't take it personally, but thought she was avoiding me. She hadn't scheduled any more interviews but didn't really need to, thanks to the snowball effect giving the PR campaign a life of its own. By the end of the second week of shooting, freelance photographers and paparazzi were regularly interrupting our location shooting, and it infuriated Joseph so much he called for a closed set. He limited access to media, which led to rumors over what *Winter Dreams* was really all about.

True to the words of warning, I'd been photographed coming out of the grocery store without makeup, wearing a red ball cap and sunglasses, my hair tied in a ponytail. I could hardly tell it was me when the photo was posted on entertainment Web sites and chatter blogs as a glimpse into the "real world" of Hagen's latest find.

I didn't have time to think about it. Loni, my makeup artist and an avid entertainment news junkie, kept me informed on the set.

With news of Luke's forthcoming return foremost in my brain, I had even less time to think about publicity. By midmorning on the next day's shoot, I smuggled my cell phone onto the set, a definite no-no with Joseph. I only did it because I was on tenterhooks waiting for Luke to contact me. I asked Loni to keep an eye on it for me.

It wasn't a distraction. Elijah and I were rocking and rolling in every scene Joseph filmed. For comic relief, I guess, and to keep

Elijah and me motivated, Joseph took to hanging up poster board signs advertising the number of consecutive days he'd been "blown away" by the dailies. That Wednesday morning his assistant, Benji, ceremoniously walked on the set, hanging up a new poster board with a bold number "8" draw on it. The motivation worked. We couldn't wait to start our next scene.

By noon, Luke's arrival countdown had crossed the twenty-four-hour mark. Over a short lunch break, I took up watching my cell phone while Loni and a cameraman joked about how in love I was. I must have looked ridiculous, staring at my cell phone at an outdoor picnic table waiting for Luke's call.

It didn't come, however, and by 2 p.m. I was going over my calculations one more time. The whole thing was impossible to fig-ure out accurately given all the variables and miscalculations I was obviously making. Disgusted, I ditched my phone back in the trailer and muttered my acceptance of the truth: "He'll call when he calls."

But by eight that night, I still hadn't heard a word from Luke, and that's when I started to worry. I tried calling him, thinking there was every chance he was having dinner in Honolulu, chewing on a steak, waiting to call when he thought filming had broken for the day. But all I got was the sound of his voice on the recorded outgoing message. I shut off the phone without leaving one of my own.

A while later, I couldn't stand it anymore and decided to call Don. I punched in the number and felt a great sense of relief when he picked up on the other end.

"Hi, Don. This is Harper. Sorry to be calling you so late, but I wanted to know if you'd heard anything from Luke. I'm starting to get a little worried."

"No, we haven't heard from him yet. He told us by radio he'd be leaving Tarajuro for Hawaii through the Marshall Islands sometime before dinner yesterday. That's the last we heard."

"Is that normal, going so long without hearing from him? Shouldn't he have reached Hawaii by now?"

Don was silent. I could hear little gasps in his breathing as he mumbled for words.

"Don … are you still there, Don?"

"I'm sorry, Harper. We don't know why, but Luke's radio went dark all of a sudden. We don't know what's going on. I'm at the office trying to find out. He may have landed on another island with a mechanical problem, or …"

"But he would have contacted you, right?"

"Harper, we just don't know. It isn't like Luke to stay out of contact, but he's flying through remote areas hundreds of square miles wide. We don't know if there's a problem. We're checking and trying not to jump to any conclusions."

Conclusions.

"Now don't overreact, Harper, but I've contacted the U.S. Coast Guard. It's out of their tactical jurisdiction, but they have monitoring radar that they're checking. I've talked with the missionaries by radio. They confirmed Luke took off around 6 p.m. our time."

"And no one has heard from him since?" I asked, hoping for a different answer this time.

Don was silent, as if until that moment the situation had been hypothetical. Saying it out loud, that it had been twenty-six hours since Luke had left Tarajuro, meant there was trouble.

"No, we haven't."

"Who do we call, Don?"

Don scrambled to answer. "It's not that easy. Luke's flying over water in an area larger than the U.S. and Australia combined. We know his basic chart course, but satellite images show there was weather in the area. He could have strayed off course, and right now we don't know if he ran into problems five hours or five minutes after takeoff."

"Do you think his plane may have …" I couldn't bring myself to say it.

"I've been in touch with the coast guard station in Hawaii. Nothing's been reported so far. I've notified them that Luke's plane is missing, but we just don't know anything."

I staggered to find a seat in the apartment, clutching the phone in my hand, doing whatever there was to do to keep myself from panicking. "What can we do?"

"At this point, nothing. We wait. That's all we can do, Harper. I'm staying glued to the radio. The missionaries are contacting some of the nearby islands for any news. They're just sick about this. When the sun comes up tomorrow, the coast guard will use one of its search planes to comb the area."

"But you said it's hundreds of square miles? How are they going to …"

"Harper, all we can do is wait."

♫

I closed the cell phone about to lose my mind. *All we could do was wait?* I couldn't wait. Waiting was like a slow death. I slid from the chair, falling to my knees to pray, feeling light-headed, faint, and gasping for air.

Lord, please ...

I waited to hear from the God who had spoken so clearly into my life over the past three months. He knew where Luke was. He didn't need a coast guard rescue chopper to search the islands. But there was nothing coming from heaven. No word, no sound.

Find him, Lord. Bring him back home to me.

Why was this happening? What was happening? I paced the floor of the apartment, my mind running wild, wishing Avril were there to help settle me down. I prayed again, crying out to God to solve this, to put things right, but there was only silence.

I called Avril, who was out on the town with friends. She answered from a Mexican restaurant not far from the apartment.

"Avril, I need help."

"What's wrong?"

"Luke's missing. His plane might have gone down somewhere. They don't know where, and they don't even know if it's happened. But no one's heard from Luke in more than a day."

"Oh my. Where are you? Are you at home?"

"Yes."

"I'll be there in ten minutes."

We drove around West LA at night in an attempt to calm my nerves. Too wound up to eat, sleep, or think straight, Avril and I headed up the Pacific Coast Highway to Malibu, praying on our way to Sydney's beach house. I wiped tears from my eyes as we drove under the starless night, an angry black ocean at high tide breaking on the shore to our left. It was past ten o'clock, but I had to see Sydney.

"Luke's missing," I said, as soon as Sydney opened her front door to find Avril and me standing there.

"What?"

"He's missing. They can't find him. Luke's plane is lost and nobody knows where he is. Sydney, I'm freaking out."

"Come in here." She held open the door for the both of us, and I stepped inside like a woman on fire. "Now, tell me what happened."

I started to tell her all the details I knew, but tears stole my words. Avril filled her in with everything I'd told her just minutes before. Sydney moved forward to hug me.

"I'm so sorry," she said. "I don't know what to do in this situation, Harper. Honestly, I'm filled with more questions than answers at this hour. I don't mean to be insensitive, but let me just go to another page of the problem. How are you going to work tomorrow with all this on your mind?"

"I don't know," I said. "I don't know how I'm going to get through the next five minutes." I paced the floor like a caged cat. "I can't get Luke out of my mind."

"Oh, Harper. Don't torture yourself."

"I know it's irrational, but I feel like he needs help and there's no one there to help him," I said, returning to tears. I collapsed onto the arm of a chair.

Sydney drew in a deep breath.

"Harper, Sydney's right," Avril said. "We don't know at this point what the story is, and you're doing yourself no good imagining the worst. We'll stay with you until you hear the next piece of news, good or bad."

Sydney agreed. "It must be *impossible*, but you have to go on doing what you're doing. That's *all* you can do."

"Luke's always been there for everybody else, Sydney. Who's going to be there for him?"

Avril and Sydney exchanged looks, and for a moment I felt like an outsider in my own unfolding story. I dropped my face into my hands, shaking my head, trying to wake myself from the nightmare. Praying for strength, hope, rescue, peace—none of which were in supply.

"Something has to be done, Sydney. What's happening now just isn't good enough."

"You just have to wait. *Pray* they'll find him."

I couldn't take sitting still another minute. I walked to the open door, about to show myself out. And then I paused to ask Sydney a question. "How do you think Joseph will react if I ask for a day off? I don't know how I'm going to work tomorrow."

Sydney grimaced. "Oh, I don't know. Joseph's got a tight production schedule. I've seen it. Most movie actors wouldn't even ask for time off unless someone …"

Sydney stopped short of saying it, averting her eyes to Avril again.

"I'm sorry, Harper," Sydney said. "I just don't know Joseph well enough to call and beg a favor of a few hours off, let alone an entire day."

Sydney shook her head at the situation, shoring herself up for my benefit. "I know this is tough, Harper, but you're going to have to go into work tomorrow as if nothing is wrong and perform like the professional you are."

~ THIRTY-ONE ~

Avril and I walked across the stiff crab grass in Sydney's front yard. It had been thirty hours since anyone had heard from Luke McCafferty. I climbed into the passenger side of the car, not sure where to go next, when the cell phone rang. It was Don. I stared at the phone lighting up in my hand, afraid to answer, numbed by the knowledge this call would be either the best or worst news I'd ever hear.

"Answer it, Harper," Avril instructed me.

"Yes?"

"Harper, we just got word. Luke's plane went down somewhere in the South Pacific. One of the nearby islands reported receiving a breaking message from Luke just before the accident. It's definitely a crash now. The coast guard will send out a plane in the morning to do a thorough search for his plane."

"What did he say in his message?"

"It was engine trouble, Harper. He just couldn't keep the plane in the air."

"Could he have made a water landing? Did he have pontoons on the plane?"

"Wheels. It would have been a violent landing."

We were both silent. I refused to believe what I was hearing.

"What are you saying, Don?"

"I'm not saying anything yet. We'll await news from the coast guard tomorrow. Luke's plane had what's called an ELT, or an emergency locator transmitter. They'll triangulate and find the source. I'm going home now. I'll pass on any more information to you tomorrow, as soon as we get it."

"Don, are you going to go down there?" I asked. "What if the coast guard's unable to find him? What if they can't pick up the locator signal? What if …"

"Harper, going down there isn't going to make any difference. Now listen, this is going to be tough to hear, but you need to prepare yourself for the worst."

Don clicked off his phone. I sat in a state of disbelief.

"Where would you like to go now?" Avril said, sticking the key in the ignition and shifting the stick into reverse.

"Just drive," I said.

Avril peeled away from Sydney's place, turning on the headlights and flooding two beams of light onto the streets. They looked like searchlights.

Had the last three months only been a dream? Was I still in Chicago languishing in some altered state, no phone call from Ben Hughes inviting me to serve as understudy, no *Apartment 19*, no click-and-meet membership plan on LoveSetMatch.com, no Joseph Hagen, no movie, and most importantly, no Luke McCafferty?

Don't say things have a way of working out until you've talked to James in Sandy Eggo. Dreams can come true, but so can nightmares. Reality is just the spinning flip of a coin and waiting with bated breath to see which side lands up.

Avril rocketed down the highway; the silvery moon loomed great over the ocean, controlling the tides. If beyond the curling tide of Santa Monica Bay, a thousand miles southwest, lay broken, burned wreckage scattered across a rising and falling sea, then what was the point? What else was there anyway?

I flipped open my cell phone and searched for Katie's number. It had to be 2 a.m. in New York by now, but I needed to talk to the people who knew God best. I needed hope.

After several rings, I heard the sleepy sound of Katie's voice.

"Hello?"

"Hi, Katie, it's Harper. I need some really serious prayer. I know it's late, and I'm sorry, but something has happened."

"What? What's happened, Harper?" Katie said. "Tell me what's going on."

"It's Luke. He's been on a mission trip to a small, primitive island hundreds of miles south of Hawaii. On his way back, his plane went down. No one knows where he is, or if he's even alive. No one's heard from him in more than a day."

"Oh, dear Lord."

"I want to go try and find him, but I have an obligation to the film. I absolutely can't leave. It would shut down production and cost hundreds of thousands of dollars. I'm just calling for prayer, because I need answers. I can't go on like this."

"Okay, Harper. Just hang in there. Are you alone?"

"No, Avril's with me."

"Let me get David on the phone. He's closer to God than anyone I know."

I heard some shuffling of the phone, and Katie telling David the gist of my struggle. A moment later they were both on the cell's speakerphone.

"Hi, Harper, it's David. We're going to pray for Luke now. We're going to ask God to protect him. We don't know where he is or how he's doing, but *God does.*"

Avril pulled her car into the parking space behind our apartment. The security gate closed mechanically behind us, a methodical, droning hum. Avril held my hands, and I closed my eyes, wanting prayer to bring medicine to my misery.

"Our heavenly Father, we come to You tonight in the most pressing of matters …"

I listened to David pouring out his requests on my behalf to the Lord. I opened my eyes. A cloud sailed past the moon on its way to somewhere.

After our prayer, Katie spoke. Her voice was sympathetic, a lifelong sister I'd known only a few months.

"How are you doing, Harper?"

"I just want to be with Luke," I said, my voice wilted and sullen.

"Then I'll pray for that, too, Harper," Katie said. "We both love you. We'll stand with you in this."

"Whatever God's going to do," David said, "I feel like it's going to happen quickly. I think you ought to try and get some sleep. You just do what you can do, and let God do what He's got in mind."

There was no sleeping that night. Avril offered to stay awake with me, but I wanted to be alone. I checked my cell phone on the nightstand over and over again throughout the night, picking it up every five minutes, hoping it would ring.

Loni gasped audibly when I lumbered onto the set and fell into the makeup chair the next morning at six.

"Harper, what happened to you?"

I told her I couldn't say. I just didn't have the strength to go through it again. I dozed off instead, a numbing slumber that ensnared me while I sat upright in Loni's makeup chair. When I awoke, Joseph was crouching down in front of me, gazing into my eyes like a boxing referee checking for signs of coherence.

"What is the matter?" he asked. "Harper, are you all right?"

When my eyes opened more clearly, I could see a trailer full of crew members worried over my well-being.

"No," I said.

Joseph turned back to the crowd gathered at the door.

"Okay, everybody. Clear out for a moment. I wish to speak with Harper alone."

Joseph shut the trailer door afterward and sat next to me. He looked concerned, but then I caught a look at my own face in the mirror and knew why.

"Okay, what's going on? You give me one hundred and ten percent for two weeks, never complain, never ask for anything. You're always cooperative, always prepared. You do whatever I ask. Today, you come in looking half dead. I know you haven't been out all night because the only time your picture is in the gossip pages is when our publicist puts it there." Joseph leaned back in his seat. "So, tell me ... what is going on, Harper?"

I drew in a deep breath, trying to pull myself up in the chair, and opened my mouth to speak.

"I love someone, Joseph, someone who's disappeared. His plane crashed in the South Pacific. No one knows if he's alive or not, and I'm trying, but I can't ... control my emotions."

Joseph studied me, slumped in the makeup chair, like he was on the set in his director's seat. He'd spent a lifetime watching actresses deliver lines that came from the depths of their souls. His heavily wrinkled face showed no emotion.

"Harper, did you ever know anything about my wife, Helena Modova?"

"Just the pictures I saw of the two of you in a magazine."

"My wife, Helena, died in a automobile accident in Munich, 1981. She was twenty-eight years old. We have two children; both survived the accident, but Helena was killed."

The quiet director shared his story, choosing his words deliberately and never showing emotion.

"I spent a year afterward working, but not working. The house where we lived together, a house of laughter and dinner parties, was like a cold, marble tomb. Eventually, I sold the house because I would have gone insane there, remembering Helena. I have not remarried in almost thirty years. It is my opinion, and my opinion is the only one that counts, that you cannot work today. You cannot be Harper again until you find out what has happened to your friend.

"I will shoot other scenes with Angel, exterior shots. You will go wherever you need to go and search for answers, okay? But I can't give you much time. You must return by Monday, or my film is in jeopardy. You must do all this in four days. That is all the time I can give you."

Joseph slapped both his thighs with the palms of his hands. The slapping sound was sharp and defining, like a hypnotist waking a half-conscious patient. We stood, and I put my arms around him to thank him for understanding, for letting me go.

He was a cold European director, with little gold statues in his award room, and a widower, too, still living perhaps in a house as cold as marble. I loved him for his compassion, something that came from his suffering, but I didn't want to become like him, someone with a story of painful loss, like James.

I collected my things from the trailer and walked off the lot without speaking to another soul. The rest of the cast and crew watched, not knowing what was going on.

Real life isn't just make-believe, it's hard. When we feel the ravages of pain is when life seems most real. There really was a Luke McCafferty, an island called Tarajuro, a call with bad news, and a real coast guard plane searching hundreds of square miles for debris from a small aircraft. It was not all just a show.

~ Thirty-two ~

At least I knew the way to McCafferty Logging in Eugene, Oregon. I rented a Jeep Cherokee at the Portland Airport and drove the hundred miles south to Eugene. I wrestled my cell phone out of my carry-on bag and flipped to Don McCafferty's number. He picked up instantly.

"Yes."

"Don, it's Harper. I should have given you a heads-up, but I'm on my way to Eugene. I couldn't stay in Los Angeles."

There was nothing, only silence on Don's end of the line for a moment. Then he spoke in a voice that was anesthetized, frozen, not the strong man who doled out accident reports without flinching, but the voice of someone who'd been awake all night.

"There's nothing more you can do here. I told you. There's nothing more you can do."

"I think there is. Is there any new information?"

"No, nothing new. I don't know what you think you being here will change. Storms in the area have impeded any rescue efforts. The coast guard won't go out until the weather clears. We won't hear anything new until then."

"I don't have any peace about this, Don. I want to go to Tarajuro and find out what happened. See if there were witnesses who might have seen Luke's plane go down. I have to have answers."

I heard an audible groan on the other end of the line.

"Harper, honey, you're taking this too far. It's one thing to come join us here in Eugene, but don't go all the way to the bottom of the world trying to bring Luke back. Where are you now?"

"I'm about thirty minutes from your office. Obviously, I don't have a plan worked out yet, but I *have* to go. I couldn't live with myself if I didn't."

When I pulled into the parking lot at McCafferty Logging, Don McCafferty stood waiting for me at the front door. I parked the rental car next to the Jeep Luke and I had taken that night we spent together in Eugene. Just seeing it in the cold with its doors locked and its lights off made me ache. I moved past it up the walkway, keeping myself busy with activity and motion. Don greeted me with an embrace.

"I'm sorry if I was rude to you earlier, Harper. Please come in." He held open the glass door for me.

"I just want to know what happened."

"I know."

A receptionist sat behind her workstation in the modest lobby, dabbing her nose with a tissue, her eyes bloodshot, looking as shell-shocked as everybody we encountered on our way into the building.

Don took me into the conference room. There was a framed poster-sized advertisement for McCafferty Logging hanging on the wall showing an aerial photo of a large company Cessna just like Luke's flying over the Oregon wilderness.

A conference table long enough to seat a dozen people ran nearly the full length of the simply furnished room. At the far end was the only modern addition, a cart holding a TV and DVD player. I saw on a shelf in the cabinet the ham radio and microphone Don had been using to talk to Luke.

The conference table was littered with maps of the Tarajuro area south of the equator, west of Kiribati. Newly sharpened yellow No. 2 pencils rolled across the table when Don rearranged the maps.

"I'd been trying to chart Luke's course using his time of departure, air speed, the flight plan he'd given me," he said. He shuffled through the charts, bringing to the surface the most detailed map of the area. Using a navigational ruler, Don drew a straight line in pencil from Tarajuro through the Phoenix Islands directly to Honolulu. He'd circled a spot on the map where he'd charted Luke's probable last minutes of flight.

"I just want to show you how inherently difficult a search mission is in this area of the world. This is where I estimated Luke went down. But here"—Don moved the tip of his pencil inches across the map—"you can see there's nothing but ocean out there." He looked at me, reading my expression. "The area is breathtaking in its size. You could look for clues down there, Harper, and be just five miles off, and never find what you're looking for."

"You mentioned one of the islands picking up Luke's last message. Which island?"

Don pulled a different map from the pile and marked a star next to the island.

"Here. Botuvita. If he was near the island, he may have already been past Kiribati and on his way to Hawaii. Luke was most likely following a shipping current, so there's no telling at what point he entered the sea, and how far the current carried the wreckage before it finally went under."

"Did he say anything else in his message?"

"Look, I know this is hard, but I'm trying to save you the heartache of going all the way down there for nothing."

Don got up from the conference table and led me to the communications center. A spiral notepad lay next to the radio's microphone, a narrow red stripe running along the side of it that I assumed was the Talk button. Don lifted the notepad and flipped through its pages.

"Looks like there are five or six pages of notes from our conversations. I tried to write down anything that seemed important."

He handed me the notepad.

"Don, I'm going to Tarajuro. I'm going to find Luke, or at least find out what happened to him if I have to search the entire Pacific inch by inch, island by island ... but I need your help," I pleaded.

"I can't go with you."

"I know. I just need you to tell me ... if you were going to look for him, where would you start?"

Don pulled the top chart toward us on the conference table and tapped the "X" spot with his thick index finger.

"Botuvita."

♪🐾

At 2 a.m. I awoke aboard a half-empty red-eye from Portland to Honolulu. The cabin lights were dimmed for sleeping passengers, and a nearly full moon cast a strip of light on the Pacific below. I was an actress traveling to the bottom of the world, playing a new role—detective.

I felt strangely calm, like the feeling you get when you surrender yourself to the inevitable. Images of Amelia Earhart and her
ill-fated flight through the Howland Islands beleaguered me. If no
one had found her in more than a half century, how in the world
was I going to find Luke? Don had given me Luke's last known
whereabouts, the charts, and notes from their ham radio conversations. Everything I thought I knew was based on mere assumptions,
and I had no concrete idea of how to conduct a search operation.

I was depending on prayer, the same thing that had kept me afloat
in the tempestuous storms of my isolation in Chicago, of Helen Payne
and Tabby Walker. I prayed that God would intervene in my search,
or that He was actually the One calling me to search for Luke in the
first place. His missionary pilot had gone down at sea. Maybe He had
called me for a rescue. It sounded ludicrous to my own ears, but I had
to go, as ill-equipped as I knew I was. I had to travel to Botuvita.

A flight attendant knelt down in the aisle of the half-empty flight
and spoke to me in a soft voice.

"We'll be in the air for another two hours. Is there anything I
can bring you?"

I felt my stomach rumble. Not eating had given me a headache.

"I missed dinner," I told her. "I hate to ask, but is there any food
on the plane?"

"We're scheduled to serve a light breakfast in the morning. Let
me see what I can turn up."

The flight attendant moved to the forward galley as I glanced
around the plane. Almost everyone seemed to be sleeping except a
man in a white business dress shirt typing at a laptop in the focused
overhead beam.

The flight attendant—I noticed her name tag read Jill—returned with a toasted bagel and two packets of cream cheese. "I also just brewed a pot of coffee for the pilot crew if you're interested."

"Yes, coffee would be wonderful. Thank you."

A moment later, Jill returned with a white Styrofoam cup of hot coffee, which I took and set on my open tray table.

"Are you traveling to Honolulu for business or for a vacation?"

"Neither. I'm trying to find someone, a pilot whose plane went down near the Phoenix Islands. Honolulu is just a stopover for me."

Jill frowned. "Is he in the military?"

"No, he was flying supplies to missionaries in the South islands."

"Is the coast guard looking for him?"

"Yes, but it's a lot of sea to cover," I told her. "I just couldn't stay in LA."

Jill's face looked compassionate, but hopeless for my predicament. I thought she'd say something not rosy, but generally positive. Instead, she just reached across the silent aisleway to squeeze my hand.

"What kind of plane was he flying?"

"A single-engine Cessna," I said, the words underscoring just how without hope my quest was.

Jill nodded again, at a loss for anything to say, the silence between us filled with the hum of our own airplane at thirty-eight thousand feet.

"How are you getting from Honolulu to the lower islands?" she asked.

I drew in a deep breath. "I haven't gotten that far yet. I'm probably going to contract a charter in Honolulu. I'm just assuming these things can be done."

"They can. My brother-in-law is a pilot on Oahu. As long as you're looking, you might want to give him a call. He's honest, a little different, but he has a fast plane."

"A little different?" I asked.

Jill's face looked like she was trying to come up with a way to explain her brother-in-law.

"Australian," she finally said. "They have their own sensibilities. He's fine, it's just that he can be a little rough around the edges."

She took a napkin out of her apron pocket, clicked the end of a ballpoint pen, and began to write on the napkin. I pushed on my own overhead light and saw the name she had written: Joel Hawthorne. She wrote his telephone number beneath it.

"Give him a call," Jill said, putting away her pen. "Good luck."

I deboarded the plane in Honolulu. Crowds of vacationers only multiplied the difficulties of finding Luke. Searching for him had seemed oddly easier in the quiet of the commercial jet miles above the island.

I hadn't slept on the plane; it was something I'd never learned to do. On a bench by a row of rental cars and hotel advertisements, I sat with my one rolling carry-on bag and took out my cell phone. The charge was strong and so was the signal. No message from Luke, but I'd come to accept that wasn't going to happen. I dialed the number for Joel Hawthorne on the napkin and listened to the phone ring. No answer. I began praying again. It was a moment of weakness. I was fighting doubt, and all my prayers seemed to fall flat before me. I shut my eyes seeking a moment of rest and oblivion from my physical fatigue and grief.

I remembered waiting at O'Hare in Chicago when I'd prayed that my plane would be on time. Arriving late in New York was once the biggest crisis I could imagine.

~ THIRTY-THREE ~

Joel Hawthorne was a man on the go. As I was hanging up on his business line, the answering machine kicked on, and I listened to the outgoing message. It was a short and to-the-point little ditty, voiced in the pilot's thick Australian accent. When the beep came, I spoke.

"Hi, Mr. Hawthorne. I met your sister-in-law, Jill, on my flight in from Portland last night. I'm looking to hire a charter plane to take me to the Kiribati Islands. Please call me if you're available and interested."

I left my cell phone number and switched off the call. I stood up from the bench and turned to face a plethora of choices for sleeping, eating, driving, or flying the adventure of the Hawaiian Islands. There were signs and airport shuttles for rental cars, helicopter tours, volcano hikes, and scuba diving. On a lighted sign of attractions, hotels, and limo drivers, was a small four-by-five-foot ad for a local island tours company. The sign read:

See Hawaii from the Air!

Hawthorne Aviation

The number Jill had written down on the airline snack napkin was listed on the ad, but there was also an address along with a walking diagram to Hawthorne Aviation and a simple but helpful "you are here" dot where I stood.

The walking course to Hawthorne Aviation was basic enough. I memorized the map, and pulling my one canvas carry-on, proceeded to look for a shuttle to the Avis Rental car counter. The directions said that Hawthorne Aviation was just a tenth of a mile west of Avis Rental.

When the Avis Rental car shuttle dropped me off at their front door, I could see Hawthorne Aviation's building next door. The structure was little more than a shack, not larger than five hundred square feet.

The day was already hot and tropical. I could feel perspiration dampening my neck and wondered how long it would be before I saw the inside of a shower again.

I stepped into the tiny building, thankful to discover the AC had chilled the room to a near subzero temperature. It was a seedy dive of a place, with plastic ferns poking out from wicker planters. A red, white, and blue banner hanging from the front counter announced the business's grand opening, though layers of dust suggested that opening may have taken place while I was still in college.

I approached the glass counter, admiring a collection of bar coasters, baseball cards, and local souvenirs displayed. Pinup posters showing off exotic locales decorated three of the interior walls, making Hawthorne Aviation feel like a travel agent's shop. I looked for a bell on the counter to ring.

An attractive woman wearing a red and white flowered Hawaiian shirt and white Gap jeans stepped out from the back. She was young, soft spoken, and relaxed in a way that suggested she lived a carefree island lifestyle. I decided to tone down my overpowering sense of urgency. I wanted to already be in the air flying to the Luke's island, not to come across as a stressed-out lunatic.

"Can I help you?" she asked.

"I'm looking for Joel Hawthorne. Is he here? I left a message earlier."

"Are you interested in booking a Hawaiian air tour?" she asked. I saw her reach for a printed form on top of the counter, but couldn't bear the thought of filling out my name, address, and the dozens of other questions in little blocks on the sheet. This wasn't the time for that.

"Something like that. I met Mr. Hawthorne's sister-in-law, Jill, on a plane from Portland last night. She said I may be able to charter a plane to the Kiribati Islands, and suggested I contact him."

"She told you I could take you to Kiribati?" an Australian man's voice asked behind me. I turned to see a tall man, six feet four or more, standing in a doorway beside the counter. He was clean shaven except for a full moustache that rounded out his upper lip. He looked more professional than I'd expected, given the decor of his office, and resembled a doctor working in a field hospital more than a pilot for a tiny aviation company.

"If you're wanting to fly all the way to Kiribati, it'll cost you at least twelve hundred dollars to take you, and probably another grand to fly you back. Course, if fuel is excessively pricey or hard to come by, you can expect those ticket prices to climb."

"How soon can we leave?" I said, in no mood to barter prices.

Hawthorne looked at his girl Friday like my coming in had interrupted a private conversation about their needing a sucker or they'd both be out of business. His eyes turned back to me.

"I can have a plane ready in two hours."

﹌

I rode the Avis Rental car shuttle back to the airport, then hailed a taxi driven by a large Hawaiian man and asked him to take me to the nearest hotel. I was already exhausted and wanted desperately to take a shower, perhaps even steal an hour of sleep before leaving for Kiribati. The driver dropped me off at the Oahu, not two minutes from the airport. There I rented a room for an unconscionable price, three hundred dollars, the most I'd ever paid for a shower and a nap, but it suited my purposes, and I put it on my American Express.

In room 304, I luxuriated under the water of a long, hot shower before falling into a comfortable king-size bed. I'd brought my travel alarm and set it to ring in an hour and placed it on the nightstand. I also made sure to charge my cell phone, not knowing if I'd have an opportunity again on the trip.

I thought about calling home to talk with Avril or Sydney, but I didn't want to hear it all again, how I was jeopardizing my career, throwing away a once-in-a-lifetime opportunity. They already thought I'd lost my mind and feared for my safety.

I just fell asleep instead, dreaming of the ocean, of islands and blue waters, white sandy coastlines, and native islanders fishing with nets. Luke was in my dream too. He was wearing cutoffs and a torn shirt, standing on a deserted island beach and waving a cell phone to me, wanting me to call him. A wall of water stood between us. I opened my phone, desperately punching in numbers, trying to find the message he'd sent. When I stared at the phone, it was under the blue water at the end of my arm. The words in his text message floated off the screen, blurred in the shimmer of salt water.

Don't worry yourself sick. I'm not in any danger.
I've only been missing forty-eight hours.

Three hours later we were in the air flying over open water. Mr. Hawthorne's powerful six-passenger Cessna cruised at an altitude of twenty thousand feet. The Pacific below us was an infinite watery desert.

After discussing the plan with Hawthorne, we agree to retrace Luke's route, going over the McCafferty Logging charts and maps that Don had given me. I read some of the journal of Luke's trip from Don's scribbled notepad, and learned that one of the Tarajuro missionaries, Eve Walbry, had said a prayer for Luke and me when she heard of our relationship.

We were headed toward Tarajuro, the island where Luke had worked with the missionaries for almost ten days before cutting his trip short. We'd start our search there. My strategy was to investigate Tarajuro, learn what I could, and move forward from there, stopping at every populated group of islands on Luke's flight path, asking anyone and everyone—pilots, fisherman, sailors—if they'd seen or heard anything about a plane going down in the waters of the South Pacific.

It was late in the day, but the sun was bright, the sky remarkably clear. Now that Luke's ocean lay a few thousand feet below us, I felt a strange sensation of closeness to him.

"How long until we land at Tarajuro, Mr. Hawthorne?"

He glanced at his instrument panel, a wall of dials and gauges.

"Before nightfall, obviously. This plane is a lot faster than the Cessna Luke was flying. We'll be looking for the airstrip about six thirty tonight."

At 6:28, Joel Hawthorne landed our plane at Tarajuro, a simple airfield marked off with orange barrels. The island was a tropical paradise. By the time Hawthorne shut off his engine near the refueling station, locals were making their way out to greet us, along with an Australian woman I took to be one of the missionaries.

"Welcome to Tarajuro," she said. "You must be Harper Gray. Don McCafferty contacted us by radio to say you were coming."

"You must be Eve Walbry," I said, wiping sweat from my hands to shake hers. Eve was in her late forties, I guessed, wearing oval spectacles, sandy colored shorts, and a sleeveless button-up blouse.

"Yes, I'm one of the missionaries working here on the island. You'll get to meet my husband, Daniel, once we arrive to camp."

"It's nice to meet you," I said. "This is Mr. Hawthorne, my pilot. We've flown here from Honolulu to find out what happened to Luke. I wonder if you'd help us with any information you may have."

"We've been praying ever since we heard the news. Luke was, well, *is* someone who loves serving the Lord. He's someone God's worked through so a hospital can be built here—and someday it will be. It's only a clinic now, but there's nothing else even remotely nearby."

Hawthorne pulled our bags from storage, and I heard him toss them on the ground. The sun was setting below the trees dimming the airfield, and I fought to rid my mind of the image of Luke stranded at sea, clinging to a floating piece of debris. Eve invited us to join her and Daniel for dinner, where she promised to tell us everything she knew. Worn out, dirty, and wishing I'd brought bug spray, I helped Hawthorne move our things from the landing strip down a beaten path that led into the jungle of Tarajuro.

"Luke was in excellent spirits when he left here. Bounding with energy, happy to see us, but ready to get back to the States."

"Did he say why he wanted to leave earlier than planned?" I asked. The four of us—Eve and Daniel Walbry, Mr. Hawthorne and I—sat around a small but proper dinner table in the Walbry's clinic and living quarters.

"Well, to see you," Eve said. "He was a bundle of energy. Once all the supplies had been delivered, repairs made, the equipment up and running, he was torn between keeping his original plans, and going back early. We could see he was in love, and so Daniel and I insisted."

Hawthorne asked, "He didn't say anything about deviating from his flight plan, did he?"

"No, not to us. He refueled late in the day, said he would make a stop on his way to Hawaii, and was off."

"Do you have any idea where he planned to stop?"

"Not really, but I took it to mean with the late hour, he might land on one of the other islands in the area and stay the night."

The four of us finished a dinner of fish and fruit, and I asked our hosts if it would be okay to turn in. I was exhausted, emotionally and physically. Eve led me to the small plank-wood-floor room where Luke had slept just a few nights before. I thanked her and closed the curtain.

In the light of a candle, I lay on the cot in the dark room, took out Don's notepad, and read where I'd left off. On the fifth page, I read this inscription, almost scribbled as a doodle on the page.

Will reach Honolulu tomorrow. plans to contact
H. once he reaches cell towers. thinks she'll
like Hawaii. wants to take her there.

I tried to maintain a grip, but tears poured down my face in silent streams. So much of our communication had come to me in written form, I felt grateful for one more message from Luke. I blew out the candle and lay back down on the cot. I turned again to prayer, knowing how God hears each one, from Chicago beds to Tarajuro cots.

♫

Early the next morning Eve and Daniel Walbry accompanied us to the airfield. After Mr. Hawthorne refueled the plane, they said a prayer for Luke and me and sent us on our way. Minutes later, we were airborne, back over expansive blue waters.

"Well, at least we know something we didn't yesterday. He had it in mind to make a stop before heading out to open sea that night. Your mate's plane may have been outmoded, but he was a sensible flier."

"So if you were leaving on Luke's flight path, and you knew it would be getting dark in four or five hours, where would you plan to stop?"

"That's hard to say with so many small islands, but I'd say one where I knew there was a reliable airfield. If it were me, I'd have shot for Sparrow Island."

"How soon can we get there?"

"By ten."

Hawthorne lowered a visor, shielding his eyes from the brilliant morning sun. I looked around the inside of the plane, our home for much of the day before and presumably this one as well. Hawthorne had removed all of the unnecessary seats but one, and in their place lay two long pontoon skis.

If only pontoon skis had been fastened to Luke's plane, I thought. *What a pointless omission.*

"Are you hungry, Mr. Hawthorne?" I asked, wanting to change the subject in my own mind.

"As a matter of fact, I am hungry, and as long as we're going to be spending all day in a small airplane, you can call me Joel."

I unbuckled my seat belt and climbed in the rear of the plane to reach my suitcase. I unzipped the clasp and pulled out a box of Super Protein bars and two water bottles. Returning to my seat, I gave one of each to Hawthorne.

"Oh, that's beautiful. This is fast becoming as luxurious as a commercial airline. Pull down that compartment door panel behind you," he said, gesturing over my shoulder.

I twisted a black knob and opened a flat panel at the rear of the cockpit. Behind the green metal door I found a coffeemaker.

"Do you know how to make coffee? There's water in storage back there, coffee, filters."

We ate in silence, sipping hot coffee at twenty thousand feet and learning how to spend extended periods of time in each other's company.

"Listen, why don't you fill me in on what we're doing out here," Hawthorne said after finishing up his protein bar. "I don't mind flying you from island to island because as long as I'm up in the air, I'm making money, but are you thinking we're going to find your mate alive somewhere on one of these small islands?"

"Luke's plane has gone down. I can't leave it at that. I love him too much to not know what happened."

"Right, but you're talking about searching at least a thousand square miles of open water, hundreds of islands, four days after who knows what happened. I'm not trying to be a pessimist, but at the same time I have to be honest. Your mate's best chances for survival are that he had some sort of flotation device aboard or that he was picked up by some passing ship, as unlikely as that is, that's making its way to Hawaii."

"They would have communicated that information to authorities."

"Probably the best we can hope for is that he somehow survived and is floating out at sea. But the only way I can do this is if we treat your search and rescue operation with some sense and realistic expectations, and not like we're a couple of Pollyannas. Luke may be fine, but I've got to tell you, it's more likely that he had engine trouble in deep sea and had to ditch the plane. If the coast guard hasn't found his ELT, that's another clue; it means it's buried too deep beneath the water."

"Mr. Hawthorne—Joel—I used to be shy about saying this kind of thing, but I have faith that we're out here for a reason. I'd like to believe that reason is because Luke's alive. I don't know what good it does preparing ourselves for the worst every mile we fly. I have two more days left to search, and I want to follow the leads we have."

Hawthorne's face soured.

"See, I don't like the sound of that, love. Your heart's in the right place, but not your head. You're working off nothing more tangible than a lucky four-leaf clover."

"Hardly, Joel. I'm working with something far more meaningful and powerful."

"And would you mind telling me what makes you think your faith will make any difference?"

I started at the beginning, telling Hawthorne my story about Bella and Christmas in Chicago, New Year's Eve in New York, and how the journey I'd been on inspired me to believe. Hawthorne listened, not because he believed any part of it that involved God, but because we were spending all morning aboard a small airplane with nothing else to do.

Joel Hawthorne was a smart, sensible man. When he forecast our reaching Sparrow Island by 10 a.m., he was right. By 10:02, we were kicking parking blocks under the Cessna's wheels on the landing strip.

A few islanders gathered around us. We asked if anyone had information about Luke's plane. No one knew anything, so we walked down a well-beaten slope toward the ocean to speak to a group of men fishing on the beach.

Malau Jonah was a local islander who spoke good English. Not only had he seen Luke land on Sparrow Island, but his cousin on a neighboring island had seen the plane crash.

"He told me, uh, the plane went down into the water," he said. With his rough, dark hands, he pantomimed the angle of decent, a sharp forty-five degree fall into the Pacific. "Were there any survivors?" I asked Malau. "Did the pilot survive?"

"The pilot killed. No survivors."

I stepped back from Malau Jonah and the circle of fishermen telling Hawthorne the news. Luke was gone, that was all that mattered. I'd been holding out hope that God had a plan and an answer for us this morning, a way to bring Luke back that might involve the island and be something only He could do. But now the day only felt hot, and Sparrow Island seemed only a fishermen's beach far away from LA.

"Did he say where the plane went down?" Hawthorne asked.

"Talk to my cousin Boli. He lives on Botuvita."

"Is there an airstrip on Botuvita?" Hawthorne asked. I was out of questions, my reservoir of hope cracked and draining.

"Yes, an airfield. It's not far from here by plane."

Hawthorne walked Malau and some of the men back to the airstrip and pulled out our maps from the cockpit so they could show us Botuvita, confirming the location. Hawthorne was ready to return to the sky.

"Come on, Harper. Be strong, girl. This mystery is coming together a lot faster than I expected. We'll get on to Botuvita and find Malau's cousin Boli. He's an eyewitness. He can tell us what happened, and we can get on our way to Hawaii."

Having the pieces all fall into place excited Hawthorne. I walked around to the front of the plane and climbed in, buckling my seat beat, leaning my head against the window. I knew the truth now: Luke was gone. I could feel my body bending toward the inevitable pull of mourning.

After refueling, Hawthorne stayed outside the airplane giving me the privacy to grieve. He didn't respect my faith, but he had the decency to respect my sorrow.

After a few minutes, he climbed in, and we taxied down to the end of the runway, still damp with yesterday's rain. I glanced through the cockpit window into the eyes of islanders, men walking back to the beach to fish, women with their babies in shoulder wraps. They seemed to recognize grief, even in the eyes of a stranger.

~ THIRTY-FOUR ~

Our maps showed dozens of small islands dotted throughout the South Pacific. Hawthorne told me many of the islands were primitive environments, sparsely populated, and absent of any modern technology. News travels from place to place by word of mouth, by boat. Family ties are strong. Islanders feast on tuna caught in nets and fruit harvested from the jungle. Modernity had little affected these places, except for the addition of landing strips to welcome planes bringing outsiders with supplies and medicine, and stories of the complicated world far from the shores of paradise.

We landed on Botuvita just as the rains descended, turning the airfield into slick mud. Hawthorne and I climbed from the plane thirty yards from a shelter and were soaked to the bone by the time we reached it. The sight of our plane circling the island brought islanders to the shelter. We were welcomed and offered a sweet papaya-like juice as refreshment.

"What brings you to Botuvita?" Chief Tonga asked.

"A man named Malau Jonah on Sparrow Island told us the story of a plane crash," Hawthorne explained. "He said we should speak to his cousin Boli. This woman is a friend of the pilot who was flying that plane."

"Yes. Boli. He is here on this island. He will speak to you."

When the rainstorm ended an hour later, a group of us marched through the jungle toward the village. We met Boli and the fifty or so islanders and were treated to a welcoming feast. I wanted desperately to interview Boli about what he knew, but first we had to shake the hands of every man, woman, and child on the island, as was their custom.

"You have come to Botuvita to ask Boli the story of the airplane," Chief Tonga finally said. He called to Boli, asking what he knew, then translated the story for us.

"My cousin and I met twenty nights ago when a fishing party left the island to go to Taki. For days we fished separately, his men on the west side of the island, my boat and friends on the far side of the island. While we were in our boat, I see a white plane with red lines flying lower and lower to the sea. There is no landing strip on Taki. The plane flew around the island but crashed into the sea close to shore. We paddled to the wreckage, but there was only the smell of fuel and a piece of the plane's tail floating in the water."

"What did you do with the tail of the aircraft?" Hawthorne asked. The chief spoke to Boli.

"We pulled the tail from the water and brought it up to the beach."

"Could it still be there?"

"Yes."

Hawthorne turned to me with an idea of how to settle our pursuit of Luke's story.

"Harper, we don't know conclusively if this is Luke's plane or not. The timing is close, but if we could locate that scrap of tail, it could have a serial number, and we can make a positive ID."

We thanked Boli, the islanders, and Chief Tonga for their hospitality, and they walked with us back to the airfield late in the afternoon. Hawthorne and some of the men from the island removed the pontoons he'd stored, preparing the plane to make the water landing on Taki that Luke was denied.

It was late again, our tour of South Pacific islands eating up the daylight hours. Hawthorne was ready to be done with this trip but driven to finish his job out of respect for a fallen fellow pilot. We were both tired when he brought the craft down beautifully in the water, as graceful as a swan dropping onto a lake, and taxied up to the beach.

I took my bag this time, lifting it out of the stowaway area and checking my cell phone for service. It was dead.

"You're not likely to get reception for that thing out here, love," Hawthorne said. "Occasionally reception can bounce off the water, or pick up a signal from passing ships, but nothing predictable or regular."

Hawthorne secured the plane to the shore with rigging, and we hiked up the only trail that led away from the beach. It would be dark in a couple of hours.

The family tribe of the Taki greeted us, offering me a night's rest in a hut I'd share with a family of six. Hawthorne slept in a separate shelter with some of the men. I prayed for sleep and found it quickly.

I awoke the next morning with a stiff neck to the sight of a three-year-old boy clamoring for his mother's attention. I felt a deeper ache, not knowing how I'd cope with going back to Los Angeles to resume work as Joseph Hagen's new girl. I prayed the shortest prayer, one from my dark days in Chicago: *God help me.*

I stepped outside the hut to wander under the umbrella of an overcast sky. A fire for cooking burned in a clearing between the huts.

Hawthorne was gone, probably checking his plane again, *his* one true love. I saw no point in rushing our island objective. We would talk to the chief again soon, tell him of our purpose, and ask to see the wreckage.

A short stump near the fire beckoned me, and I fell onto it, lacking the energy to do little else. From behind me I heard a voice.

"You are cold?" I turned to see the chief standing there. He was an older man, blind, his face as radiant as an angel's. I looked him over, lost in a world of grief.

"No, the fire's warm," I said, turning back toward the campfire. "I'm not cold."

"I am very happy today. Happy to see you."

"Thank you," I said, wondering if I should stand out of respect but lacking the strength to rise.

"But you are sad. Why are you sad?"

"I have lost someone very special to me. I cannot see him again, and my heart is sad."

"Do you have medicine?"

"There's no medicine for this. Only time can help."

"Do you have medicine?" he asked again. I reached for a stick to poke the fire.

"No, I have no medicine."

"Do you have medicine on the plane?"

"I'm sorry," I said, turning to look back at the chief so he could understand. I pulled my cell phone out of my pocket and set it on my leg. Hawthorne appeared from the brush trail, sweaty from work and the long, hot walk.

"Have you asked him?" Hawthorne said.

"Not yet."

"Well, what are we waiting for? Let's see what we came here to see and get back on our way."

Hawthorne was impatient, but then again he was right. We'd chased down all our leads, and our time for searching had come to an end.

"Do you have medicine?" the chief asked Hawthorne.

"Why do you need medicine?"

I powered on my cell phone for no other reason than to escape the nonsensical conversation. It powered up and a moment later vibrated in my hand. The screen noted three missed messages. I was amazed. Hawthorne had been right; there *were* times you could get a signal off an island.

"There is … sick. The man is sick here," said the chief.

I pushed the button to retrieve my messages, expecting to see a text from Sydney or Avril or even Joseph asking for an update. The first message, however, sent shivers down my spine.

Halp

"One of your people is sick?" I heard Hawthorne say.

"No, not my people. *Your people.*"

I shot up off the stump, knocking over the log, and it rolled into the fire.

"Where is he?" I shouted.

"The man is sleeping on the hill."

My eyes roamed the hillside, searching for a narrow break in the thick foliage. There were hills everywhere, thickets of rain forest, dense overgrown jungle. Where? Which hill? Then I saw it—the corner of a building higher on the hillside reflecting the sun's rays off its tin roof. I sprinted toward the building.

"Harper, wait!"

Following a winding trail no wider than the tire of a wheelbarrow, I stumbled and fell once, twice, three times but kept on climbing. I followed a twisting stretch of footpaths that curved and curled up and around the slope. Finally, the path widened as I turned. I could now see the open door of the bamboo hut, its tin roof looking like the tin man's coat rusting in the woods.

I slowed to a walk, afraid and hopeful at the same time about what I might find inside. I poked my head in the doorway, my feet firmly planted on the other side of the threshold. My beloved was lying on a plank on the floor, his head bandaged with a bloody cloth, his feet swollen and his eyes closed.

I crept into the hut, alone with him, and knelt down beside him.

"Luke?" I said, softly, watching his eyelids for movement. How long had he been here without medical care?

His eyes opened, perhaps from a dream, and I waited to see recognition in them. He spoke my name, "Harper," in a sound less than a whisper. I bent down and kissed him.

Luke McCafferty was alive.

~ THIRTY-FIVE ~

I held Luke's hand as Hawthorne and some of the island men transported him, using the wooden plank as a stretcher, down the narrow trail to the beach.

"Harper, I haven't been able to refuel at these last island stops," said Hawthorne. "To be honest, I wasn't expecting we'd be adding an additional passenger."

"Is there enough to get us back to Honolulu?" I asked.

"I don't know. We'll have to lighten the plane somehow, and there aren't many options."

I stopped in my tracks. "You aren't thinking that one of us needs to stay behind?"

Hawthorne was silent.

"What are the other options?"

"Strip the plane. Everything nonessential will have to go. I mean everything."

I remember nodding my head in agreement. Time was our enemy; we had to move Luke off the island for medical treatment without delay. Within the hour the plane had been stripped bare, and Luke had been secured with straps in the back of the plane. He didn't look well at all, and I began to worry that we'd found him alive just in time to watch him die.

Hawthorne splashed through the shallows of the lagoon, climbing up into the plane. He slammed the door shut behind him and wriggled into his seat, binding his safety harness across his chest.

"Hang on," he instructed.

The plane's engines roared to life. Hawthorne throttled the plane forward in the water, turning it around for quick departure. I watched the men and women of the Taki village waiting to witness the miracle of flight and prayed for a miracle of a different kind.

The thrill of acceleration gripped me as we skimmed across the water. We shot past the islanders, Hawthorne pulled on the wheel, and we lifted off the surface. We flew for a moment just a few feet above the open water, then Hawthorne quickened our speed and we ascended into the great blue sky.

"We're pointed back toward Honolulu, Harper. You keep an eye on Luke, and I'll work on getting us there in one piece."

"How tight are we on fuel, Hawthorne?"

"I'd rather not think about it. We're going to fly in a straight line in the thinnest air I can find. Let me mind my work here, love."

I kept quiet after that. Praying, watching Luke wince in his sleep. Offering him sips of bottled water whenever his eyes opened.

"I had a vision that I'd find you," I whispered once when he opened his eyes. "Now we're headed back to Honolulu."

"I was praying you'd find me."

♫

Forty miles south of the island of Hawaii, we heard a sputter from the engine.

"What was that?" I asked.

"We're out of fuel. Hindsight being twenty–twenty, I should have kicked off the pontoons. The weight's dragging us down, but I just couldn't take the risk."

"Are we going to make it to Honolulu?"

"Not likely."

The engine sputtered again, and I felt the airplane shimmy from side to side. A moment later a deafening silence fell upon us as the engine shut off.

"We're officially a glider now," Hawthorne said.

"For how long?" I asked.

"For as long as we stay airborne."

I rushed to the cockpit. "And exactly how long is that?"

"Give me a minute, and I'll give you a rough, quasi-scientific guess. We're at approximately fourteen thousand feet, traveling at a speed of one hundred and forty miles per hour, and descending rapidly. According to my calculations, adjusting for wind speed, which is at our backs, we'll be a flying airplane for the next ten minutes."

"That's not long enough," I said.

Hawthorne opened a communications channel on the radio.

"Mayday, mayday. This is Cessna 4331J22 sending out a distress call. We are out of fuel, heading northeast and going down. We have pontoons so we can land safely, and we are carrying the missing pilot Luke McCafferty."

Hawthorne glanced back at me.

"And also the lovely Hollywood actress Harper Gray. Any assistance by ship or by plane would be appreciated."

He switched off the radio and let out a sigh of surrender.

"It's out of my hands now, love. I've played all the cards I have."

"Thank you, Joel," I said. "You've earned your fee today."

"After this, I'm going to have to raise my rates."

The plane continued falling as Hawthorne steered it left and right, keeping us airborne for as long as possible.

"Mayday, mayday," he repeated over the radio. "We are Cessna 4331J22 soon to make an emergency water landing about thirty miles southwest of Oahu. We have an injured man aboard, missing pilot Luke McCafferty. Requesting assistance."

I looked out the cockpit window at the endless ocean. We were about to land in the middle of it. I looked back at Luke, thanked God for allowing us to find him alive, and prayed fervently for our rescue.

"Hold on, we're going in," Hawthorne said, pulling the headset off and tossing it on the floor of the plane.

I went to the back of the plane and locked Luke down to the floor with the weight of my body. The impact of the pontoons skidding across the choppy waves shook the airplane violently. Bottles of water flew from my open bag and bounced around the floor. Hawthorne's coffee cup smashed against his tool kit, and he let out a yell. Luke recoiled in pain from the brunt of impact, and I tried to calm him with my voice. Finally, the plane came to rest, bobbing up and down like a small boat tied to a dock.

"You're praying, right?" Hawthorne asked.

"And believing," I said, just seconds before the radio cleared.

"Cessna 4331J22, this is the U.S. Coast Guard, do you copy? We are sending a rescue medical chopper. Expected ETA, thirty minutes."

~ Epilogue ~

"Harper, that's the most amazing story I've ever heard. Maybe someone should turn your life into a movie."

I smiled at *Entertainment Tonight* producer Benton Stuart in my living room at the beach house. "I'm just glad you were willing to take a day to come over and hear it."

Benton set her Pellegrino glass down on the coffee table, next to the lunch plates we still hadn't cleared. "And roll tape. As much fun as this has been for me, I think our viewers are going to love hearing this interview. Especially since your reviews for *Winter Dreams* are glowing, and sitting where I am across from you, I have to say you are too."

I looked down at my growing tummy and sighed.

"It's been quite a year since our adventure, which brings me to the announcement I told you about. I've decided to take the next year off—and maybe the next twenty."

The doors to the back deck slid open, and Luke stepped inside, bringing with him the sounds of the ocean. Benton turned to look at him.

"Sorry," Luke said. "I thought you might be done. I'll come back."

"You're fine," I said. "We're just finishing up."

"Harper," Benton asked, "are you telling me you're retiring? Rumor has it after the success of *Winter Dreams* you're being offered more A-list scripts than you can read. One assumes these are worth a boatload of money. Even your good friend and *Apartment 19* co-star, Avril LaCorria, just signed a two-picture deal worth millions. How can you just walk away when you're being given everything Hollywood has to offer?"

"I don't think of it as walking away. It's more like … running away to an island in the South Pacific. There's an opportunity to help build a hospital on Tarajuro."

Luke sat next to me on the arm of the sofa, placing his hand on my stomach. I watched how the television lights made his wedding band sparkle. White gold, with the tender words I'd had engraved hidden inside.

"God's already given me everything," I told Benton. "There's no counteroffer Hollywood can make."

My cell phone chimed on the table in front of me with an incoming message. I saw it was from Avril and opened it.

can't believe you talked me into a blind date.

In sandy eggo! call me to tlk. i'm weirdly excited.

I smiled.

"You know, this is only going to make you more in demand," Benton said, raising one perfectly plucked eyebrow.

"They'll have to find me first."

Benton cued the cameraman and he turned off the lights, returning the room to normal. It felt good to finally have their heat off me.

"You're warm," Luke said. "Let me get you a glass of ice water."

"No, don't go."

The baby kicked, and Luke and I felt it together, his hand still on my belly.

"You see, she doesn't want you to go either."

"Oh, it's a girl. Do you have a name yet?" Benton asked.

"We're going to name her Bella."

"That's beautiful," Benton said.

"That's what Bella means, *beautiful*. It's from Isabella, meaning 'God's promise.'"

Luke leaned in, softly and sweetly planting a kiss on my cheek.

"Kind of sums it all up, don't you think?"

... a little more ...

When a delightful concert comes to an end,

the orchestra might offer an encore.

When a fine meal comes to an end,

it's always nice to savor a bit of dessert.

When a great story comes to an end,

we think you may want to linger.

And so, we offer ...

AfterWords—just a little something more after you

have finished a David C. Cook novel.

We invite you to stay awhile in the story.

Thanks for reading!

Turn the page for ...

• An Interview with the Author
• Manhattan: Lonely Island
• Which Character Would You Like to See in a Sequel?

An Interview with the Author

In *Screen Play*, Harper and Luke get to know each other long distance through the online dating site, LoveSetMatch.com, text messaging, and emails. In the spirit of *Screen Play*, best-selling author Christa Parrish (*Home Another Way, Watch Over Me*) and Chris Coppernoll dialogued with one another through email on the themes, message, and meaning found in *Screen Play*.

CP: **Screen Play** *is your third work of fiction. Why is this novel so important to you?*

CC: *Screen Play* is important because it comprises all the themes that inhabit my novels: isolation, singleness, sudden and unexpected fame, and God's mysterious hand working on our behalf. I like this story. I love how Harper's this beautiful, young woman who, at the time she finds herself crossing the line from her twenties to her thirties, goes through a bewildering series of circumstances that leave her friendless in Chicago. Her acting roles have dried up. Her best friend, Avril, is gone, and her boyfriend, Sam, abandons her for his new life without her in Los Angeles. The story basically opens with Harper emerging from an unsettling year alone. An acquaintance we never meet in the story, Bella, has invited Harper to a mission outreach church in the city, and she's given her life to "the Rescuer." In God's perfect timing, Harper's phone finally rings, and she's invited to join the cast of a Broadway revival in New York. For me, that could be the entire story, but I wanted to tell a story about how quickly God can change our circumstances, and everything can change for the good.

CP: Chris, did you find it difficult to write Screen Play *from a woman's perspective? What were some of the challenges? Some of the surprises?*

CC: Yes. The biggest surprise was that I did it. ☺ I think *Screen Play* had to be written from Harper's viewpoint because we need to hear her tell the story. I wanted readers to sit on those hard subway seats and feel the emotions Harper feels at the Carney Theatre and everywhere else her journey takes her. Harper is one of the most complex characters I've ever written. Writing in her voice was the most challenging part of the novel and the decision I questioned most (because it was a stretch), but it was the truest way to tell the story. I think God gives most novelists an affinity for understanding people, the way an attentive actor watches someone famous and then imitates their character on screen. I worried about whether readers could accept Harper's voice, knowing it came from a man, or if they'd be distracted. I had to trust that readers could be swept up in the story and it wouldn't be an issue.

CP: At one point, Harper writes to Luke, "It's part of bigger story God's telling in my life. Sometimes I feel as much a spectator as a participant." Why did you choose to write that? Do you ever feel this way?

CC: Sometimes life feels just that way. We say, "What will be will be," or "If it's meant to happen, it will happen." Writing *Screen Play* occurred at the same time I was experiencing changes in my personal life that felt God-orchestrated, like God was involving me directly in His plans. Some of my personal experiences influenced Harper's story because there's a parallel.

CP: Harper remembers the loss in James's life and thinks, "I wondered if he felt like God had suddenly realized He'd dealt him too many blessing cards and decided to take one back." What would you say to someone who also felt this way when his or her life has been touched by pain?

CC: It's easy to write pat answers when life deals a difficult blow, but all of us go through challenging times. I'll simply tell you what my experience has been. Everything painful in my life has come from one of three sources: someone's sin against me; the consequence of my own sinful choices; or God's providential decision to change me through trying circumstances. Whatever life challenges we face, God can reveal the goodness inside when we turn to Him.

CP: "It struck me how in a city the size of New York, those I was getting to know best I was connecting with through a computer screen," Harper thinks. How do you see technology playing a role in the fellowship of believers? Are you ever concerned it can be a replacement for true community?

CC: As icky as the two words sound when used together, community and technology can work together. I'm thinking of the Twitter community—a Web site that allows people you've selected from anywhere in the world to exchange their brief thoughts online—and how friends where I live in Nashville were recently able to mobilize hundreds of believers to pray for someone in an emergency. Social networking sites like Facebook work like a small-town newspaper. They provide only the news our community chooses to post whether they are the community next door or a community far from home.

CP: In Screen Play, *we see the ups and downs of trying to find "the one," from Harper's relationship with Luke to Avril's relationship with Jon. As someone involved in singles' ministry, what advice would you give to the millions of people navigating the world as single people but desiring to have a partner in life?*

CC: Wait upon the Lord. Should God have someone for you, He will make it clear to the both of you.

Manhattan: Lonely Island

An Essay on Community

I began work on *Screen Play* with a poignant image in my mind, a picture of Harper surviving in the empty Chicago apartment, then relocating to another lonely place, the crowded island of Manhattan. And still feeling degrees of separation.

In my other life as a speaker and teacher, I often give talks on the importance of living in a fulfilling and sustainable community. It's something I believe is God's intentional design for us, and I encourage others to join their lives in community. But what exactly is it?

A group of singles was chatting on Facebook, posting comments that tried to answer that question about what it means to be a part of community. "Community," one wrote, "is my network of family and friends." "Community is a place where I feel accepted." "Community is where I belong."

How can something be defined that looks so different to each of us? Something that can mean everything from the clubs we join, to the friends we have, to people living in cooperatives and our grandparents' nostalgic neighborhoods from a half-century ago?

Wherever and however we find community isn't as important as what happens to us when we're engaged in it. As we encounter a true experience of community, we recognize its perfect shape for filling that vacant space in our lives. In meaningful community, a social DNA exchange takes place among us. When we gather with those who love us and whom we love, community bestows to us its resources—things absent from a life lived alone. Community is where we receive the gifts of profound and fulfilling fellowship, and where we practice our own God-given spiritual gifts.

Community happens everywhere, and forms anywhere and forms quickly, but surprisingly, it doesn't happen every time a group of people get together or even when Christians meet.

For example, in high school I sang with five guys in a vocal harmony group called Northshore. We experienced real community and remain friends today. However, when I worked in a "Christian" company for three years, an environment where you'd expect a certain degree of spiritual community, community never happened.

Pastors understand the importance of community and therefore encourage their flocks to meld into close community. Small groups are formed with the best of intentions, meeting to study God's Word, share a meal together, and fellowship with one another. But following months of study and discussion, regular meetings, and coffee cake, some groups may have yet to experience even a spark of community. Why?

In his groundbreaking book *The Search to Belong,* author Joe Myers says communities need to flow together spontaneously, not be pulled together by the force of their being simply "a good idea."

If Myers is right, churches that insist on small groups as the critical model for bringing about spiritual growth and connectedness may become frustrated even as they multiply their numbers, because they still fall short on building authentic community.

My favorite community Facebook post read simply, "We can't live without each other, and we cannot live without God!" As Christians, we're called to live in unity with God, made possible through Jesus Christ, and in unity with one another. Inside the sphere of community is the access point to the beauty and riches God has enclosed in the skins of His people. It's the place where we can experience the truest expression of ourselves. In community, we engage in active relationship with one another. We live out Jesus' calling to be one as He and the Father are One (John 17:22).

WHICH CHARACTER WOULD YOU LIKE TO SEE IN A SEQUEL?

Readers often tell me when they've enjoyed one of my characters. Sometimes they say they've enjoyed them so much, they'd like to see that character return in a sequel. Have you ever felt that way? I'd enjoy hearing your thoughts. Take a look at the list below of some of the most popular characters from my first three novels. Send me your favorite pick for a sequel at chris@providencebook.com, and who knows? Your vote may just lead to an all-new story! I look forward to hearing from you.

Providence	*A Beautiful Fall*	*Screen Play*
Jack Clayton	Emma Madison	Harper Gray
Jenny Cameron	Noel Conner	Avril LaCorria
Erin Taylor	Michael Evans	Helen Payne
Peter Brenner	Janette Kerr	Ben Hughes
Arthur Reed	Christina Herry	Luke McCafferty